DEATH OF
A PROTOTYPE

DEATH OF A PROTOTYPE

THE PORTRAIT

VICTOR BEILIS

Translated from the Russian
and with an introduction and afterword
by Leo Shtutin

ANTHEM PRESS

Anthem Press
An imprint of Wimbledon Publishing Company
www.anthempress.com

This edition first published in UK and USA 2017
by ANTHEM PRESS
75–76 Blackfriars Road, London SE1 8HA, UK
or PO Box 9779, London SW19 7ZG, UK
and
244 Madison Ave #116, New York, NY 10016, USA

Original title: *Smert' Prototipa*
© Victor Beilis 2014
Originally published by Glas, Moscow, 2005
English translation copyright © Leo Shtutin 2017

A CIP record for this book is available from the British Library.

ISBN-13: 978-1-78308-672-6 (Pbk)
ISBN-10: 1-78308-672-6 (Pbk)

This title is also available as an e-book.

CONTENTS

ACKNOWLEDGEMENTS

I'm grateful to Victor Beilis for his unwavering support over the course of my work on this translation, and for his patience in the face of my rather slow progress. I must also express thanks to my mother, Irena Shtutina, for always being on hand to help whenever I was stumped by some literary allusion or linguistic difficulty (which happened all too often!), and to Patrick Vickers, who read through the entire text and offered valuable comments and suggestions.

TRANSLATOR'S INTRODUCTION

Give me your hand, gentle reader –

This is the first work by Victor Beilis to make it into English since the single-volume publication in 2002 of a duo of novellas – *The Rehabilitation of Freud & Bakhtin and Others* – translated by Richard Grose. Beilis remains virtually unknown in the English-speaking world as a writer of literary fiction (although his output as a scholar of African folklore is familiar to specialists in that field), and I hope that this translation of *Death of a Prototype* – his first, and so far only, novel – will serve to generate an awareness of his wider literary oeuvre.

You won't be frightened, will you now, of the secluded little spots that I intend to show you?

Much like the novellas that preceded it, *Death of a Prototype* is a hyper-allusive and self-consciously 'difficult' work: Beilis delights in intertextual play, inviting the reader to unravel a complex web of quotations, references and paraphrases. This represents a considerable challenge for non-Russians (and non-Russianists), hinging as much of it does on the reader's familiarity with the literature, culture and, to a lesser extent, politics of that country. Nevertheless, the author engages no less closely with an entire spectrum of Western European cultural traditions, from classical antiquity to twentieth-century postmodernism. Unsurprisingly given its subtitle, the visual arts play a particularly important role in the novel. So too visuality in general: seeing and being seen, acts of perception and observation, gazing, glancing and glimpsing.

X

How I should like to observe the changes in the expression of your dear face as I tell my story, but —

The reader is also confronted with an intimidating array of literary styles, all jostling against one another. Alongside several dialogue-heavy chapters — not all that different stylistically from much contemporary fiction — we encounter poetic, archaicized prose, self-referential literary analysis, Joycean stream of consciousness, and so on. The novel, then, is structurally heterogeneous and fragmented, with styles, genres and narrators succeeding one another at great speed. And yet it is also highly balanced and controlled, in some ways recalling a contrapuntal musical composition and abounding in thematic echoes and correspondences. Plot has been largely subordinated to texture, so readers expecting a rollicking thrill-ride will, in all likelihood, be disappointed.

— alas! — I am compelled to walk a little ahead of you, the better to show you the way. Denied the joy of gazing upon you face to face, I shall abandon myself to the delight of storytelling, for to present my history to you *— whoever you might be —*

And yet, *Death of a Prototype* is a novel that not only challenges but also rewards the reader, especially one attuned to fine-grain detail. What initially seems incidental and offhand can prove to be of crucial significance many chapters later — so keep your eyes peeled! You'll find some supplementary information at the back of the book ('Explanatory Glosses and References'), but, ultimately, being able to grasp this allusion or that is of lesser importance than opening yourself up to the pleasure of the text as a whole. The text — I guarantee —

— is happiness indeed.

Leo Shtutin
February 2016

PART ONE

Notice

Recently I received by post a weighty package without a return address. Affixed to the manuscript inside was a note advising me that, upon reading the text, I might do with it what I wished, according to my own discretion: discard it or publish it, either under my name or under that of the real author, whom without doubt I would recognise after reading not two of the lines that follow these preliminaries.

I did, of course, recognize the author immediately, without even looking at the first page. N. – an initial will suffice. I haven't yet decided whether to reveal his real name, although in all likelihood I will – I cannot seriously consider publishing his work as my own – but later, not now; now it would be of little consequence. He did, after all, send me his opus anonymously and even proposed (the scoundrel!) the surrogacy of his creation – well, let the question of authorship remain open for the time being. I do not wish, however, to lead anyone into confusion by giving all this the air of a whodunit: the name plays no role whatsoever in the story, or, to be more precise, in the account, set down below. For certain reasons of a personal nature I do not wish to reveal the identity of the creator. Those with more than a surface knowledge of his books will recognize, as I did, the hand of the writer, but, in any case, I cannot withhold the true author from other readers either. And that's that – so don't expect any dead ends or garden paths.

But a few words about N. He was the first professional littérateur I became acquainted with as a young man; in fact, he wasn't so much the first littérateur – by the time I made his acquaintance I was already friends with several unpublished young poets and ceaselessly versified myself – N. wasn't so much the first littérateur as the first member of the Union of Soviet Writers with whom I unashamedly maintained relations, paying no mind to those among my friends and compeers who condemned any association with engaged literature. N. had a marvellous knack for getting love stories printed in Soviet journals and the biggest state publishing houses of the country despite entirely emancipating their narratives from questions of ideology or industrial production. My poet-friends smiled derisively, but their secret respect was clear to see. Yet I was never a particular admirer of his art: rather, I liked him for what he was – for his utterly undemanding independence, or, put another way, for that particular kind of firmness which, fully self-aware, affords infinite patience and – *softness.* An unfortunate choice of words, perhaps, but that's the best I can do.

At any rate, the story of our interactions has nothing to do with the matter at hand. It only remains for me to tell you about A. Really, there's little point in keeping her hidden behind an initial – in the manuscript she is referred to by her full name: Adele. This is also the name of the heroine in many of N.'s stories – his polymorphous, capricious, irrepressible, underhanded, tender-hearted, angelic, diabolical heroine. It was through me, a long while ago, that they became acquainted, and for a long while N. (God be his judge!) suspected that she and I had been having an affair that we did not discontinue even when she, a married woman, briefly became his mistress. The episode with N. seemed to be of little significance in her rich and vigorous existence; for him, however, who could hardly be called inexperienced, who had been both popular and successful with women, Adele became nothing less than an obsession, an unceasing passion, an idée fixe, a source of joy and unrelenting pain – in short, she became everything that a woman can possibly become for a man in the prime of his life.

The ebb and flow of their relationship, or rather, the brief history of their involvement, invited a variety of interpretations and gave rise to numerous novellas, stories and plays whose heroine, though invariably named Adele, came to be endowed with such divergent character traits that you'd never suppose she could be one and the same woman – or, indeed, that she could be a real person at all. N. was simply getting even, avenging himself, marvelling at her, falling in love all over again, killing her, playing might-have-been scenarios over in his mind, harbouring suspicions, throwing fits of jealousy, asking for forgiveness, condemning her to death, begging for mercy – and thereby prolonging their long discontinued affair.

My role in this story also encompasses the fact that I was the first to learn of Adele's sudden death and emailed N. to inform him – I hadn't the courage to let him know over the telephone. She died in the Eternal City, just by the Trevi Fountain, at the moment when, facing away from it, as per tourist custom, she was throwing a coin over her shoulder into the water. This action proved to be the very last of her life, though it wasn't realized fully – the coin never left her hand, while Adele herself just slid, *lightly and freely*, to the ground; her husband, who related these details to me, read this conduct as yet more of her tomfoolery and didn't even rush to help her up. It was of Rome, of Rome alone, that she had always dreamed, and this visit was her first: she spent two carefree weeks there …

And that's more or less all I have to say by way of preface to the publication of the manuscript in question – it follows below:

Koretsky

The guests were many, their liveliness ever increasing. Almost all of those present were long-time friends, and if someone did happen to be new to the fold, the stresses and strains of striking up a new acquaintance would quickly be overcome.

The conversation was general. A few jokes, a little gossip; then, not unusually, the men proceeded to poke fun at the fair sex, while the women, cheerfully defending themselves, evocatively portrayed male shortcomings. But the evening's tone grew ever more serious; some imperceptible turn in the discussion brought literary examples, mythology and archetypes into play, raising the question of male and female principles.

This subject was taken up with great enthusiasm by the previously laconic Koretsky, and everyone's attention was soon focused solely on him. With his monologue in full swing, the lady of the house introduced another guest into the room and, for the benefit of those unacquainted with her, announced:

'This is Adele Volskaya!'

Koretsky started visibly and looked up at the newcomer:

'You're really Volskaya?'

'What's so surprising? That's just my maiden name.'

'It's odd,' muttered Koretsky.

'What's odd? Explain!'

'You see, it just so happens that for half a year now I've been enthralled by a certain phrase from one of Pushkin's prose fragments: "… *the hall door swung ajar, and Volskaya traversed the threshold*".'

'And why were you so captivated by it?'

'I believe it is the most energetic expression in all of world literature – and just listen to the play of sounds: *vls, vrs*! But now I was struck by something else: the moment you trav – er, came in, it was as if the phantom of Pushkin's phonetics swished over my head, and then your name was announced, which, as you say, is your maiden name, and which, as I can see now, is the one name you could possibly have.'

'But even so,' Volskaya said in a fluster, 'you must forgive me for interrupting! You were talking about something interesting, I heard you even before I came in. Please, continue!' And, taking a seat next to an old acquaintance, 'Who's that?' she asked.

'Oh, but don't you know? That's Maxim Koretsky. You must've heard of him: he's much renowned for his erudition and – take care now – no less so for being a lady-killer!'

'Oh yes, yes, I have! So that's him then?'

'In the flesh!'

Koretsky, meanwhile, had returned to the original topic of discussion – an intense preoccupation of his, it would appear.

'Just like Jupiter and Juno,' he said, turning to Volskaya, 'we were wondering whose lot in life is the sweetest, a man's or a woman's.'

'Let's start with Jupiter. What did the Olympians contend?'

'This is what Ovid has to say about the matter in the *Metamorphoses*:

> *They say that Jupiter, soused with nectar,*
> *Put aside his grave concerns and joking around*
> *With an idle Juno said to her, "Your sex's pleasure*
> *Is clearly greater than any felt by males."*
> *She said no, and so they agreed to ask Tiresias*
> *His opinion, familiar as he was with either sex.*
> *…*
> *Chosen as arbiter of this lighthearted spat,*
> *He confirmed Jove's opinion.*

'How interesting! But please explain, what does it mean when it says that Tiresias was familiar with either sex? Did he swing the other way? But in that case he wasn't in any position to judge.'

'I think Tiresias was no stranger to homosexual experience either, but that's neither here nor there: the point is that for seven years he was a woman. It happened like this. Once, while on a woodland wander, Tiresias happened upon two copulating serpents. Repulsed by this spectacle, he gave the serpents a good going-over with his stick, was bitten and immediately turned into a woman. The male guise was restored to him seven years later when he launched another attack on the amorous serpents. Which is why Tiresias's competence as umpire in this contest was beyond doubt for the Olympian couple: he'd been *both* a man *and* a woman. In reply to Jupiter's question Tiresias declared a woman's pleasure to be *nine* times as intense as a man's (everything's been quantified!). In retribution, Juno blinded the umpire – *don't give away women's secrets*; yet Jupiter bestowed upon him the gift of second sight – *dig deeper*. It seems to me that in his role of soothsayer Tiresias espoused both masculine and feminine traits. And we might add that in the European tradition the image of the poet-prophet in general is characterized by masculinity, valour, the mantle of responsibility – but also by feminine features and an androgynous appearance. Then again, the Eastern tradition doesn't particularly differ in this respect from the European: not only do sorcerers, witch doctors and seers invariably prove to be women's most intimate confidants, they also perform specifically female functions. But I should like to turn yet again to Tiresias – may I?' said Koretsky, appealing to the guests.

He had their undivided attention.

'Please do, please do!'

Koretsky continued:

'My curiosity compelled me to discover the nature of Tiresias's first prophecy. This too can be found in Ovid, and it concerns the destiny of Narcissus:

When Tiresias was asked if this boy would live
To a ripe old age, the soothsayer replied,

"If he never knows himself." The seer's words
Long seemed empty, but the outcome—the way he died,
The strangeness of his passion—proved them to be true.

'Self-desire – a desire that is neither masculine nor feminine – is unheard of. Strangely enough, Hermaphroditus, too, is neither a man nor a woman, while it seems he should be both.'

'Well then,' Volskaya's neighbour interjected, 'it's clear enough now what Tiresias thinks, but let's hear what Koresias has to say for himself.'

'I'm undeserving of your pun,' Maxim replied. 'I have none of Tiresias's experience, nor am I possessed of his expertise or his wisdom.'

'Now-now,' said a guest, mockery in her voice, 'don't put yourself down!'

Koretsky paid these words absolutely no attention and simply darted a glance at Volskaya as if she were his only interlocutor.

'I can say nothing about the intensity of a woman's pleasure – I cannot contrast it with a man's. And I don't think homosexuals – whether men or women – seek entry into the mysteries of the opposite sex. Now, lesbianism is femininity squared, or, better yet, circled or looped, characterized at the same time by a disavowal of the most important thing of all: childbirth. And, when comparing themselves to women, it isn't pleasure that men most commonly focus on (as far as I can judge, they're quite content with what's been handed to them in that department), but childbirth. Jupiter's no exception, what with him sewing children into his thigh or producing them from his head. Artists often speak about the "gestation period" of their creations, about "giving birth", about their "babies". Finally, if you recall, *"I'm not impartial to a pregnant man."* And they say a substantial cash prize was announced some time ago in America for the first man to get himself pregnant.'

'You haven't laid claim to this prize, have you?' The same sardonic guest – with venomous undertones.

'If I could give birth,' Koretsky said earnestly, 'my happiness would be greater than any prize. But I think that perhaps I've wearied everyone, though, of course, the subject hasn't been exhausted.'

'Please, continue,' Volskaya entreated. 'You speak well.'

'Thank you.' Koretsky pressed his lips to Adele's hand and looked up questioningly at his derider.

'But have you never considered the conventional means of begetting?' she asked, persisting with her taunts.

Koretsky was silent for a while, then quietly intoned:

'If by that you mean the act of copulation, then it is not unfamiliar to me; but I have no children to speak of ... But all this isn't about me, after all. As the mythologies of various peoples bear witness, male deities have frequently sought out unorthodox modes of procreation. One of them is self-impregnation. It'd be interesting to learn whether this was ever attempted by the self-desiring Narcissus, but the answer, I think, must be no: auto-eroticism does not tend toward the production of offspring. One who attempts to impregnate himself is but a step away from coition with his own kin, be it with his sister or his mother. The beginning of creation is almost always triggered by self-impregnation or incest. It's an interesting one: does total asceticism pave the way for self-impregnation? And what, in this regard, is sublimation? The birth of thought, the birth of spirituality – these are the fruits of male self-impregnation.'

'Self-impregnation? Sounds like you do nothing but!' Another barb from the sharp-witted lady (who, come to think of it, requires no anonymity – she'll eventually be identified anyway: Marina). 'Can I ask, do you only sublimate one energy into another or do you indulge in an occasional hushed-up lapse into vice as well? Oh!' – clasping her hands together suddenly – 'could it be you're in need of some perking up? I think I'd be fit for the job.'

'Are you sure you'd know how?' Maxim muttered, struggling to maintain his composure. Marina laughed.

'God knows there's only one way of doing it!' she said. Stepping right up to him, she cupped his nape, drew him to her and gave him the generous gift of a long kiss.

A hush immediately fell over the room – the type of strained silence that's always difficult to endure.

'You're too magnanimous,' said Koretsky, lowering his eyes.

'I'm just magnanimous enough,' countered Marina, fixing him with an unblinking gaze.

'Well, I think the ladies have come away with a resounding victory, not that there's any change there,' Adele's neighbour cheerfully concluded.

'Tonight's victory doesn't seem as clear-cut as all that,' said Volskaya.

Koretsky, thanking her with a look, objected:

'In fact, everything I've said was intended to acknowledge female superiority once and for all.'

There was no more general conversation for the remainder of the evening. Marina confronted Volskaya:

'D'you need him?'

Volskaya shrugged.

'Give him! I want him, so drop him, all right?'

'Take him … if you can.'

'Volskaya!'

'Yes, Marinochka?'

'Look …'

'Yep … Here he is now.'

Koretsky was coming toward them, ready to address Adele as if he could see only her –

'It's stifling in here,' said Volskaya preemptively. 'I'd be better off listening to you outside.'

'Wise move,' observed Marina, and withdrew.

When they were outside he said, 'No one was there tonight but you.'

'Not now – you'll ruin everything. Hail a cab, then, don't dawdle!'

Not another word was uttered till morning, though it's doubtful whether anyone would've ventured to call the night a quiet one.

In the morning she said, 'I need to go home. My happy Kamper's due back today.'

'Camper? What camper? Why a camper? What's a camper got to do with anything?'

'Kamper's my husband, you silly thing.'

'Why do you refer to him as a camper?'

'Because that's his surname.'*

'Will you … sleep with him … tonight?'

She giggled.

'Unless he's been especially heavy on the whoring around over the last few days, he'll have most likely worked up a healthy appetite.'

'Naturally, it's a woman's charitable duty to attend to the cravings of any thirsty man.'

'It's not my duty – I'll attend to them with pleasure: I have missed him, you know.'

Koretsky was looking at her dumbly. She laughed.

'You're a strange one, aren't you? Nothing extraordinary about any of this! Now look: this is my hand. D'you know how many times a day it gets shaken by other people's? Or how many strangers (including the ones just waiting to try it on) brush past my legs, arse and breasts? Or how often I can feel myself getting eyed up and then mentally undressed to boot? Just feel here – the skin on my hand's the same quality as on my tits, not a bit rougher. See? Only the epithelium here's a bit softer. Go on, kiss it! And what about this,' she added, her words complemented with a gesture, 'd'you remember what Goethe said about "the biggest finger", the one you have "in addition to the other ten"? It's just a "finger" – nothing more. I don't see the point of offering easy access to one part of your body and keeping another under lock and key when the source of pleasure is in the very part you've stashed away. And isn't it better that way for all concerned? You wouldn't be a happy bunny if I left you hanging for three months only to get cold feet and do an about-turn purely for the sake of propriety, would you now? Well, would you? Why aren't you saying anything?'

---

* Naturally, this surname is a fabrication. In all probability, there is no such surname in existence. (N.'s note.)

Maxim's eyes were glazed over and dead, and unquestioning and automatic the manner in which he obeyed her orders to touch, stroke, kiss, look. He did all this mechanically and without pleasure, almost, it would seem, without grasping the meaning of the words themselves, as if he were simply moving in accordance with the dictates of his motor impulses. For the first time in his life he didn't know what to say, and made no attempt to find the right words. Koretsky felt he was a shell inhabited by a nauseating absurdity, an absurdity that was now rising in his throat.

'Please, wake yourself up – I need to go,' said Volskaya, gathering up her clothes from different corners of the room.

'Will we see each other again?'

'Well, I'd say our paths are bound to cross now we've made each other's acquaintance.'

'But are we really acquainted?'

'You don't remember my maiden name, then? I did mention my husband's surname as well.'

'Oh yes, your south Coaster, or wait – your Trecker? No, that's not it either. Something to do with holiday-making, was it?'

'Indeed: Kamper.'

'Does that mean Camper is your married name? Or is it Camper-Volskaya?'

'Last night you were a more self-assured speaker.'

'I simply considered it desirable and perhaps even necessary to intensify our acquaintance. Oh, I'm tired of this buffoonery … When will you come?'

'I don't know … Don't be angry, I like being with you, but I really don't know. Everything came together perfectly last night, but now we have to wait for the next opportunity.'

'But how – '

'Oh, you poor thing, you need perking up again, don't you?'

'Not "again" – it's only now that I need it at all.'

'But, sweetie, Marina and I arranged everything last night. And you know what, here's my advice: don't turn a blind eye to this arrangement. She's a catch, is Marina, you'll see what a catch she is. Afterward you'll be able to do some comparing, and I have to say I'm not too sure of myself. This kind of rivalry is bound to hurry along an opportunity for our next rendezvous – unless you forget about me, of course.'

'Are you insane?'

'No, just a bitch, but don't put all this on ice – phone Marina today.'

What did Koretsky do? Eh? What did he do? Well? What was it?

He picked up the phone immediately, in Adele's presence, at seven-thirty in the morning.

'Marina,' said Maxim, 'I've just nailed Volskaya, but I didn't float her boat and now she's off. Still fancy perking me up?'

'Come right away,' croaked the sleepy voice at the other end of the line.

'But the night's wiped me out.'

'We'll see what we can do about that,' said the voice, somewhat less sleepily. 'Send Volskaya my love and get yourself over here.'

'Give it here,' said Adele, snatching the receiver away from him. 'Marinochka, hi! ... Yes, just as you wanted ... That's right ... Yep ... And that ain't the half of it ... A proper he-man ... Yep ... Bye!'

Volskaya and Koretsky left the house together, but then they went their separate ways, as planned: Adele headed home, and Maxim paid a visit to Marina.

Oh, I won't go into the details of what happened there. Koretsky scarcely managed to prevent himself from becoming hysterical, but Marina succeeded not so much in perking him up as in setting him ablaze, and he gave another good account of himself, which is always the best remedy for a man who's down in the dumps.

Marina ... she deserves her own novella, or even a novel, but let's say no more about her. Koretsky paid her further visits, and not infrequent ones, but she never played any real role in his life. He never even tried to describe her in his literary endeavours, as he often did with his friends or acquaintances, making full use of their stories, turns of phrase, blunders and jokes.

His meetings with Volskaya were few and far between, and Maxim understood that neither woman belonged to him alone: in Marina's case, this was even preferable, but the knowledge that Adele offered other men 'easy access' to her erogenous zones made his blood boil with rage.

Adeles Major and Minor

On the very first day of their acquaintance, once he'd returned from Marina's, Koretsky absentmindedly scrawled down on paper the lines he'd been turning over in his head:

Play on, my sweet Adele,
And know not grief or dread:
The Charites and Lel
Festooned your silky head
With diadem of laurel
And rocked your cradle-bed.

He reflected for a moment, and then added fiercely,

And in that bed, at last,
They took you hard and fast.

The poem surged onward, ribald and thoroughly obscene. It featured a 'frisky boy' who, 'in a trice, / Froze his poor finger into ice' – 'he goes ow-ow / She laughs, and how!' And it ended like this:

Depart that worldly throng
And heed these words instead:
The years, Adele, grow long—
Oh let's away to bed!

This proved to be the first poem of an extensive – endless, even – cycle revolving around Adele, who lent her name to a new genre: 'adeles' (plural). As Pushkin 'read his Noels', so Maxim read his adeles.

Truth to tell, in the beginning he didn't actually do a great deal of reading: he had the adeles circulated via samizdat under the pseudonym of I. Dzherkoff. The adeles began to bring Dzherkoff a degree of fame, and soon after the start of perestroika the author was to be found giving frequent public recitals of his poetry; accompanied by Dmitry Aleksandrovich Prigov and Timur Kibirov, he was occasionally applauded no less rapturously than the other two men.

Hard on the heels of the poetry came Dzherkovian prose. It too seemed to organize itself into cycles which, in contrast to their verse counterparts, came to be known as 'major adeles', for their heroine was the selfsame Adele, her patronymic alone changing from story to story, and sometimes even within the course of a single tale.

For instance, according to the story where a certain N. receives his *éducation sentimentale*, Adele Ivanovna was considered a 'Russian beauty'; the idea of this appealed to N., but then he found out that Adele was a cultured and intelligent woman and, as such, had no legitimate claim to her title, since by rights only a common woman could be thus styled. Adele Ivanovna did have light brown hair, but only on her head; she had a braid as well, but not like the braid of Venichka Erofeyev's beloved – hers ran 'from neck to bottom', while Adele's sprouted from her very arse and was black as a raven's wing. At first this appealed to N. as well, and he even began bringing Adele Ivanovna coloured ribbons and braiding them into her hair, but then he realized that something wasn't quite right, and suddenly it hit him: the real name of this fraud was Adele Isaakovna! This upset him, for in that moment he was in the midst of an intense spiritual quest: in identifying his Motherland with a slit that absorbed and swallowed up everything without exception, he had discovered a symbol (or a metaphor, perhaps?) for Russia. Whenever he went to see his woman, his celebrated Russian beauty, he would hasten to inspect the slit, at his complete disposal in those hours, and imagined he was looking down into the bottomless depths of his native country. But Adele Isaakovna! She couldn't possibly be N.'s Motherland, and he peered once more into the formerly beloved slit, thinking he was doing so for the last time, as a gesture of farewell. Then he noticed that the slit was moving and could immediately make out a string of sounds which, though incomprehensible to him, certainly didn't seem to be gibberish either. A man of tenacity, N. set about learning Hebrew, in keeping with his idea. Soon he was able to communicate quite effectively with the slit, which fully confirmed his suspicion that its mistress was really called Adele Isaakovna (at least according to her birth certificate, if not her passport), but this was no longer an issue for our protagonist who, goaded on by the slit (now his to enjoy again, though in a different way from before), walked into some hospital and brokered a deal with an experienced Azerbaijani surgeon to have himself circumcised. Having parted company with his foreskin he was taken in up to the very hilt by the ravenous slit, but Adele Ivanovna was enormously disappointed, declaring her preference for uncircumcised men and saying that she 'never would have thought that N. was actually a Jew.'

In another story Adele's patronymic was 'Alguacilovna', in a third it was 'Mitsubishievna' and so forth. Her name remained the same, though her partners did not: poor N. was to feature in only the first instalment of the 'major adeles' cycle.

Koretsky showed neither the major nor the minor adeles to the woman who inspired them, but the samizdat circulation was doing its job: the author's fame grew, as did the number of copies being passed from hand to hand; Volskaya would now always introduce herself anew each time she met Maxim:

'Adele Themistoklovna …'

'Adele Usfazanovna …'

'Adele Raschidovna …'

'Adele Ruprechtovna …'

And each time she would conduct herself in accordance with her patronymic of choice: if she happened to be called Adele Asmodeyevna that day, well …

Their meetings, though, were becoming rarer and rarer …

Kiryushin

I n the Bolshaya Polyanka apartment that had been home to Tatyana Tolstaya and her family since their move from Medvedkovo, guests were expected for a housewarming. Adochka Vilkina (or Adelaida, as she'd long been called by Tatyana), a fellow wordsmith and a fellow Leningradian living in Moscow, unexpectedly happened to phone after a while off the grid. She was invited over immediately and agreed to come, though she'd arrive a little late, she said, and leave early: her husband was away and the journey back home wasn't a short one.

'Oh, I'm sure we'll have no trouble finding you an escort, Adelaida: since when has that been a problem for you?' chortled Tatyana.

The party was picking up and blazing spiritedly into life. Only, involving everyone in the same conversation proved impossible: nobody was silent, and nobody was listening. Even stammerers did more than their fair share of talking. Adochka arrived just as one of the guests — occasionally glancing over at Andrei Lebedev, renowned for his research in the field of classical philosophy — was struggling to retain the attention of his audience after bogging himself down in the minutiae of Ancient Greek mythology.

'Who's that?' Vilkina asked Andrei, who'd come over to greet her.

'You mean you can't tell? Only Kiryushin can spout such nonsense. What perissology! Sorry: to put it plainly, he's blathering on. Listen — now it's Tiresias he's on about, in a second it'll be transvestites … Ah yes, there he goes … Ye gods! he knows the word *androgyne*. This is more than I can take.'

'Don't be like that! He's perfectly pleasant. Look how sad he is.'

'Want to perk him up a little?' interjected Verochka Malinina. 'I think we're on the same wavelength.'

'You've always been quick on the uptake,' smiled Ada, and darted a glance straight at Kiryushin, who, overpowered by the din and an avalanche of off-topic remarks, was now floundering clumsily.

Kiryushin picked up his glass and came over.

'Are you Ada?' he said. 'How incredible!'

'What's got you so excited?'

'But that's the title of Nabokov's great novel, isn't it!'*

'Oh, so that's what it is!'

'That the one where the brother and sister spend all their time screwing?' asked Verochka Malinina. 'Yes, spunky little book, that. You read it, Adelaida?'

'I have,' replied Vilkina and, paying no heed to the provocative tone, added, 'I'm not a fan of Nabokov.'

'Pasternaktsvetayevamandelstam?' said Malinina.

'You understand everything perfectly, Verochka.'

'Now there's audacity for you!' marvelled Andrei Lebedev.

'What's that, Andryusha?'

'Nowadays confessing your aversion to Nabokov is even worse than renouncing "our everything", that is, the very "sun of Russian poetry".'

'You're not going to turn me out of doors for that, are you? Though, come to think of it, you might as well: I've got to go.'

'Sit you down as if you'd never stood,' intoned L. S., and, producing an index card from a small satchel (his 'little man-pouch', as he called it), jotted down a note.

---

* N.B.: In those days Nabokov wasn't published on one-sixth of the world's landmass, and *Ada* could be read only in English (N.'s note).

'No, I'd actually better get going, Lyovushka,' said Ada.

'Don't speed ahead – best to call a cab instead,' declaimed Lev Semyonych (this was, of course, Rubinstein), and produced a second card.

'Maybe a taxi really would be my safest bet?'

'But that taxi may well never come,' continued Lev Semyonych. 'Best if someone saw you home.' And he filled out his fourth card.

'I'll see you home,' said Kiryushin, hurriedly offering his services.

'I won't say no to that: I live very far away – pretty scary walking around there alone.'

'It's an ugly world we're living in,' spluttered N., who'd already lost control over his tongue, 'when lovely ladies like that are the first to leave.'

'Yes, it's a mad, mad, mad, mad world,' put in two drunk conceptualists, endorsing N.'s assessment.

'And beautiful and fierce, too?' said Verochka Malinina, half affirmatively, half interrogatively.

'Yes, but still beautiful, beautiful, beautiful!' Tatyana proclaimed confidently. 'You shouldn't be running off like this, Adelaida. See, even an escort's turned up for you.'

'The escort deserves a bit of sympathy as well, you know.'

'Oh, my tender-hearted one!' purred Verochka and, coming up to Vilkina, quietly added, 'Sympathy's not the name of the game here: perking him up a little'd really be more advisable.'

'That an assignment?' said Ada.

'More like a prediction,' Malinina rejoined. 'You'd better get that taxi.'

'Kiryshin's sitting pretty yet again,' N. muttered enviously, and was promptly corrected:

'Sitting pretty, riding tall,' said one of the conceptualists.

'Riding tall in his saddle through old Moscow streets,' said L. S., and made a note on an index card.

Long story short, the two quit the abode of the poets.

They'd almost reached Ada's road when Kiryushin asked, blushing like an adolescent, 'May I kiss you?'

Ada silently offered him her mouth and, when his lips brushed against hers, ran a hand, impish and swift, over what needed no warming up.

'You keep yer busy hands to yourself, mister,' she said folksily, wagging a finger at him. 'Well, off with you then – end of the line.'

But then she glanced up at Kiryushin, and her heart softened:

'Oh, all right then, come on up: we'll have ourselves a cup of tea, shall we.'

They went in, and Ada, inviting Kiryushin to make himself at home, disappeared into the kitchen to fetch the tea. Kiryushin looked about him, examining the photos on the walls – and recoiled suddenly: above the bed hung a handsomely framed reproduction of a picture attributed to the mid-eighteenth-century artist Antonio Bartolini. Since a fine copy of this very picture was to be found at Kiryushin's parents' flat, he could remember it perfectly, down to the tiniest details – and not least because the peculiarity of the picture had tormented Mstislav even as a child, when his attempts to unlock the mysteries encoded on the canvas coincided with the fiery yearnings of puberty. The picture was far from being widely known; at any rate, Mstislav's enquiries went unanswered, and his parents had no sound explanation to offer either: they knew only that the copy – created, according to legend, by the serf artist of Count Razumovsky when he was studying in Italy – had come down to them from Mstislav's paternal grandmother, born Kazarnovskaya. As for the painting's author, they scarcely remembered his name and couldn't say with certainty that such an artist had ever actually existed, suspecting an old and now long-forgotten hoax.

'What's that picture above the bed?' he asked.

'You like it?' Ada called out from the kitchen. 'Well, that's the thing, you see – no one seems to know what it is, and we can't even be certain who created this reproduction, when, or where. When we got married, my husband brought it over from his parents' place and hoisted it up over the bed. Ever since, we've been shifting it from flat to flat, and it always gets hung in the same place.'

'And what's your husband's name?'

'Yasha.Yakov. Why?'

'And your surname – is it your husband's? Is he Vilkin?'

'No, his surname's Kazarnovsky.Why d'you ask?'

'No reason, no reason. Kazarnovsky!'

'Again you seem stupefied somehow. Is that as signifi-cant as my being called Ada? Would you want me to be Ada Kazarnovskaya?'

'Not by any stretch of the imagination!'

'I think you regard names as having this power that isn't proper to them. Enunciating a name – that represents a kind of divination for you, am I right?'

'Looks like it,' said Kiryushin laconically, his gaze returning to the reproduction.

The artist had evinced his predilection for mannerism and simultaneously anticipated the *World of Art*; he was somewhat reminiscent of Watteau, Greuze – and Somov, with a hint of the decadent mysticism characteristic of the beginning of the twentieth century, and not at all of the eighteenth. Winking mischievously and pressing plump fingers to their lips, frolic-some little cupids ahover in the upper reaches of the painting clutched a transparent gauze that descended to conceal in a most tantalizing manner the lower torso of a young creature whose gender could be neither discerned nor divined – even less so because the slight swell of its chest was simultaneously suggestive of a young girl's underdeveloped breasts and the soft inchoateness of an adolescent. The hairless pubis was, so to speak, *smothered* in a fabric almost invisible and yet opaque at the same time. Its young penis might have been tucked coquettishly (not bashfully) between its legs – or, equally, it might've been altogether absent (for natural reasons). And the entire figure seemed to proceed out of a sort of haze, its dark brown eyes agleam as if illuminated by a secondary source of light, its full bow-shaped lips pursed. An attempt to penetrate deeper into the picture could transform it into an obsession, which, in fact, is exactly what it had been for Mstislav ever since his teenage years.

'Why've you gone all silent?' asked his hostess as she came in with the tea.

Kiryushin took the tray from her, set it down on the table, turned around and strode purposefully towards her. Guessing his intentions, she sidestepped him and said coldly:

'Tonight I'm only serving tea.'

… In the morning, Mstislav – exhausted after having slept al the nyght with open ye – phoned Verochka Malinina. She was pleased and invited him over …

There was coffee and – well, all the trimmings besides.

The Portrait

A *throng of recollections has, like a swarm of gnats, enveloped me of late. Although I could review the fleet and wingèd form of all the mottled memories I see, I shall inform the reader of a single episode that, contrary though this might be to sense, has come to exert a profound influence upon my life. Every event, of course, is wont to leave a trace: the shackles of his past, be it serene or sad, no man escapes scot-free, nor race of men; we're all fast-clenched. But when the incident in question occurred, I must have been—well, I cannot reckon exactly. Suffice to say that it took place before I had even reached my teens, at the age of eleven or twelve. In the years that have elapsed since then, we have witnessed a metamorphosis most profound!*

One might think, indeed, that an entire century had passed, so great have the changes been. The world's been turned upon its very head! In truth, it is all very simple; so simple, I would venture, that— But no! that's another story! In those days, we occupied a stately, yellow-façaded house. I have oft remarked that the patriotic heart finds pleasure in this yellow colouration; we Russians veritably itch to ochre our fire towers, temples, spital houses and gaols—an obsession that highly ranked officials, for their part, regard as evidence of loyalty. Unswerving lines are the very quintessence of elegance for us. Inheritors of Mamai and Batu, we have learned to subjugate the eye: between square and steppe we see a correlation, and, seeking beauty in the trite and crass, desire to glimpse the distant Tula directly from Tambov.

Contrast, if you will, our tastes of a century ago: in that epoch, our aristocrats favoured eccentric curves and useless garlanded pilasters; they preferred medallion-decorated façades, and roofs bedecked with cherubs. We have newly recreated our forebears' style, exceeding silly though it is. In my youth, however, our tastes were rather less unruly: the barrack style was deemed to be bon ton, *and a quartet (or octet) of columns was duly marshalled beneath the regulation Greek pediment of each façade. In France, it was Napoleon who, in his age of bellicose plebeians, instigated this magnificence; in Russia, meanwhile, its foundations were laid by Arakcheev.*

Our own façade, too, followed this fashion. Indoors, contrariwise, the house maintained an old-school, eighteenth-century complexion, and two or three of its apartments might well have drawn an interjection of amazement from a connoisseur. The anteroom retained its bronzen lanterns, and, although little versed in art, I had a predilection for the rich ceilings of our rooms, and the mouldings on their walls.

As regards my parents, I saw them seldom: social engagements made great demands upon Mama's time, and Papa, too, was endlessly busy. Having no brothers or sisters (but grumbling aunts aplenty!), I began to roam the house uncompanied, and filled every room with fancy's flights, imagining myself the author of heroic deeds—each worthy of a novel—when but a chit, from the earliest of ages.

Reality … from boyhood on, I have found it insupportable and nauseating. Life's humdrum stream, ever flowing about me; its so-called sober, serious affairs; its prosaic pace, neither rising nor abating—all this I instinctively detest! But if I'm incorrect in this position, that is simply the nature of my temperament.

Divers and sundry plants stood in our rooms: golden-orange wallflowers, hyacinths, and—But, oh! the hyacinths, blooming azure and crimson, pallid yellow and light blue! I drank blissfully of their perfumes, in search of worlds fantastical and new, and upon each distinct aroma seemed to float the strains of a low, enchanting music.

On other days, upstarting from a spell of reverie, I remarked a withered flower nestled between my fingers. I could never recall when it was that I had plucked it, but splendid visions, conjured by its smell, enthralled me. My imagination's power transformed our house into a magic world—but life, meanwhile, pursued its wonted course.

Reality—a seasonless procession! The same old settings; the same décors; the same array of teachers, visiting in swift succession … My dancing master, positively brimming with ballet, gambolled in every Thursday, to scrape upon his shrill violin and flit about the room, all for my benefit. As for Latin, that was taught me by my domestic tutor. This pedagogue was Teutonic to his very toes: disciplined, erudite, staid and relentlessly self-critical. If ever he spied ink stains upon me, I would receive a tart reprimand. But the profundities of what he said, I confess, I understood but partly, not least when he endeavoured to disclose the meaning of the term Ideal.

He relished Strabo, esteemed Pliny, was disgustingly au fait *with Horace, and keenly fêted all flowerings of art—a penchant so seldom in evidence to-day. The principle of S-shaped lines, he affirmed, was the prerequisite of beauty; to convey his system by example, my tutor sipped and supped in an eminently serpentine manner. He was always decorous through and through, with Form his principal preoccupation:* 'Das Formlose—*zis simply vill not do,' he would oft repeat, invariably indignant if any one should fail to hone or, worse, wilfully eschew, exactitude in Form. And he portrayed Form's beauty in a histrionic manner.*

'Observe!' he would say: 'by way of illustration, I shall assume several antique poses. Now this is Zeus, as described by Homer; this, as per Praxiteles's interpretation, is Eros; and here is Milo's Venus; but, to close, I shall presently assume Apollo's shape—'

The simian likeness was unmistakable.

It is not difficult to see, Reader, that I could hardly be contented with this state of affairs; Nature, moreover, had endowed me with a sense of beauty all my own. The term may have been beyond my grasp, yet I could feel the power of a different, fresh Ideal. Although I sought it out with a great eagerness of soul, our house was less than fertile ground for such a pursuit: my pedagogue was anything but stately, and my ancient aunts had never been blest with loveliness. No wonder, then, that I dismissed these models as fundamentally unbecoming. But there it was, true beauty: my fancy found it, hung in the great Hall.

A portrait of a youthsome girl, most lithely poised. Its colours had dulled—or perhaps the light that filtered through the window curtains merely made it appear so. Upon her shoulder fell a powdered curl, her breast was adorned with a bouquet, and she clutched the taffeta trimming of her rose-filled pinafore.

'Mere decadence,' some will declare. 'An empty beauty, ruled by trite convention!' Perhaps, perhaps, and yet I was enraptured by

every fold, one subtle feature in particular teasing my brain like a riddle: although her eyes were filled with sorrow, I fancied that her lips—all rascally and cunning—were quirking upward, their edges curling wryly. The expression of her face, to my amazement, was predisposed to constant variation. I spied these metamorphoses of guise several times a day: the elusive colour of her eyes fluctuated ceaselessly, the meaning conveyed by her lips' mysterious configuration was never the same, and her gaze alternately expressed reproof, entreaty, tenderness, and coquetry.

What fate befell her, I do not know to this day: was she, perhaps, a French marquise who—alas!—met her end upon the guillotine? Or was her native city our splendid Petersburg, and did she while away her evenings at the ombre table, cordial and sharp-witted, and, thriving under Catherine, attend Potyomkin's glittering, resplendent ball, her beauty, sun-like, charming every one about her? I never voiced these questions, but had good reason for such strict discretion. Back then, I could not quash my furtive shame, but shall now discard it for good, and confess, effortlessly enough, that I was aflame with passion for the picture, somewhat to the detriment of my Latin. Love's first hello is Wisdom's last goodbye!

Korzunov

When Kirill Korzunov began to speak of the arcane nature of nudity, he had an idea about the affinity between the arcane and the sacred. Sacredness is serious to a great – to the greatest – degree. Yet it is only possible to understand the essence of the arcane in a state of revelation. Exhibition of the naked body can simultaneously engender transports of delight and paroxysms of laughter. Does comicality hide itself away in the depths of the serious, or is it the unendurableness of the sacred emanation that gives rise to the paroxysmal reaction? The cavalier tenaciously persists in looking down his lady's dress for he absolutely must catch a glimpse of her nipple as well. And that same fella laughs his head off in the disco when a skirt's (oh so longed-for!) rack spills out of her top during a dance.

O Amaterasu, resplendent in the heavens! When, after a quarrel with Susano'o, the sun goddess took refuge in a cave, the world was plunged into darkness, and not a single one of the gods' ruses could lure her out of her hiding place; but then one resourceful goddess launched into a dance and disrobed before the entire assembled pantheon! How the gods laughed! The Japanese gods were laughing Homerically! So loudly did they guffaw that curiosity got the better of the aggrieved Amaterasu, and she peeped out of the cave after all.

Let us indulge our own curiosity: what is the explanation for their laughter? The sight of a woman in the buff is hardly remarkable, especially not for the gods, and especially not in

Japan. And even if (let us assume) it really were an unheard-of wonder, why exactly is it funny?

'Dear friend, why do I have to laugh?' (This is from Thomas Mann.) 'Can a man employ the traditional or sanctify the trick with greater genius? Can one with shrewder sense achieve the beautiful? And I, abandoned wretch, I have to laugh, particularly at the grunting supporting notes of the bombardone, Bum, bum, bum, bang! I may have tears in my eyes at the same time, but the desire to laugh is irresistible – I have always had to laugh, most damnably, at the most mysterious and impressive phenomena. I fled from this exaggerated sense of the comic into theology, in the hope that it would give relief to the tickling – only to find there too a perfect legion of ludicrous absurdities. Why does almost everything seem to me like its own parody? Why must I think that almost all, no, all the methods and conventions of art today *are good for parody only*?'

Parody, Korzunov continued, is absent solely from the art of socialist realism, which only now, by dint of the efforts of others, has come to be regarded as one great big grimace, comical and yet almost painful as well. The seriousness of this art could never become sacredness, though it was precisely toward sacredness that its creators were striving; and for this reason the comicality revealed in it by the conceptualists and the hyperrealists is not inherent to it – rather, it has been introduced from without and will not bring forth the Homeric laughter of the gods.

'So that means parody is a kind of divine striptease?' asked Innochka Panina, her words accompanied by a coquettish, let-me-just-tear-this-dress-open gesture.

Kirill slowly proclaimed, after a moment's hesitation, 'That's actually the very crux of it.'

'Oh, what a serious evening this has been!' sighed Yadya Izvitskaya.

'And it simply must be rounded off parodically,' said Innochka, cheerfully chiming in. 'I suggest appointing Korzunov organizer of the concluding striptease!'

'I'm afraid I'd be underqualified for that: I'm a graduate of the School of Socialist Realism,' said Kirill, backpedalling.

'Yes, you seem to be lacking in lightness,' Yadya remarked.

'I know, I can feel a lack of inner freedom.'

'Is it manumission you're after? Need the bonds of serfdom loosened?'

'No: inner freedom cannot be bestowed, you can only be born with it, like Mozart … But how come you're known as Yadya? Are you Jadwiga?'

'Full name's Ariadna. So Adya'd be closer to the truth. Yadya's a nickname I've had since I was a child: hints at my Polish heritage.'

'D'you think the name Jogaila would suit me?'

'Oh, only if the great god of details approves.'

'Could you call me by that name?'

'I could, should the same god persuade me of the need to do so.'

'Yadenka, what's got into you?' Innochka put in. 'Call the man what he wants to be called. Forget Jogaila: I think I could even style him Agathon.'

'How generous you've been today, Innochka. You even wanted to show him your arcana. But you've got to agree that stripping off in front of Agathon's one thing, and baring all for Jogaila's quite another.'

'Doing it in the company of a Lithuanian grand duke isn't any harder. Well, go on then, ask him over: I've been meaning to do something like this for a good while now.'

'I think you've gone mad.'

'Have not. Look how meek he is. Right then, we'll get it all arranged now. Korzunov, do you agree not to lay claim to the role of Jogaila tonight?'

'I feel like a complete ass, but if that's the way it has to be, I swear I won't transgress the bounds prescribed for Agathon this evening.'

'In that case let's get into a cab this instant.'

'Hold your horses, Innochka,' Yadya quietly entreated, but it was obvious that the devil's dance had already begun in her eyes and that the hare-brained scheme concocted by Panina and unfathomable to Kirill was beginning to entice her, too.

No more than twenty minutes later the three of them were pulling up to Izvitskaya's. As soon as they were inside, Korzunov opened his briefcase and triumphantly produced a still-corked bottle of champagne he'd filched from his hosts' kitchen on the way out. In the same instant both his cheeks were smudged with the gratitude of the lady to the right and the appreciation of the lady to the left.

Yadya went to fetch the glasses, Innochka sat herself down on the sofa, while Kirill, feeling rather ill at ease, began pacing the room — only to freeze before a little picture that hung over the sofa. This was a reproduction of an old work Korzunov wasn't familiar with, but the more he scrutinized it, the more acutely he felt the pangs of recognition. The feeling was vastly more powerful than any déjà vu: he could've meticulously described any given detail with his eyes closed. There was a hint of affectation about the picture — but most importantly, it *tantalized* profoundly and unmistakably, exuding a sort of satanic charisma that titillated and aroused, almost physically tickling the erogenous zones and simultaneously inducing a feeling of actual nausea. Biondetta! Kirill recognized (or recalled) the name immediately. Gaze capricious; eyes appearing to've shed tears only a moment ago; lips pursed as if to blow a kiss; hemispheres of the breasts no more than hinted at; nipples tiny but fully protuberant; pubis hairless, not so much concealed as emphasized by the transparent fabric clinging to the model's hips and forming a most entrancing pattern of folds on her body. Korzunov was suddenly horrified for some reason: perhaps the name was not Biondetta, but Biondetto? On the other hand, who gives a devil's damn!

'Did you say something?' asked Yadya.

'No, nothing.'

'Really? Methinks you made mention of the devil,' laughed Innochka. 'He's admiring Biondetta,' she explained to Yadya, who was bustling about in the kitchen.

'Come again?' said Kirill, flabbergasted.

'*Biondetta* – that's what this picture's called, and that's all I was told when I bought the reproduction in an antique shop. The artist's name's something like Casini or Corsini – oh yes, Bartolommeo Corsini – that's it, I think.'

'Innochka gave me this reproduction the year we first met, five years ago now,' said Yadya, who'd come in with the tray. 'You like?'

'I'm n-n-ot sure …'

'Seems to me, though, that this is exactly the sort of thing you were discussing earlier on: seriousness and parody.'

'Yes, perhaps, were it not for the sly little grimace. What if the goddess in front of Amaterasu's cave hadn't suddenly flung off all her clothes? What if she'd merely lifted the hem of her skirt? Who'd laugh then? That wouldn't get you more than a smirk. Then again, there really is something sinister and ill-boding about the picture. That wicked snigger – there's a whiff of fate here, and it augurs ill. That smile isn't God's, it's the devil's – Innochka must've read that word off my lips.'

'I didn't *read* anything: unless you can throw your voice, you pronounced the word "devil" quite distinctly.'

'Well, enough about that,' said Izvitskaya. 'Open the champagne, if you would.'

'Quietly or with a pop?'

'What's champagne without the flying cork?' Innochka snorted. 'Pop away.'

Kirill shook up the bottle. The pop was magnificent: the cork hit Biondetta, while Yadya's face and chest were drenched by the powerful foamy spray. Korzunov was flustered, the ladies creased up.

'I find myself compelled to emulate the actions of the goddess in front of Amaterasu's cave,' Yadya announced. 'Laugh away, now.'

This, in fact, she had already done, her words offered not in apology but in explanation. She was sitting at table in bra and knickers.

'Go on then, do the honours, if there's anything left in the bottle.'

Enough was left for a glass each. They began to drink, their sips long, languid, yet not overly large, matching the glances they exchanged – there was something not so much languorous as lethargic, almost exhausting about it all.

'I feel awkward looking at you,' said Innochka, turning to Yadya.

'Is something bothering you?'

'Yes, this dress.'

'Let me give you a hand with that.' Yadya went up to Innochka, unfastened the zip on the back of her dress and pulled off the dress herself.

Innochka was braless, and now it was Yadya's bra that was bothering her.

Korzunov tried to join them in their shenanigans, but was prevented from doing so with a stern reminder that tonight he must not stray beyond the confines of the role of Agathon.

'Ah, so that's what that name means,' said Kirill dejectedly. 'And there I was, thinking Agathon simply implied a good man. Then again, a good man and a martyr, that's really much of a muchness, isn't it?'

'Oh, come off it! What wouldn't more than a few of tonight's guests give to endure sufferings like these! Sit yourself down in that armchair, Mister Theorist. And seize the moment.'

They fondled each other, abandoning themselves to a frenzy doubtless fuelled by the novel element in this situation – the presence of an onlooker.

Staying put in the armchair wasn't an easy ask, and Kirill leaped to his feet on several occasions, only to hear 'Down you sit, Agathon!' each time.

Now more exhausted than if he'd played a part in the wildest displays of passion, Korzunov eventually zoned out and began to reflect on how he'd got here and why, on how weird and wonderful this experience had proven. The curiosity he'd previously felt about this aspect of the life of the fair sex was indulged entirely − excessively, even − while the image of a three-way convergence that had flickered in his mind's eye earlier on lost its allure. But what he did feel, what he became most acutely aware of, was an unquenched and ever-intensifying desire for one of tonight's leading ladies, and − this needs to be double-checked, I still cannot say for certain, but it seems to me that ... devil take it! that she's Biondetta!

The waning attention of the onlooker sapped the energy of the players, and, bringing the spectacle to a muddled close, they both approached Kirill's armchair to thank him for his wonderful (impromptu) performance in the role of Agathon.

'I'd ask you not to offer me this role again,' said Kirill.

'And what *would* you ask for?' Yadya enquired.

'I've already mentioned the character,' Kirill reminded her.

'Don't you understand? We're only putting on one play, and Agathon's involvement in it is unnecessary (tonight for the first time), while any other dramatis personae are categorically unwelcome: they'd change the meaning of it all.'

'Ada,' said Kirill, 'this is Inferno. Yadya, why can't you be Jadwiga for a while? I mean, your name already is Jadwiga!'

'No, no, I'm not Jadwiga, I'm Ariadna − that's a whole different kettle of fish. Tell me then, did you laugh Homerically?'

'If that was a parody, it wasn't a funny one.'

'Does that mean you don't consider it sufficiently serious?'

'I'm struggling to engage with its sacredness. It's like someone else's religion: it can be grasped to a degree, but you can't take it into your heart.'

'Agathonchik,' purred Innochka, 'sweetheart, d'you want me to put out for you right now?'

'Stop it, Inna,' barked Izvitskaya, cutting her off with unexpected brutality and firmness.

'Agathon is dead!' proclaimed Korzunov, similarly resolved.

'And I'm ready to serve as instigator of the killing of Jogaila as well, said Yadya, smiling charismatically.

'I'll try and see to that myself,' Kirill said doubtfully.

When he was leaving, his ladies each gave him a kiss: first Yadya on the cheek, then Innochka on the lips. Back at home Kirill discovered in his jacket pocket a scrap of paper on which I. Panina's phone number was scrawled in a hasty hand. Korzunov reflected for a moment and copied the number into his notebook.

The Portrait
(Continued)

*U*nhappy with my academic floundering, my tutor sighed; his brow began to cloud. I absolutely was not ailing, he said, ascribing my condition to mere sloth and soberly affirming that 'Wer will, der kann!' And he persisted with his criticisms, and windily proclaimed that we're endowed with reason so we may control our will, and leash our errant selves with ever-growing proficiency. A devotee of Kant, if I recall, he had forgot his idol's proclamation that phenomenal forms of Dingen an sich lack free will; as for me, I soon came to believe that our wants are the result of prior ordination: despite my best and most strenuous efforts, I couldn't will myself to will what I willed not.

'Parse zis!' he demanded. I parsed ... her facial fluctuations. He gave me zeroes and admonished me; I grew accustomed to his rebukes—for diligence I've never been renowned, and, as regards the conjugations of beauty, it was not till much later that I discovered their meaning. O classicism, you do not come easily to me!

I am, in fact, a champion of classical schooling—but I do not believe that merchants, greasers or ticket boys on trains should be forced, by some arbitrary decree, to cram their brains with Virgil, say, or Homer. That era has now passed. To maximize our economic gains, we should, on every possible occasion, create more Realschulen. Yet I shall declare, too, that no glass retorts or engine steam can ever enlighten us—to this end, we can but discipline our thinking, engaging in gymnastic cogitation; and only the heavy plough of classical education is capable of turning up the virgin ground so that the seeds of learning may be sown. It is all a question of degree.

But I digress—let us return to our muttons. Unwise, imprudent boy that I was, I felt the habitual urge to probe the picture's shifting forms, and *wondered, while undressing before bed, what air the girl's metamorphic eyes would don next morning, and in what fashion they might welcome my gaze. They tempted me as an icy streamlet tempts a desert rover.*

I rose at seven; at two, having taken my daily dose of Latin and ennui, I glorified God! We then took luncheon, served at half past three, but by this time, the day was all but over; in January, the light is quick to die—a cheerless dusk is falling by four. Putting my books away, I dusted off my collar, smoothed down my hair, washed my hands, and headed picture-ward ... for observation. It was on the sly, of course, I wended there, feigning wholehearted indifference to the manner in which my charming girl might gaze upon me to-day.

A half-darkness veiled the empty Hall, but the ingle's quick, unsteady light was slung across the frescoed ceiling, and specked the wall where my dear beloved canvas was hanging. A barrel organ, whence, if I recall aright, the strains of Mozart's cavatinas always proceeded in that era, was playing in the street. Against its swirl of sound, I gazed, unblinking, at the picture. These tunes, or so I fancied, held the keys to the girl's perplexing traits. Desire rose through my soul, and rapturous delight was blent with sorrow in my breast. A slave to youth's tempestuous decrees, I scarcely understood this vague longing; and half-whispers would issue from my lips until at length the bell for luncheon rang.

At table, my face doubtless bore an expression of inanity; I daily grew more reticent and shy, incurring a deal of mockery from my parents. But my greatest apprehension was that someone might take it in his head to speak—or even to make a passing mention—*of the picture; I would far sooner face execution than broadcast my iniquitous desire. Even the most innocuous of allusions to the previous century, to Catherine's court, to* robes rondes *or powder, lace or panniers, made me quake with anxious dread.*

O, those distant, shimmering days! This is a time when, as yet uncomprehending of our own souls, we speculate brazenly, our minds fraught with endless questions, and when the merest swish of skirts excites a tormenting titillation. Mad dream of virtue with a hint of sin! I hearkened to this inner tumult; and I suddenly bethought myself that she was not entirely indifferent to my love, and now regarded me without any trace of a smirk. In this new mien of hers, I began to detect encouragement, compassion and concern ...

Kazarnovsky

Yasha Kazarnovsky was on his way back home from the resort. He was mulling over the events of the fortnight he'd spent in the south – all those flirts, all those trite conversations, Asenka, ever eager to pull at the heartstrings with a pitiful story about herself and promptly cry her eyes out afterward.

Kazarnovsky remembered that, when first setting out for the resort, he'd been firmly resolved to succumb to temptation should the opportunity arise: the time was ripe, he believed, to treat himself to a little intrigue with the merest dash of conjugal infidelity – there'd be no explaining to do later, and it'd make him and Ada quits (he had his suspicions).

He reflected miserably on his failure to act on these intentions despite having everything on a plate: the temptation itself, the availability of said temptation, the allure of the south, the gleeful spark of exhilaration – to say nothing of the fact that, if he'd felt so inclined, he could've always indulged in the theatrics of the lady with the little dog (Asenka again).

Yet it was all in vain, it was all spurned by Kazarnvosky – and not because he didn't desire it, but because he'd been incapable of overcoming a barrier of sorts constructed inside him by some higher power. His head would reel like a drunkard's and his hands hankered for female flesh, anticipating its familiar contours – but then his eyelids would close of their own accord, and, a curtain thus drawn over the scene, temptation presented itself to his mind's eye, an incomparably more powerful temptation that immediately loosened the spell of the moment, shattering it into a thousand pieces.

Curiously enough, this temptation sprang neither from the image of his wife nor from the memory of the first time he'd possessed her, youthful, pneumatic, temperamental, able to anticipate all of his movements in advance, but – so to speak – from a fiction, a vapour, a phantasm, a flight of fancy, and someone else's at that, conceived long ago: from a picture hung over the bed in their room which depicted a boy looking every inch the delicate adolescent – unriddled with acne, but replete with the sweetness and effeminacy becoming of his awkward age ('Gentle youth and lover tender, / Mine forever, have no shame').

All this bore the hallmarks of a glamour; Kazarnovsky began having serious doubts about his orientation and wondered whether he belonged to the sexual minority, though all his previous experience, coupled with his ever-fresh desire for his wife, gave the lie to this ultimately laughable hypothesis. He'd more likely undergone some psychological shift connected to the hyperbolization of his internally imposed injunction against extramarital relations – a shift now manifesting itself in extravagant fashion.

Yasha's thoughts turned to his imminent reunion with Ada, and he noted with satisfaction that no phantasm could've prevented him from relishing the prospect of intimacy with her, even though this intimacy would be achieved under the very eyes of the 'gentle youth'.

He'd just slipped his key into the front door when it swung open – no time even to rotate his wrist, as if Ada had been standing in wait for him on the other side. An embrace, then a whisper: 'The bath's been run, the bed's been made.' This was their playful watchword – a phrase from a popular East German brochure on marital hygiene designed to welcome the quick-witted husband home from a business trip with a word to the wise: your missus, it implied, has spent this entire time yearning for your return, longing for a rekindling of intimacy, but she can bear to wait fifteen minutes while you get your hygiene up to scratch. By way of reply Yasha had to enquire whether the missus herself had fulfilled her hygienic duties, and Ada anticipated his question with a dazzling smile: 'I've just had a bath myself,' she said, and let her robe fall open slightly.

She doesn't half know how to welcome you home! Yasha thought, exultant, as he climbed into the foamy bath. His thoughts and desires had already hurtled off to bed, and he was rushing to join them there. Glancing at the fresh linen readied for him, he dismissed it with a wave of the hand and, without dressing or even properly drying himself off, burst into the bedroom: Ada, heeding the advice of that same progressive East German doctor, lay waiting for him, naked bar a pair of knickers. Kazarnovsky had been conferred the sweet privilege of plucking this last line of defence from the fiery loins of his wife. Her knickers, he remarked, were slightly torn, asking to be ripped asunder, and he promptly did so, roaring with ardour and exhilaration.

'Oh! you brute!' she cried in mock fear, receiving his vigour with palpable pleasure and eagerly sharing in his ardency. Having slaked the aggression of their initial skirmish, Yasha changed position: in the heat of love he enjoyed watching his wife play the Amazon, mesmerized by the mystically beautiful cadences and fluctuations of her body. Which allowed him, without lessening the intensity of the moment, to draw out their entanglement and delay the final paroxysm – hotly desired, of course, but terminal nonetheless.

Squeezing Ada's hips, Kazarnovsky surrendered to the rhythm of her movements and, despite her ever-growing fervour, gave himself over to contemplation for a time. His sense of touch somewhat dulled, he squandered the chance to bring their duel to a simultaneous finish, deferring its already postponed finale.

'I see the resort's done wonders for your health,' laughed Ada.

'I've just been saving my strength.'

'And you've not been exerting yourself, not even a little?'

'The choice on offer out there left a lot to be desired.'

'Honest to God?'

'I swear!' he cried, and, without interrupting said exertions, raised his eyes up to the heavens.

And in that moment his glance slithered over the painting that hung over the bed – the very one that deterred him from whoring around at the resort even as it hinted at some hidden perversion. Wonderingly he eyed the tender youth, and some mesmeric effluence instantly radiated toward him from the vice-ridden boy. Kazarnovsky realized at once that he was growing limp and that there'd be no getting out of this situation with his dignity intact. And his fears would've proven correct if, literally that very second, Ada hadn't said, 'Sorry, honey, I need some time out.'

'Is something wrong?' he asked anxiously.

'You've just worn me out, you sexual maniac you,' she grumbled, changing from an Amazon into a reclining *maja*.

Kazarnovsky never did find out what had really spared his blushes that night: was it Ada's exhaustion, or was it her supernatural tact?

'Time to get up,' she said.

'Spare me a few more minutes,' he entreated.

'I can't, have to get something ready for supper: we've got guests coming.'

'What guests?'

'Mstislav Kiryushin. I met him at Tanya Tolstaya's, engaging sort of chap; he saw me home afterward, wanted to meet you – I said you'd be coming back today and asked him over for tea this evening. I reckon he might know something about you: reacted sort of strangely when he heard your name.'

'Now that *is* strange. Come to think of it, I may've come across that name somewhere before: Mstislav Kiryushin, sounds familiar.'

The Portrait
(Continued)

I began to detect encouragement in this new mien of hers. Her gaze spoke compassion and concern: 'Enough despond,' it said, 'be strong, our time is come! For we've sufficient power, you and I, to cast aside the burden of our fetters; this canvas is my prison-house, while you are treated by all as a mere child; they hound you so, and yet I have long known that you are ripe, that you were meant to come to my assistance. Help me, I entreat you! I shall trust you with the truth of my being: I'm more than paint, I cogitate and breathe! It shan't be hard, if you've enough tenacity, to gain me, tangible and fleshly-real, the fond companion that your dreams have spun—you need only finish what you have already set about doing!'

A miasmic pall descended upon me, there to remain for two whole days. How, I asked myself, bewildered, was I to act upon her entreaty, and rescue her? Where would I gain the requisite expertise to perform such an exploit? Poor wretches in the throes of febrile disease have, on occasion, been crazed by murky riddles of this ilk. 'I'll save her,' I repeated. 'But how? If she could only send me some sign!'

At the sacramental hour of twilight, while the barrel organ played under the window, I stole, observed by none, into the empty Hall, the better to meditate upon the feat I must accomplish. I racked my brains, yet fruitlessly; in the heat of my passion, I could very well have dashed them against the wall—when, all at once, the vigour of my young imagination put a speedy end to this exasperating circumstance.

Flecked by the dancing ingle-light, the girl seemed animate: she trembled, and her gaze appeared to alight upon me, eyes glistening, imploring. She abased her lashes, and her gaze, shifting now, came to settle on an ornamental clock, as if commanding me, 'Look thither!' I looked; the hour was precisely three.

And then I understood. She would never dare, amid diurnal clamour, to adorn her form with flesh and sinew. But night—oh, night's a different beast! For it's in nightly shade that miracles are born! Why had she fixed the clock with an unswerving stare? To counsel me, of course: at three that coming morning, with the entire household aslumber, I must creep downstairs and meet her clandestinely. No doubt remained: I had speculated aright! There was no limit to my ardour's power! I would clothe in bodily attire what for so long had ghosted through my sight! How had I not hitherto divined that the portrait sprang to life only under cover of darkness? And at this thought I felt an icy fire; a chill sensation danced up my spine, sweet yet eldritch, ghastly yet blissful.

Kiryushin

Kiryushin arrived at the appointed time with a bouquet of flowers and a bottle of vodka. As he was introducing himself to Kazarnovsky, he fixed him with an unblinking stare.

'Kazarnovksaya,' he said, 'was the surname of my paternal grandmother.'

'Oh, is that so! We must be related, then. Genealogy isn't my strong suit, I have to say, but we'll have to look into this, it's an interesting one. Now I realize I may've heard your name mentioned by someone in the family — and they were saying great things about you, too.'

They sat down around the table. Yasha chose his seat so as to avoid looking at the picture that had been encroaching so powerfully upon his existence; Mstislav, in contrast, chose his the better to see it, and didn't take his eyes away till a glass or two of vodka finally decided him to begin asking questions. Kazarnovsky explained that the picture — or possibly not the picture itself, but this reproduction — bore relation to some family history or other; about this history he knew virtually nothing, but he did remember that for whatever reason this particular picture was very dear to his parents and that they'd instructed him not to remove it from this particular frame. The original was the work of a little-known eighteenth-century artist, an Italian or a Frenchman named either Bartolomeo Casini or Bartholomeus Cazène.

'And what's got you so interested in this picture?' asked Yasha.

'The thing is, I'm quite familiar with it, or rather, not with the picture itself, but not with a reproduction either – I actually know it from an excellent nineteenth-century copy that used to hang in my parents' flat; there was no getting away from it when I was a kid. Back then its mysterious depravity was a source of torment for me, but now I can appreciate something about it that I was oblivious to during my troubled adolescence.'

'So what do you see in it now?' probed Ada, inflamed with curiosity.

'You know, this may sound strange, but I've become aware of this indefinable tenderness in it – a direct, unequivocal, undisguised sort of tenderness that isn't weighed down even by the slightest suggestion of irony. Yes, there's a hint of scorn or mockery in it – that can't be denied – but this is directed entirely at the viewer. As for the subject of the painting itself, this ambiguous, enigmatic subject, it's categorically scorn-free and serious to the greatest degree.'

'So you're trying to say it's devoid of the parodic quality we've become so accustomed to through our exposure to twentieth-century art?' This from Ada and Yasha both, talking over each other.

'Exactly. But I'd like to point out something that I think could escape the attention of the twentieth-century art lover. I'm not sure whether I can say what movement the artist belongs to, because of course what I'm getting at isn't a movement at all, it's simply an inclination, if that's the right word – an inclination common to artists affiliated with all sorts of different schools but united in their orientation – their sexual orientation, I mean.'

'No need to spell that one out – it's obvious.'

'Right. Anyway. The artist, courageous enough to speak openly of his unconventional orientation – and to speak of it in exactly the context where travesty is possible, and where comicality thus lurks – emphatically renounces parody and becomes inconceivably serious and tender. And so, with this in mind, I literally froze when I came across the following pronouncement in Jean Genet's *Miracle de la rose*: "For I tear my words from the depths of my being, from a region to which irony has no access, and these words, which are charged with all the buried desires I carry within me and which express them on paper as I write, will recreate the loathsome and cherished world from which I tried to free myself." This is astonishing not only in its compulsion and audacity to do away with irony but also because it represents a *stance* – a stance that's been carefully thought through, reflected upon, clearly formulated, and which, it seems, has gone completely unnoticed …'

Kazarnovsky listened to Mstislav with rapt attention, as did his wife. The topic seemed to captivate all three, although each of them engaged with it in his or her own way.

We really are relatives, this Kiryushin and I, mused Kazarnovsky. Seems to me we understand each other well, and our sexual preferences must be similar too, no doubt – And he tripped over his own thoughts, recalling that it was Ada who'd invited this stranger round tonight – a stranger who, expounder of homosexual tenderness though he might be, was nonetheless sneak-peeking *at her* from time to time, and whose words concerning the seriousness of feeling untainted by parody were doubtless unwittingly addressed *to her*.

Yasha suddenly felt as if his insides – his blood vessels, his bare viscera – had been cruelly lashed by stinging nettles. His belly shrank back at the sharp pain before disappearing completely, and all his appendages grew limp – particularly the one that had already let him down once today …

The Portrait
(Continued)

I spent the remainder of that day on my best behaviour, revising
my verbs without a single sigh and attentively reviewing all of
Latin's cases, together with the prepositions that governed them;
in an attempt to hold the least suspicion well at bay, I generally strove
to insinuate myself into the good graces of the adults. We were entertaining guests that evening, and convention dictated that I must show
my face at table. I was tormented by their dreary discussions, until at
length the time came for me to take my rest. To bed, to bed—an end to
my detention! I said good-night and sped upstairs with glee, followed
by my pedagogue.

I lay me down and straightway shut my eyes as if mightily wearied, but he remained a long time awake: I heard him pace before
the looking-glass, his forehead furrowed, and saw his German 'bacco
glowing red as he inhaled in solemn cogitation. Finally, snuffing out
the candle, he too clambered into bed, and presently drifted off—contentedly so, I should imagine—while I was stricken by a bout of fever.

But time advanced. Our visitors, perforce, must homeward now: the
drivers began to bustle about in the yard, and rivulets of light coursed
the ceiling as the carriages departed. The last of them gone, silence fell
upon the house, but the hour of my tryst was distant yet.

I shall now fall in the estimation of the ladies, shall lose all claim
to their sympathy; I know not how to excuse my conduct, and submit
myself, therefore, to their mercy, realizing full well that my reputation
stands to suffer. I cannot say why I should blunder so shamefully, but
as I awaited my hour of bliss, I fell asleep—a dream enveloped me.

That base, unseemly dream has now all but vanished from my memory,
yet what could I have been dreaming of, but her, by whom my inmost

core had been invaded? Afflicted by ennui, the girl was upbraiding my torpor; guilt weighed so heavily upon my soul that I awakened with a violent start.

My fingers quivering with agitation, I struck a match, remorseful and aghast; shadows leapt and flung themselves about the room, but my pedagogue, thank God, lay profoundly asleep. To my delighted astonishment, the designated time had not yet passed: five entire minutes remained until the stroke of three.

I dressed hastily and, a burning taper in my hand, sped from my apartment, scarcely breathing, lest any one should hear. How raucous were the pulse beats in my breast, and how dizzying the lightness in my head, as I traversed a lengthy suite of rooms, not daring gaze at a single looking-glass!

I knew the house well, knew its every room and nook—but now, enveloped in the silent pall of night, it wore a strange, uncanny aspect. My own footfalls sounded alien to me, while overhead, eccentric, fractured shadows scurried up the walls, hooked their claws into the ceiling and, never still, descended anew. Striving to pay them no attention, I proceeded ever onward.

The omened door already loomed ahead; a single step further, and my fate would be clinched! Yet I was stopped unexpectedly dead. Disbelieve me, Reader, if you must, but, by my troth, I heard a whisper in my ear. 'Retreat now, boy,' it said, 'while you can! But if you choose to enter the Hall, you shall emerge an innocent no more.'

Was this the voice of an angelic guide, or else the whisper of some furtive fear? I stood conflicted: passion and dread collided within me, even as desire was being stoked by guilt… But no! It was clear what I must do, and the hairs on my nape rose at the prospect: I made a pledge to her, and by that pledge I would abide, braving whatever trials might impend in the Hall. And so, with wrist aquiver, I rotated the handle of the lock. The door sprung noiselessly ajar; I was greeted by half-darkness, but there was pallid radiance among the gloom, a bluish glintering created by a crystal chandelier that softly swung upon its chains and conjured up the image of leaf-borne dew trembling under the light of the moon.

Then, heralding some mystic visitation, a fresh aroma wafted through the Hall: was it a trick of fancy, or was I drinking in the sweet perfume of roses? I felt a chill of trepidation, but, overcoming my body's quavering, advanced decisively toward the portrait.

Edward

As it turned out, Kirill Korzunov phoned Innochka Panina as soon as he recovered from the night he'd spent with her and Yadya Izvitskaya. This didn't happen immediately, for the impressions that night had made on him were extremely complex and needed to be carefully chewed over and digested. His mind scorched by flashbacks of the role he'd been assigned, he pored obsessively over the scenes looping in his memory – only to realize that, in fact, he was seeing nothing but Yadya. If he were called upon to reprise the role of Agathon, however, it would've driven him insane. And yet it occurred to him that he might be able to get to Izvitskaya through Innochka, as Innochka seemed keen on striking up a more intimate acquaintance – or at least that's what Korzunov concluded upon finding the scrap of paper with Panina's hastily scrawled number in his jacket pocket.

When he called her up Innochka made no attempt to conceal her joy: laughing happily and calling Korzunov her sweetheart – and not her Agathon, thank God – she immediately agreed to a rendezvous. For some reason, it wasn't at her place they'd be meeting, but at a venue he knew only too well – Izvitskaya's (she being out of town that day).

At the appointed time Kirill, bouquet of flowers in hand, stood outside Yadya's door. No sooner did he ring the bell than the door swung open, and his hand held out the flowers, but immediately shrank away: in the doorway stood a lad of fifteen or sixteen whose resemblance to Izvitskaya was so astonishing you couldn't've failed to recognize him as her brother. He scrutinized the visitor unsmilingly for a moment, then with a gloomy nod invited him inside, announcing in a voice that sounded more like a child's than an adolescent's that Innochka had told him Kirill would be coming, that she'd be a little late, and that she had asked him, Edward (he pointedly called himself by his full name), to entertain her guest awhile in her absence, though he honestly didn't have the faintest how to go about it, this being the first time he'd had to do such a thing.

Despite his self-confessed inability to entertain guests, Edward talked nineteen to the dozen, boasting slyly to Korzunov that Innochka and his sister let him in on all their secrets, convinced that a young boy could only benefit from familiarizing himself with adult life and learning to understand women at the earliest possible age: that way, he wouldn't come to regard them as creatures of mystery, which they were far from being.

Kirill listened in indescribable astonishment as Edward chattered away, pacing the room and gesticulating. Comparing the boy to Yadya, he couldn't help but marvel at the similarity of their gestures and expressions, at the identical grace of their movements; and there was a certain effeminacy about Edward, one that he found more endearing than irritating.

Even his rump is feminine, he thought.

Then his gaze fell upon the picture that had astonished him the first time he was here. He remembered the name Biondetta bursting from his lips – and *Biondetta,* it turned out, was precisely what the picture was called – remembered, too, how he'd conjectured that the title should perhaps be slightly different – not *Biondetta,* but *Biondetto* – and which today's acquaintance strangely confirmed. Examining the picture once again, running his eyes over the folds of the transparent fabric clinging to the body of its mysterious subject, Kirill suddenly felt himself being assailed by a devilish temptation: wouldn't it be something to wrap the torso of the proud-rumped boy in a gauzy fabric and, in so doing, to test the hypothesis about the creature portrayed on the canvas?

Edik-Biondetto, meanwhile, was still prattling on, but Korzunov, totally engrossed in his own thoughts, didn't hear a word, until he realized that Edward was waiting for him to answer a question.

'Sorry, what was that?' he said.

'I was just saying that Innochka's about to get here, and I'd like to arrange a little surprise for her. Would you help me out a bit?'

'And what's the surprise?'

'You've probably noticed how similar I look to my sister. I want to dress myself up in her stuff – when Innochka first sees me she'll definitely think I'm her, and after all she's asked you over because my sister's out today: can't imagine Yadya'd be too happy about you coming here. So I reckon Innochka'll be totally thrown when she sees you here with Yadya.'

'What do I have to do?' laughed Kirill.

'Give me your advice, that's all. I'll get myself dolled up, and you'll say yea or nay each time – simple as. Agreed?'

'Agreed.'

Fishing his sister's things out of the wardrobe, the boy periodically disappeared into the bathroom before emerging to perform an impression of a woman's gait while somewhat exaggerating the techniques of female coquetry, which fact was pointed out to him in no uncertain terms. On several occasions Kirill was ready to give his choice of outfit a resounding stamp of approval, but Edward, never entirely satisfied, continued with his rummaging regardless. Then he suddenly announced that he knew what'd really work, and retreated once more into the bathroom. He emerged wearing a flimsy little dressing gown and a kerchief, as if he'd just had a shower. The skirts of the dressing gown were open: the bottom button was undone. He now looked almost identical to Yadya.

'Well, how do I look?' asked the boy, smiling craftily, and, coming up to Kirill, turned his back to him and wiggled his hips.

Oblivious of what he was doing, Korzunov thrust his hand under the robe and stroked Edward's silky soft rump. It took

him some time to realize the boy wasn't wearing any under-
wear and that he must've known all along how this would end
up – and more than known: he'd actually been adding fuel
to the fire! Edik swivelled back round, and Kirill immediately
shut his eyes, horrified at what he'd done – nothing like this
had ever happened to him before.

When he opened them, he saw Edward looking at him
intently, his nostrils aquiver – though not with rage, Korzunov
twigged, and not with desire, but with an inner laughter he was
struggling to stifle.

'Yadya!' cried Kirill, finally recognizing her, and shut his
eyes again, consumed by shame and despair.

'Oh! I'd thought as much!' spluttered Yadya, convulsing
with laughter. She was speaking to Innochka, who'd emerged
from the bathroom. 'He likes boys: he's like a brother to us,
Innochka.'

The Portrait
(Conclusion)

*T*he portrait was glowing, as if bathed in moonlight. I could discern the slightest folds in the girl's attire, her face's every feature. Her eyes were replete with love and sorrow, the lids languorously rising; and, though filmed with tears, they were simultaneously afire, radiating a certain restrained power as I had never glimpsed in light of day. Afraid no more, I fell beneath the sway of luscious torment: ardent yearning blurred with languor, intermixing in such a fashion—so fathomless, so chasmic—that no word in human language could ever convey this feeling. I thought I heard some muffled call sounding forth from afar, and foretasted the Empyrean even as I sensed the looming of a black Abyss. My thoughts, meantime, ran thus: they were no lie, your promises of love! This morning you shall gain a fleshly form. I'm here! I wait! But why must you tarry so? Do you not see that I have come for you? I sought to catch her eye—and passion shuddered through my every vein, while raging jealousy (but God only knew of whom) revealed itself amid my mental throes.

But why is it that you stand stock-still! I've failed to grasp, perhaps, the implication of your glances. Too young, am I? Unworthy, in the end, of complete trust? I'm childish, then! Or, but Heaven forbid! have you surrendered to another man's advances? Who was it stole your love? And by what right? Disclose yourself, interloper, and I shall handle you!

I writhed, in waking dream, under the torment of my heart's inferno. O god of love! You're youthful as the spring, and yet your ways are ancient as creation!

But in that moment, a hissing filled the chamber, the wall trembled slightly, and a triple ding rent the night's silence in twain, compelling me to swivel and look round. What sudden transformation! The air yet heavy with the echo of that final chime, the nocturnal pall was lifted, extinguished was the lunar gleam, the lustres burst alight; the antique Hall, ashine and aglitter, was ready, it would seem, to host some dazzling gala or grand ball. Old-fashioned but somehow refreshed, it stood possessed anew of its former beauties: I saw distinctly, beneath the lustres' blaze, the new-born splendour of a bygone epoch. Was this, then, a dream? And was I still abed? But no! for my fingers were, in that very instant, running over the picture-frame: undoubtedly, I was in the Hall. And then, a scraping of sleigh-runners in the street, a trickle of plaster from the ceiling, a creak of panels, a sudden silken stirring—

I raised my eyes—and caught my breath in worshipful astonishment.

Still in her wonted posture, she was now … she had almost left the limits of the frame. Her breast, illumined by the lustres, was heaving—I plainly saw its steady fall and rise. She fought for absolute release from the picture's confines, but as yet to no avail; I sensed her every atom implore, O, will my liberation! Will it harder! I willed her free with every fibre of my frame; my fervid gaze animated her figure to an ever greater degree, instilling it with vital force. As feather grasses undulate in summer's gentle breezes, so her frilled attire streamed: I heard it swish, and saw, distinctly, the shudders of her pinafore.

'O will it harder still!' the dewy eyes beseeched. With fervour springing from my inmost core, I longed for her release. The girl grew ever more unhindered in her movements; and her fingers suddenly released her pinafore, which dropt open and disgorged a flower-fall—a flood of roses gushed into the chamber. Uncrumpling her finery, and stepping clean beyond the frame and onto the parquet, she gave the air of a damsel of sixteen who, desirous to drink the scents of May, abandons the veranda for the garden. But was this truly she? I could not say for certain, and simply stood there, struck dumb with joy yet frozen with terror. And thus we gazed upon each other, saying naught.

If I were a colonel, had I ever donned the vest of an hussar, I would surely have collected all my senses and artfully exprest my ardour, plying her with adroit compliments. But I had not, alas, been granted the gift of swagger and, embarrassed and dejected, knew not if I must halt, or else advance—yet duty goaded me to act. And so, recalling my dancing lessons, I advanced two paces, readying to bow. Unforcedly, as through its own volition, one foot drew close against the other; arms hanging loose, as per tradition, I bent before her like some pliant bough. The instant I unfolded my torso, she made me an arch curtsy.

It is all too evident, in retrospect, that a misunderstanding had taken place between us, and that she had taken my old-school bow for an invitation to a dance. I was mightily taken aback, but my bashfulness prevented me from disabusing her of this erroneous impression; and thus, all in a fluster, I offered her my hand. No sooner had I done so, than there issued forth a distant music: faint phrases of an antique minuet evocative of billy witches winging circles high above a linden tree at dusk, their thrum redolent of cellos and bassoons. My fingers scarcely touching hers, maintaining a decorous distance, we tip-toed slowly forth, solemn and unspeaking. But after two brief turns, she pulled away abruptly, in apparent expectation, and from her fresh, vivacious lips there fell a lilting laugh.

By this comportment I was much offended, and abased my eyes to maintain a semblance of dignity. 'Don't be cross, now, my friend!' she exclaimed, 'and, pray, do not chide the flippancy of my manner! You're droll! Believe me, in all my days, I've never set eye on any like you! Was it for this you blazed with such unearthly passion? You desire nothing more than a dance?'

Knowing not what to answer, I was filled with bitter anguish: what did she want, then? Why was she discontented, and displeased with me? Where, precisely, had I blundered? She made me dance! And I, her devotee, began to weep. I'm 'droll', am I? I thundered inwardly, searching for some sharp riposte and thinking myself ready to detest her. My blood grew turbulent with indignation; suddenly, however, she pressed her visage to mine and assuaged my ire: I felt the flame of a fleet and teasing kiss upon my cheek, and, to my delight, heard the whispered words, 'Don't cry! I love you!'

Flooded by unfathomed bliss, I tenderly was clasped, all faint, against her alabaster breast. My thoughts grew dim, reason and consciousness gradually receding. I felt her embrace, the live touch of her young shoulders. My circumstance occasioned not dismay, but sweet *delight in me; I relished this fading out of life, and slowly, pleasure-drunk, I lost myself, and fell into a swoon or slumber …*

I forget how I regained possession of my senses, but day had already broken by the time I came to. I was lolling on a divan in the Hall, relations bustling all about me. Racked by the throes of fever, I burned and quivered, straining to breathe, my thoughts confused and disordered— but all the while, I held a withered rose …

A telling token of the night's events! A mad, frenetic dance began within my chest, and I stole a furtive look at the picture. I detected a phantom about the girl's lips—the ghost of a smile; and her bouquet, I fancied, was a little crumpled. Yet she had resumed her previous pose: her lissom form, which I had so often scrutinized, was immobile, her fingers clutching, as they had always done, the taffeta trimming of her pinafore.

My relations, meantime, were pondering the nature of my malady. Mama insisted on measles, but my aunts preferred a different diagnosis: scarlet, surely! As for my pedagogue, he was arguing vigorously with our physician; but I caught nothing of their debate, save for two frequently recurring Latin terms: somnambulus *and* febris cerebralis …

The Artist

The artist Yakov Novodomsky gazed fixedly at the wall of his studio: as often happens, he had gleaned from the pattern of the wallpaper a fragment that resolved itself into an altogether extraordinary figure. The only peculiarity was this: while the curious image usually tends to disintegrate as soon as the beholder's gaze is averted, here it was actually possible to approach it for a closer look, even have a go with a magnifying glass! Novodomsky tried all manner of things. He made an effort to isolate an example of the same phenomenon on the opposite wall, but no matter how hard he looked, he could find nothing of the kind; then he experimented with turning round suddenly and walking along the wall, altering the angle from which he could see the fragment and making sure not to focus his eyes on it, but not even affected absent-mindedness could prevent him from discerning the picture in evidence on the wallpaper. Furthermore, this picture was possessed of some sort of illusionistic effect: at times it would curl up and become quite tiny, as if it had been sucked into a funnel, with little eddies round the sides, no less – the absolute likeness of a whirlpool – and at others it unfurled to such an extent that it appeared to leave the confines of the walls – a whirlpool turned inside out.

Yakov had already been persecuted by this glamour for several weeks, and he decided to break its sway by means available only to people of his profession – he would commit the image to canvas. It was then that the lady on the wall (for it was a lady) betrayed another of her quirks to him: she was loath to take on the role of sitter. No sooner did Novodomsky take up his brush and raise his eyes to look at the 'model' than he lost sight of her, just as the photographs he tried to develop revealed nothing more than an unremarkable bare wall, even if the fragment in question was enlarged many times over. It was clear, then, that he must paint from memory, a circumstance which ultimately he didn't consider all that undesirable for the work at hand. He'd felt the great intensity of the initial impulse, which would be followed by creative freedom, inspiration, and, if luck was on his side, revelation – that is to say, all the suffering and pleasure engendered by artistic toil. What more could he want?

And he was willing with the kind of inner willingness that customarily permitted him to withstand, without breaking down, a considerable period of the most severe pressure, during which he devoted his days to rendering on the canvas a species of actuality, transfigured from something essentially phantomic: precisely what amateurs take for the material of life, or pure and absolutely objective reality.

He was disconcerted only by an obstacle of a – well, of a *theoretical* order. Novodomsky never copied anything – he acted on nebulous impulses to create something artistically distinct, but what needed depicting in this case had been assigned or simply gifted to him in advance (by whom, for God's sake? by whom?). Everything had been arranged and predetermined, and it seemed somehow improper to make use of it (abuse it?), like furtively appropriating someone else's belongings. In vain did Yakov recall that all creators exploit such gifts of fate without compunction: they *eavesdrop on a shard of music / And dub it, jokingly, their own*, while *verses fluently dictated / Alight upon the snow-blank page.* The feeling of disconcertion did not pass.

Then he thought that untimely self-torment would serve no purpose whatsoever – in the words of Napoleon, 'on s'engage et puis on voit'. He had to grasp the nettle now and wait until later to discover whether his was the path of the copier or whether his creative ability would carry the day. Nobody was forcing him to imitate: could he not treat the wall like any ordinary material, even if he had no idea who was responsible for its provision? But there was the rub, for the lady on the wall wasn't indifferent to proceedings – she unquestionably possessed volitional authority, and her power over Novodomsky became manifest when she began to subject him to demands he found quite incomprehensible.

For one thing, he felt the need, for reasons unknown to him, to christen this wall-creature, this 'signora', as she initially appeared to him, and Yakov promptly named her Henriette, although he could've sworn that never, not for love or money, not even in the most extreme of circumstances, would he be able to recall of the existence of such a girl's name – it simply wasn't in common usage, and, in view of the lady's exoticism, he was far more likely to style her Antoinette, Diana or Bianca. It was unclear which epoch Henriette belonged to and whether her array was masculine or feminine: she was wearing either flesh tights, or close-fitting trousers, or simply modern leggings. Either a page's finery or sportswear. Her hat resembled a loose beret, supported by her right hand, on the fourth finger of which a ring set with a large diamond was plainly visible. A complete absence of style, and perhaps even taste, at first glance, but something told Yakov that everything here was a sign waiting to be deciphered, that none of it was arbitrary, and that it all constituted a well-defined system whose every single component was articulate and functional.

It followed, then, that until these hieroglyphs and this idiom could be deciphered, he might as well forget about the very notion of creative freedom – if he did not, the result would be deceit and arrant nonsense. Novodomsky studied the image on the wallpaper, attempting to memorize it as precisely as possible, took up his brush and – The image disappeared. Overcome either by relief or by exasperation, he would mutter over and over again the words, 'You shall forget Henriette, too', which infiltrated his thoughts relentlessly although he couldn't say where he'd come across them.

And forget her he did! But no, not quite: he managed to summon her to mind – and simultaneously failed to do so.

It seemed to him that he knew her every trait and gesture, knew, too, the attitude of her head, and yet his hand hung help-lessly over the canvas, unable to make even so much as a stroke. Novodomsky set his brushes aside and resumed in pencil. But his sketches were weak and clumsy and utterly ineffectual, and not only did the artist tear them to shreds but − if it is not indecorous to say such a thing − he pounced upon them with sadistic cruelty and roared:

'Have it! Have it! Up yours, Henriette!'

In those moments he thought that if the same thing had happened to him in the presence of a model and he was simi-larly incapable of completing a sketch, he wouldn't think twice about killing the model, throttling and disfiguring and dismem-bering her. To the bin with you, where you belong! Calm and controlled. That's the only way. Let's try again. That curve there, yes, that's it. This is tasteless rubbish, that's what it is! Worthy of the brush of Ayvazovsky! You pillock, have you completely lost the plot? This isn't rocket science! Right, that's it.

Novodomsky put his work aside. He had to concentrate. Or rather, take a break and concentrate afterwards. This situa-tion gave rise to two possibilities. He could (1) go down to his watering hole, or (2) go down to the museum − either while away a few drunken hours in the company of sympathetic tip-plers or stroll around looking at other people's work (which translated to convincing himself of the veracity of his principles versus picking up a fresh idea from an unfamiliar colleague). And nothing was stopping him from paying a visit to both venues in turn − the exhibition first, and on to the watering hole later.

Right then − to the museum. To the Pushkin. Old Italian masters on display there at the moment. Just what the doctor ordered.

That was indeed a wise move. The exhibition showcased many magnificent portraits he'd never seen before, not even in reproduction, and he devoured them all with the entirety of his being. He stood before Sebastian del Piombo's *Dorotea* − he was captivated by the gesture of the young woman in the guise of

Lucretia on the canvas of Lorenzo Lotto ... Parmigianino ... Pontormo ... And that's – but that's –

Novodomsky began to choke: he'd swallowed the wrong way, and he broke into a fit of coughing. He turned scarlet, his eyes goggled and his hands snatched frenziedly at the air, and then someone helped him find his way to the toilet, where he spent several minutes struggling to overcome the paroxysm suffocating him. Returning to the room, Yakov made an immediate beeline to the offending painting. The name of the artist was not certain – it was presumed to be Giovanni Giacomo Bordolini, a second-rate mannerist. At any other time Novodomsky would've walked past without even pausing to look. In the centre of the canvas was a man in late middle age, his squint-eyed gaze seemingly directed toward some unseen object, and superimposed onto the semidarkness of the background was the bright little form of a signora who – what's the simplest way to put this? – who, to all intents and purposes, was Henriette. The painting was entitled *A Portrait of the French Nobleman Henri de la Maisonneuve.*

Nothing could deter Yakov from meticulously examining – and, above all, above all, committing to memory! – this already rendered image of Henriette. The painting had attracted no attention but his own, he stood beside it alone, and when, now enlightened and in no doubt as to what he must do, he tore himself away from the canvas and saw standing before the *Madonna with the Long Neck* a young woman wearing close-fitting trousers and a loose beret, this image corresponded so closely to his newly devised plan to track down a live model that he almost choked once again. The woman approached and, speaking rapidly as if she had finally found a suitable pretext to accost him, asked:

'Do you need some help? I've got some menthol lozenges handy.'

'Have we met?' said Yakov by way of reply.

'No, but I know who you are – you're the artist Novodomsky, aren't you? I've seen you once before, at a *vernissage.*'

'Why didn't you make yourself known then?'

'That time I didn't have any lozenges to offer.'

'Did I swallow the wrong way when I saw you, like I did just now?'

'In point of fact you did.'

'What an inane oldster I am.'

'Go easy on the self-deprecation, please.'

'All right then, we'll replace the word *oldster* with a phrase that sounds similar but means something else entirely: *bold satyr*.'

'I agree, that works better. But that means the next move is yours.'

'You really know how to boost a man's courage, don't you? Well then: will you be my sitter?'

'There's no one I know of who could snub Novodomsky if he made such a proposition.'

'I have to tell you, though, it wouldn't be a portrait of you: only I need a model for something I'm working on at the moment, and you'd be just the ticket.'

'Your wish is my command.'

'Excellent. And — a slightly belated enquiry, I know — but what might your name be?'

'Ariadna. But you can call me Adya.'

'Adya, what say you we go down the boozer? Are you sure you can stomach an oldster's company?'

'Again you're — '

'All right, all right: you sure you're not afraid of a satyr's society?'

'Just the thought of it makes me giddy with joy — and curiosity.'

'How about the Central House of Artists? No, no, of course not. Let's go to "Petrovich's".'

They set off on foot toward Myasnitskaya. Novodomsky bought some flowers by the Rumyantsev Library and presented them to Ariadna together with hyperbole no less florid. She accepted the flowers with pleasure, but winced a little at the compliment:

'Let's try and keep the triteness to a minimum, shall we? All we have to do is pretend we're husband and wife, long since divorced, but old friends nonetheless.'

'I'd rather be a new friend, and as for divorce, I'd prefer to consider that a future possibility, and even then only on account of our difference in age.'

'That's no ground for divorce as far as I'm concerned.'

'Does that mean our union is to live on?'

'For ever and ever. And I hope enough's been said to stop us posturizing in front of each other from now on. Look at me: there's no need for equivoques or euphemisms in my company. As for my own antics, which you'll soon see – well, they're in my nature: it all stems from my flawed character, and not from any desire to clown around.'

These deliberations took them all the way to 'Petrovich's' with his immutable 'Petrovich is glad to see you.' And indeed, a good few patrons acknowledged the newcomers with a word or two of greeting – some saluted Yakov, some Ariadna, and some even saluted them both. Novodomsky's attention was drawn to two gentlemen who'd raised their glasses to Adya – one big and bulky and bearded, the other small and scrawny and bearded.

'Who's that?' he wondered aloud, sympathetically eying the comic pair.

'The big one's Beilis.'

'Don't know him.'

'And the little one's Lev Semyonych …'

'Rubinstein? So that's what he looks like, then.'

'Hava Nagila' began to play – Hanukkah was approaching, and the Russian people sought to congratulate the Jews present in the room on the occasion. Everyone leaped up to dance, with those of a Slavic appearance pulling off the turns and twirls most expertly of all. Ariadna was asked to dance by Beilis, who, despite his corpulence, moved fluently and not without a certain elephantine grace; he chattered away without taking a breath and something he said made her burst into heady laughter. When the dance was finished, Beilis escorted his lady back to her table, ceremoniously expressed thanks to Novodomsky, and Ariadna gave him a farewell kiss on the cheek.

'You've known him for long, then?'

'Oh, ages. We're friends.'

'Does he joke a lot?'

'Not always. But just now he was saying that music like this is a good accompaniment to Jewish anecdotes, and he told me a few – really funny stuff.'

'His eyes seemed sad.'

'You noticed, did you? That's right, they are, but even so, he likes a bit of fun and he's easy to be with.'

'Won't you introduce us?'

'Of course I will. But not today, if you don't mind: I wouldn't want you two to strike up a frivolous, what-are-you-drinking sort of acquaintance. He's familiar with your work and talks intelligently about it. As a matter of fact, it was through him that I first heard about you.'

They drank some vodka, ate a couple of Petrovich's fancily named Chicken Kievs, and fell silent, for the music was loud, the turns and twirls were becoming ever more frenetic and they found it impossible to talk without overstraining their vocal chords. They looked at each other. Bending to his ear, Adya shouted:

'Are you matching me up to your canvas, or is it the canvas that's being matched up to me?'

'It's odd: that's how things *should've* played out, but, if I'm being honest – and I've surprised myself, actually – I've completely forgotten my work in your company, which is unheard-of for me, especially considering the brainwave I had the moment I saw you: there she is, I thought, there's my model.'

Another lengthy silence followed – the kind of silence that ensues when everything's been said and the merest half-word or half-gesture ensures complete mutual understanding. Which is precisely what engrossed them now: they were interpreting, intuiting, investing.

Novodomsky called over a waiter and paid the bill. They waved goodbye to their acquaintances, climbed the stairs and stepped out into the street. Yakov glanced questioningly at Adya.

'I'll do everything the way you want it,' she whispered, sliding her arms around his neck, 'but I won't go to bed with you, at least not while I'm your model. And not at all because I don't want to, quite the opposite: women are less restrained in their desires than men, and I'm no exception. But I know this is the way it has to be, and don't ask me how I know, or why. If you see fit to insist, I won't be able to deny you, but please, have patience, don't rush in: spend the night alone and think it over.'

Not a single one of these words surprised Yakov: on the contrary, he was almost waiting for them to be expressed. He kissed her eyes and said, 'I did warn you, I'm an oldster and I'm in no hurry to get anywhere – I really do need to spend tonight alone thinking things through.'

He saw Ariadna into a cab and headed home himself, reflecting on the events of the day, on how much had happened. He mechanically removed a long dark thread from his jumper and, realizing it was from Ariadna's outfit, didn't discard it, but began coiling it round his finger like a young man bent on discovering his beloved's initial. 'A', he said, and twined it once, 'B', twice, 'C', thrice, and so on until he reached 'H', and twined the thread a final time. Yakov repeated the procedure: the result was the same. He broodingly wound it and rewound it all the way home and, when he was getting out his keys at the door, it slipped out of his fingers and he decided not to pick it up.

Wasting no time, Novodomsky produced his pencils and paper, intent on encapsulating what he remembered of the day. He worked with abandon until five in the morning, and there she was, Ariadna, peering up at him from the sheet, for in those hours Novodomsky entertained thought of nothing else. He was about to put the drawing aside when some impulse compelled him to look up at the wall – and he saw that Henriette, whom he'd all but erased from his mind, now occupied the entire space from the floor to the ceiling.

Novodomsky had just enough time to think, My hour has come, and with an already altered hand he annotated the drawing with the wholly incomprehensible words, 'You shall forget Henriette, too.'

PART TWO

Notice

Such was the manuscript in the envelope.

What can I say about it? I was struck by the combination of unmistakable professional know-how and an ultimately touching helplessness vis-à-vis the organization of the material: the ragged composition; the excesses of emotion, inadmissible for an experienced littérateur; the inability to get to grips with extra-literary – or, put simply, everyday – allusions; the constant insinuations of certain circumstances which I (*I*, rather than anybody else; *this*, at least, I've understood) must puzzle out.

This unquestionable challenge, whether to a contest of literary craft or else to a personal (male) joust, ought without doubt to be taken personally, and I do, of course, accept it, though as regards literary pretensions, I have none, or almost none, in the present case: this isn't my province and, furthermore, a certain prescriptiveness about the task frightens me – I'm not a kid any more, am I now, to go in for literary exercises.

In picking up this gauntlet, though, am I preparing for an ordinary duel, or am I merely firing off gruff rejoinders to dainty barbs? Well, I wouldn't want anybody to jump to either conclusion: I haven't the slightest animosity towards N., and nor do I take offence at his barbs, if only because they're invariably wide of the mark, although their target is, it has to be said, a very specific one – or at least I've recognized myself as being precisely that target.

The constraints I'm going to impose on my own text shall, I think, be related to the role of commentator, which I shall endeavour to fulfil and whose bounds I'll overstep only rarely and in cases of extreme necessity.

As I have already made clear, N. wrongly suspected that Adele and I were involved. Not so: we were simply long-time friends – I knew her before she was married – and at times I was called upon to play the role of her confidant and advice-giver. I cannot say this role came easily to me or that I willingly set about performing it, but I almost always took pride in the fact that Adele's choice had fallen on me. I was devoted to the extraordinary freedom that breathed in this woman's soul, and always grew enraged when quipsters riposted to my rapturous remarks by joking that a stranger's soul is always obscure, but as for *bodily* freedom, well, she certainly had bags of *that*. Everything she did radiated freedom, and I cannot recall any occasion when her lightsome gait failed to turn the head of every passer-by as she walked across town.

In the first episode of the manuscript sent to me by N., Adele's surname is given, not incorrectly, as Volskaya – but this was her married, rather than maiden, name, while the ridicule poured by the author on that of her husband ('Kamper') stems from nothing more than the fact that he really was holidaying somewhere in the south at the time. I myself was entertaining guests on the day N. met Adele, and it was over at mine that the dinner party described on these pages really took place; ditto the (sometimes pretty accurately recounted) conversation. Only Koretsky's monologue consists of remarks made by several different interlocutors, including N.'s and, naturally, my own. I remember that the question of male-female opposition engaged me as much as it did N., and we spoke of it often, citing examples from antiquity and alluding, as erudition permitted, now to Aristophanes's *Lysistrata*, now to Lucian. Koretsky – in whom one cannot fail to recognize an attempt at self-portraiture on the part of N., but whose character is undoubtedly also suggestive of yours truly – infuses his speech on the subject of male and female principles with a certain tinge of metaphysico-existential sorrow. And it is this sorrow that N. transforms into a foundation for a love affair, thereby predetermining both the character of the nascent liaison and the denouement of this as yet embryonic relationship from the very outset. And so Adele – I mean Adele the literary heroine, not my friend Adele – was induced into the type of behaviour described in the manuscript by the author of the text, the qualities of the prototype notwithstanding.

It's plausible that something similar happened between real people, too. I'm in no way attempting to stand up for my friend, I'm merely pointing out that there's no more wilful intent or female infernality to be found here than a predeterminedness or apriorism brought about by a somewhat unexpected male self-abasement on the part of N. An immediately declared capitulation cannot become a solid basis for a love story. It can only be a story of defeat, or a whole string of defeats. A man whose face speaks of a need for consolation will never find that consolation in the places he seeks it, only elsewhere – but is it really consolation? Fortunately, N. understood this at least as an *author* (he should, in fact, have grasped it earlier on with his *male* intellect; to be honest, I cannot conceive how, given his substantial life experience, he could have still been ignorant of this by the time he met Adele).

And so, flitting around Adele we have Marinochka, Verochka, Innochka, all eager to console and take care of the poor wretch ('sufferer' would be much too inappropriate in this context). I have to affirm, though, that I myself could reel off a dozen-odd female names linked with N.'s this whole time – he's guilty of no truth-bending in this instance. But how exactly he has managed to overlook the pitifulness – as opposed to any tormentedness – of his character, remains a mystery to me. The author, I suppose, identified too strongly with his protagonist, or, put more precisely, burdened him all too heavily with his personal problems.

Adele, as per her old habit, took me into her confidence at the very beginning of their short-lived liaison, and didn't neglect to speak with me later, after she'd definitively deflected his outpourings. I cannot say, of course, that I know the 'ultimate' truth, but I have, in any event, heard out both sides. And – given N.'s extremely loud and shrill lamentations – I'm compelled to give the floor to our heroine. Damn it, how infectious is this state of being entangled in real-life events – you can't help but start confusing character with prototype! Not only N. but I myself am now calling my friend a 'heroine' instead of using her own name. What, in fact, is the need of giving characters real-life names! Granted: characters can, in some measure, *represent* real individuals – but they're not the individuals themselves! What purpose does it serve, anyway? How're disguised characters any worse? The disguise, moreover, can be reduced to a veil of such transparency as to make an open secret of the author's intentions, while observing the conventionality essential to any work of art. Though younger than N. and, I daresay, a better judge of modernist art, I'm prepared to fight until the last to observe certain conventions, even if I'm labelled a fuddy-duddy conservative.

N., though, doesn't even suspect what sort of blow I'm capable of dealing him (and deal it I shall!). Or, more accurately, he has no idea about the surprise concocted for him by Adele herself. After she died, you see, a large folder was discovered in her desk drawer; in a note attached to the cover and addressed to her legatees, Adele instructed that the folder be given into my keeping, its contents left undisturbed. I have therefore come into possession not of *one* manuscript, as N. supposes, but of *two* – with identical rights over both!

In my view, Adele's literary prowess is beyond question. Her sense of style, the balance of the composition, the well-proportioned parts; even the raggedness of the sections creates the impression of rigorous forethought. Whenever the text masquerades as a diary, it is evident that Adele, for her part, never deluded herself even for a moment about the limits of 'candour' and 'sincerity', fully aware that, ultimately, your diary is never written for yourself, no matter how intimate it may be or how secret you keep it. Adele, I believe, was vaguely regarded by N. as a potential writer. It's not for nothing that one of the episodes of his opus describes her as Adochka Vilkina, a friend of Tatyana Tolstaya's and a 'fellow wordsmith'.

No, I'll never be able to keep my overhasty promise of remaining faithful to the humble role of commentator. Not even close! Am I really supposed to content myself with the task of a lowly interpreter or corrector when I have texts like these in my possession? Not on your life! And bearing in mind that N. himself has challenged me to a literary duel ... Well, I'll happily oblige!

Having accepted N.'s challenge, I was – truth to tell – tempted by the idea of using Adele's writings without revealing their authorship. My initial intention was to make it seem as if I were employing novelistic devices, and, now in character, riposting to his fabulations (and speculations!) with my own inventions, devised to make things all the more painful for N. by dint of revealing, or rather, retrospectively prophesying, the real events of his story. Then I decided that this would be departing somewhat from the gentlemanly code of conduct; as well as admitting to direct quotation of Adele's writings, I must, however, also declare that I have ceded to the temptation of fleshing out scenes omitted by my friend, whether due to her modesty or else on account of her literary taste and sense of tact. Let N. himself figure out which one of us has authored what! This is how I have chosen to take up his gauntlet! Each of his novelistic episodes shall be counterpoised by another episode whose authorship and co-authorship shall remain undisclosed.

Come to think of it, though, there's no avoiding a number of explanatory notes: certain parts of N.'s manuscript are so obscure that they require spelling out, and sometimes you're even subjected to the old nudge-wink routine – Get to the bottom of this, man! N. seems to be saying, or don't you have what it takes? In one case, I have to admit, I really was stumped, or at least semi-stumped. I'm referring to those sections of the manuscript which, composed in the stylized language of the mid-nineteenth century, recount an early adolescent experience involving an animated female portrait. At first I was much taken with this stylization, thinking it highly accomplished and masterfully crafted. Then I began to 'doubt some foul play', and the longer I considered the matter, the more justified my suspicions appeared to be. Scrutinizing the visual dimension of the text, I noticed what amounted not so much to a regularity or rhythmicity as to a certain uniformity of paragraph length, and it was then that I hit upon the idea of a stanzaic structure. Might we be dealing with a narrative poem here? But why would anyone compose a poem only to write it out in prose, and such antiquated prose at that?

My thoughts, however, were already moving in that direction, and a series of none-too-tidily concealed rhymes soon came to my notice. Let's consider, shall we, the very first paragraph of the text. By way of reminder:

> A throng of recollections has, like a swarm of gnats, enveloped me of late. Although I could review the fleet and wingèd form of every mottled memory I see, I shall inform the reader of a single episode that, contrary though this might be to sense, has come to exert a profound influence upon my life. Every event, of course, is wont to leave a trace: the shackles of his past, be it serene or sad, no man escapes scot-free, nor race of men; we're all fast-clenched. But when the incident in question occurred, I must have been—well, I cannot reckon exactly. Suffice to say that it took place before I had even reached my teens, at the age of eleven or twelve. In the years that have elapsed since then, we have witnessed a metamorphosis most profound!

My suspicions were aroused by the following phrases: *enveloped me—memory I see—contrary though this might be; like a swarm—wingèd form—I shall inform; be it serene—must have been—reached my teens.* I believe, too, that *trace, race* and *place* may constitute a triple rhyme. Isn't that a few rhyming possibilities too many? I'm convinced the source text has a rhymed form. But I must confess that I've not managed to identify it: I couldn't find the original in any book, and do not assume that anything comparable is to be found in the oeuvre of N. himself.

Admittedly, only the first paragraph of this strange text offers such a wealth of concealed rhymes; subsequent discoveries may be written off as far-fetched speculation or conjecture. Is N. dropping a hint of sorts, or is it that, being new to this game, he initially keeps his verse 'translation' too close to the original prose, honing the requisite flexibility only later? This question is one I cannot answer.

Thinking back, though, I do remember N. once telling me a story about an antique chest he'd inherited from someone or other, and which disgorged a certain manuscript into his keeping. If I recall, N. then came up with the idea of a kind of literary game, intent on roping not only writers but professionals across the humanities – historians, psychologists, sociologists – into playing. He would read the manuscript aloud, either in its entirety or in part, and offer his listeners the task of reconstructing the end of the tale, or else that of delineating the character of the author and the era of composition. The piquancy of the subject matter also presupposed a psychoanalytic approach to the homework. It's possible that he had this very narrative in mind even back then. I don't know whether N. accomplished his undertaking in some literary salon or whether he saved the material to be used in this game for later, employing it in the manuscript I was sent. If I've understood N.'s intentions correctly, I have, in all probability, become his sole opponent in a contest that is already underway, and must, therefore, assume the roles of all the expected participants, including the psychoanalyst. Well, looks like I'm going to have to pick up this gauntlet as well!

But this rationalization is becoming too long-winded for my liking – it's almost as if I'm trying to justify myself to someone. And yet I don't consider myself in the least at fault. *Quod scripsi, scripsi!* And that's enough!

Adele

The guests were many, their liveliness ever increasing. Almost all of those present were long-time friends, and if someone did happen to be new to the fold, the stresses and strains of striking up a new acquaintance would quickly be overcome.

The conversation was general. A few jokes, a little gossip; then, not unusually, the men proceeded to poke fun at the fair sex, while the women, cheerfully defending themselves, evocatively portrayed male shortcomings. But the evening's tone grew ever more serious; some imperceptible turn in the discussion brought literary examples, mythology and archetypes into play, raising the question of male and female principles.

For a short while everyone's attention was fixed on Maxim Koretsky, but his manner of speaking was too literary, and the ladies, who tolerate no abstractedness in these questions, could not conceal their disinterest; then one of the wiser – or perhaps simply one of the more enterprising – gentlemen slyly struck up a playful discussion with a neighbour. This localized flirting soon infected almost all of those present, until Adele Volskaya alone continued to persevere with Koretsky's theorizing, supplementing it with singularly subtle and well-thought-out questions and astounding him with her unexpectedly broad scholarship both in the field of classical mythology and in provinces considered to be exclusively male. It seemed to him, at any rate, that what's known as male nature held no mysteries for Adele, as if she'd not only known many men, and known them well, but had, if only fleetingly, belonged to the opposite sex herself.

'It's stifling in here, don't you think?' said Maxim.

'Yes,' Adele replied, 'all this flirting does rather take your breath away ... Shall we pop out?'

They slipped inconspicuously from the flat. When they were downstairs, Adele asked:

'Have you ever worn a moustache?'

'Why d'you ask?'

'A slightly silly look's never done a handsome man any harm. And besides, a moustache is so nice and prickly.'

'Whereas I've heard it described as ticklish and distracting,' said Koretsky, already drawing her towards him.

When they managed to break free of each other, Adele wryly observed:

'Looks like we can't leave the flirting behind even here.'

'What, you feeling breathless here as well?'

'No, but I'm all shivery – wouldn't mind taking refuge somewhere with four walls.'

Before she could finish, Koretsky flagged down a car and gave the driver his address.

'Shall I put the kettle on?' he asked when they came in.

'Do you want warming up ... or ... cooling down?' quipped Adele.

She'd hit the nail on the head. Koretsky was indeed putting off the moment of intimacy. Something was bothering him. Either he believed that it was she who'd been calling the play from the outset, which was certainly the case, or he was simply unsure of himself that evening – and, as it soon transpired, justifiably so. He was hesitating, and not because he'd planned an unhurried, tormenting sort of love which would gradually build into a frenzy, as he'd done on previous occasions, but because he felt somehow disquieted, completely bewildered and incapable of rising to the occasion. He failed to regain the upper hand, and even when it came to the unbuttoning of his own shirt, Adele attended to it herself.

'Adele ...,' he whispered.

'Shhh,' she breathed, pressing a finger to her lips, 'I'll handle it, I'll handle it ...'

She certainly did handle more than her fair share ...

Ada

Kiryushin had spent hours wandering the rooms of the Pushkin, engrossed in an exhibition of works by the Italian masters of the High Renaissance that had been brought to Moscow from museums across the world. He'd lingered by Pontormo's *Woman with a Small Dog*, from the Frankfurt collection; he'd pored over the magnificent portraits of Parmigianino, literally spellbound by the 'magical hyperrealism' of the *Madonna with the Long Neck* from the Uffizi, and even more so by the portrait of a young woman known as *Antea*, from Naples.

But Kiryushin had been captivated most of all by the work of an artist whose name he'd never encountered before, and which, try as he might, he couldn't remember afterwards. It might've sounded like a cross between Bellini and Bertollucci, or perhaps it absolutely didn't, but it certainly began with a B. This was a portrait of a signora executed with an utterly astounding degree of undisguised and, it might be said, nonchalant, or better yet, insolent, conventionality, on one hand, and with a verisimilitude verging on the terrible clarity of a mirage on the other. The background was an even gold, the figure seemingly flat as a result, but at the same time protruding menacingly beyond the confines of the canvas. The lady was portrayed full-length, her left flank turned towards the beholder and her face shown in three-quarter profile; her left leg was bent at the knee, as if she were taking a step forward and simultaneously hiding her shame, even though this was already partially obscured by a diaphanous veil that twisted eccentrically around her body and clung to her slight breasts with their barely protuberant nipples. Knees disagreeably pointed, fingers and toes extraordinarily long and curving upwards, recalling in their strangeness the anatomy of a grasshopper's extremities. Right hand extended, thumb and index finger pinched together as if clutching the abdomen of a newly caught butterfly – but no butterfly to be seen! Little finger, tapered implausibly at the (clipped!) nail, tending affectedly outwards and upwards. Gaze concentrated on a particular point, so steady and unchanging that the light-brown eyes have filmed over. Head almost disproportionately large, with a rounded, prominent brow, not unlike those to be seen on the canvasses of Botticelli; neck stretched forward, its curve hinting somewhat at the model's humped back, or at least at her slouching posture.

Over its 'heralding of truth', which is often said to be capable of 'touching' and 'influencing', Kiryushin preferred and particularly valued art's capacity to presage mystery, and he gazed almost amorously at the mystically-beautiful paint-ing, experiencing something approaching ecstasy – juxtaposed with a sensation of vexed disquietude. And now his aesthetic awareness was being intensified, enhanced, and perhaps it had even been engendered by – how shall I put this? – by a certain incident, coincidence, occurrence – I cannot identify the cata-lyst precisely.

For when Mstislav headed for the painting, half-turned before it was a woman who, just like the model in the portrait, stood with her left side towards him. She looked like she was doing an impression of the figure: she'd bent her left leg at the knee, and her right hand, which held a bouquet of yellow flowers, was extended slightly. But she wasn't posing for any-one: she was alone and, to all appearances, fully engrossed in contemplation; the concentration of her gaze was comparable to the languorous look in the eyes of the signora on the can-vas. Kiryushin had never overestimated his understanding of women, but he knew enough to know that no woman could even for a moment refrain from keeping track of nearby males' wandering eyes; and his own attentions, he supposed, had probably not gone unnoticed either. But whether these attentions were focused on the lady in the portrait or, conversely, on the lady before the portrait, shall remain a mystery for all concerned, including the author of the present account, who's supposed to know everything without exception.

Mstislav stopped; he approached the painting only after the space in front of it was clear, and an intimate, one-to-one discourse between himself and the work, which he could enjoy without fear of being caught in the act, became a possibility – as far as such a discourse is feasible in a public place. But now he was struggling to make up his mind: had he arrived at an independent judgement of the painting, or would his view of it forever be distorted by the initial adventitious presence of the visitor to the museum who bore such a striking resemblance to the model?

After he'd examined the painting from all possible angles and scrutinized it in detail, as his artist-friends had taught him to do, Kiryushin settled down in an armchair in the middle of the room – a little further away from the canvas but without unfixing his gaze. This was a masterpiece he'd heard nothing about, just as he'd heard nothing about its author, and yet, strangely, it wasn't the painter himself, but the woman portrayed, who preoccupied Mstislav's thoughts: he was trying to fathom out the nature of the connection between the two. Her image – realized with such predilection that Mstislav doubted not for a moment that this was a portrayal of a real-life subject – radiated rapture, yet seemed to exude a vengeful sense of dominion seized over that subject within the confines of the frame, alongside the artist's bitter resentment of his own impotence before the model, or rather, the impotence felt by the *man* when faced with this boundlessly imperious and insuperable woman. This was a dethronement attempt that had ended in complete human failure, but it represented a resounding creative victory for the artist nevertheless – for he had created a monument. All his bitter sarcasm was transfigured into a powerful means of odic glorification; not without reason did Kiryushin recall the words 'Godlike Princess of the

Kirgiz-Kaisak Horde', which popped into his head when he'd only just approached the painting, and which he initially dismissed as a somewhat outlandish chance association. But then, Kiryushin was certain that the lady's praises had been sung by a man who endured exquisite torment at her hand, and in whose life she was passion and woe supreme. The artist had possessed her – that much was clear – and yet her surrender brought him not joy, but misery. Kiryushin went so far as supposing that even the first time she succumbed to him must have resulted not so much in the artist's pleasure as in a sensation of resentment and unremitting anxiety. '... *the woman we are destined to enjoy, / Having first endured her torments,*' he muttered, marvelling at what a contrast these words made to his reconstruction of events. Far from delivering the artist from his sufferings, the realization of his desire to possess the signora must – of this Kiryshin was certain – have marked the beginning of a grave and incurable affliction.

Kiryushin felt weary – the kind of weary that took hold of him more quickly during engagement with art than when he read poetry, for example, or listened to music. Realizing it'd be beyond him to fully appreciate the exhibition's other paintings, he left the museum and headed towards Rumyantsev Library. Heedless of the whys and wherefores of what he was doing, he bought some flowers, smelled them, and carried them with arm outstretched as if intent on handing them to someone three paces before him.

And then he saw a woman he truly would've liked to offer the bouquet to, though I can give you my word that he hadn't anticipated doing any such thing. It was the same lady who'd stood in the museum between him and the Italian painting he'd been so astounded by. Now then, what could she've been doing when Mstislav picked her out in the crowd just by the entrance to the metro? Go ahead, have a guess! You've got it in one: she was, of course, throwing away the selfsame flowers she had in the museum. Without thinking, Kiryushin ran up to her and said, 'I beg you to take these flowers in exchange for the ones you've just thrown away.'

She regarded him calmly, thanked him, then enquired, 'You didn't like them either, then, those other ones?'

'I already hated them back in the museum.'

'You've been following me all the way from the museum?' she asked, taken aback.

'Absolutely not,' said Mstislav, struggling to sound unruffled, 'but those flowers stopped me from getting a proper look at the painting.'

'You mean the one of the signora with the butterfly?' she said, half affirming, half questioning.

He wasn't surprised, but noted nonetheless, 'There was no butterfly to speak of.'

'Oh, I know, I know, but surely it's implied that those slender fingers of hers are clutching something?'

'You're right,' agreed Kiryushin, 'a butterfly wouldn't go amiss there. On the other hand, we should be grateful to the artist for sparing us a scene of torment: *"A very hunter did I rush / Upon the prey:—with leaps and springs / I followed on from brake to bush."* Then again, there's more than enough torment in that painting as it is, wouldn't you say?'

'I would. If you ask me, there's a dark history concealed in the subtext, and I think I can put my finger on what it's to do with: the model is obviously the artist's lover (and certainly not his wife, don't you agree?), but … she's also his sister.'

'You presume we're dealing with incest?' asked Kiryushin, marvelling at this hypothesis.

They fell silent for a moment, and then he said fervently, 'I absolutely have to know right away whether or not you're my sister because I think my father may've had children on the side.'

These words, contrary to his expectations, didn't make her laugh, and she simply introduced herself:

'My name is Ada Vilkina.'

'Oh God, but this is devilry of the highest order!' he exclaimed.

'Devilry?' she repeated, uncomprehending – and smiled suddenly: 'What, could it be that you're a Vilkin like me? Should we refrain from mingling our bloods?' she added pluckily. 'Are you going to do a runner?'

'I wouldn't do a runner even if that really were the case,' he replied, unsmiling, 'but just judge for yourself what a cornucopia of Nabokoviana we've got on our hands: butterflies – incest – Ada – it's all a little too much.'

'Yes, I agree: it's all excessive somehow, contrived, even, though I couldn't possibly say by whom. And besides, I don't even like Nabokov. The pun isn't exactly the most elevated form of wit, and a novel that's just one gigantic punundrum (you'll have worked out, of course, that I'm talking about *Ada, or Ardor*) can't be anything other than pure pretension.'

'But Ada, dearest Adochka, how are we to extricate ourselves from this tangled web, woven – let us suppose – by mere chance?'

'We'll acknowledge only that the finger of fate is pointing at us – everything else is but a series of signs sent our way so we don't overlook what really matters. Incidentally, I know a lot about you already, but I have to admit, I won't be able to guess what your name is unless you drop me a hint.'

Kiryushin did so. Ada laughed:

'So it's *your* brain I've been wanting to pick about this for so long:

> *O Cypris! Into thy rites I've been inducted,*
> *With thy benevolence I'm blessed,*
> *Yet shall my path to thee forever be obstructed*
> *By androphobia that springs from sweet Salmacis' breast?*

Mstislav was flustered:

'You've read my poem?'

'Yes, and ever since I've been trawling through all my dictionaries for the word "Salmacis": the meaning of the lines is lost without it.'

'Salmacis is the nymph who became one with the ill-fated son of Hermes and Aphrodite.'

'So that means the poem is hinting not only at the unre-quitedness of desire but at something more universal as well?'

Kiryushin suddenly felt overwhelmed by a burning impatience. He put an abrupt end to the literary discussion with a question:

'Adochka, where are we going?'

She reflected in silence for a minute. Then she made up her mind and said determinedly, 'We're going to yours.'

Kiryushin promptly displayed his practical savvy and business-like manner:

'Let's pick up some champagne then, shall we?'

'And something to eat as well,' she added. 'I'm sure you know all about female ravenousness. Though men, as far as I can tell, get serious munchies themselves after a bout of loving – correct?'

We're going to love each other! he thought, exultant. Those were her words, not mine.

Never before had he needed so little time to achieve intimacy, and yet these were circumstances where a quick success seemed almost inconceivable. What he felt as a result resembled an extreme disquiet. He grew jittery and jabbered on without cease, while she was collected and – composed.

Her next words were delivered slowly, almost sluggishly. 'You see,' she said, 'it's strange, and things don't happen this way, but somehow I'm certain I love you. And I'm not afraid to say it out loud. Can you explain why?'

'Yes!' he cried. And suddenly, his face sinking: 'Or rather, no. But I do know that women don't make up their minds about this question right away, or at least not before physical intimacy, but only *afterwards*, which is the exact opposite of what happens with men. And that's why you can believe in the sincerity of *my* confession now, but I shall take your words as a guarantee, as a promise of things to come. You'll repeat later what you've said just now, if you still can.'

'I think we're talking too much,' she muttered peevishly, taking him by the hand. 'Let's go, let's go!'

They didn't even bother opening the champagne. They were caught in the grips of a fever that cut short their first encounter, but, letting loose simultaneous cries of dismay, they segued into the next without the slightest hesitation, and concentrated all their efforts on drawing *this one* out for as long as possible. Their caresses were as tender as they were blissfully tormenting; they couldn't take their eyes from each other, consciously, and not unwittingly, aware that their bodies were perfectly coordinated, almost made-to-measure for each other, and the one thing that remained incomprehensible to them was why they'd been brought together only now, and why Nature hadn't accelerated such a complete and comprehensive convergence.

By the time it was over, he'd clean forgotten having asked her to repeat the words she'd spoken earlier – not that there was any need for her to do so. Neither of them felt any desire to speak. They uncorked the champagne without dressing and drank it in large, languid sips. The twist of their eyebeams grew tight as an intergrafting of hands; they felt their connection enduring and deepening, their gazes penetrating to such depths that not only were all verbal signs rendered inadequate, they simply became unthinkable. And yet, Mstislav had scarcely regained his senses when his tongue began to move, slowly, sluggishly, though in all likelihood he was oblivious to the sounds it was producing: *It could be that whisper was begotten before tongue, so too that leaves in treelessness had eddied …*

'I have to go,' said Ada finally.

'You want to leave? But why?'

'I have to. Kazarnovsky's back in the morning.'

'Kazarnovsky? Why Kazarnovsky? Who's Kazarnovsky? Whence Kazarnovsky?'

'Woah, that's a lot of questions all at once! What's got into you? Kazarnovsky's my husband.'

'But that's just not possible!'

'Not possible? What's so extraordinary about that surname?'

'It's the maiden name of my grandmother on my father's side.'

'You're kidding me! So the spectre of incest really is haunting us, is it?'

'Some joke that is! What's your husband called, then?'

'Yasha. His name's Yakov. And you say he's related to you?'

'I've heard nothing about him – I mean, I've no cousins by that name, but I can't say I've looked into more distant relations.'

'I'd like to introduce you two. Perhaps your combined efforts will be enough to establish how closely you're related.'

Kiryushin pictured himself saying hello to Kazarnovsky and flashed back to his nosedive to earth on learning that Ada had a husband – the sound of the surname alone had distracted him from the pain of his terrible fall, but the problem was exacerbated by the possibility of kinship.

'What kind of relationship have you got with him?' asked Kiryushin.

'Not an easy one, Slava, I'd call it muddled and confused. That is, we loved each other, and even now we're still very caring and attentive to each other's needs, but for a while now things have been falling apart, and I suspect that Yasha' – she paused briefly, then continued with difficulty – 'that Yasha has discovered himself to be otherwise oriented.'

'Ada,' said Mstislav, 'listen to me: don't go home, stay here. Are all the portents we've been sent today really not enough for you?'

'I can't,' she rejoined firmly. 'Just imagine what'd happen if he came back and I wasn't there. All this isn't as easy as it might seem to you now.'

'But will you at least tell him about us?'

'I – I don't know, at least, not straight away … But you absolutely must come over to ours tomorrow night. I'll tell Yasha I met you at Verochka Malinina's: you do know Verochka, don't you?'

He detected an arch little undertone in Ada's articulation of that name and realized that she was familiar not only with his poems but also with certain facts in his biography. Which was hardly surprising, though, if Ada and Verochka were friends.

'Will you talk to Verochka yourself about keeping up the cover story,' he asked, 'or will you entrust this to me?'

'Darling, the last thing I want is for you to end up in hot water because of me, and besides, a conversation like that with a girlfriend is pure pleasure for a woman,' she said, with the same archness as before.

She couldn't've hinted with any greater tact, thought Kiryushin, at being privy to the details of his liaison with Verochka, at his obligations to her and, equally, at the fact that their new relationship was complicated no less by the presence of Ada's husband than by the involvement of yet another party, clean forgotten by Mistislav the moment he saw Ada. And, to make matters worse, it'd turned out that his ladies were good friends – and that he and Kazarnovsky were potentially related! Kiryushin felt like some biblical sinner being stoned to death in retribution for the triumphant glee he'd first felt at the effortlessness of it all. The path to Cypris is tortuous and bristling with thorns – he'd discovered as much for the thousandth time; yet the bitterness of this thought somewhat stifled the sorrow he felt at his sudden separation from Ada, who plucked her flowers from their vase and, asking him not to see her out, quietly left the house.

The Portrait
(Abelone)

Evgeny Vitkovsky, poet, translator, connoisseur of literature, responded as follows:

I have neither the inclination nor the time to concern myself with intertextual connections or to investigate the
plot involving an animated female portrait. In my opinion,
its proposed elaboration is somewhat clumsy and inelegant,
although it masquerades, not without affectation, as Russian
nineteenth-century Romantic prose. Yet its actual source is,
I believe, not Russian at all, but German. I shall sketch out here
only my initial thoughts on the matter; some proper digging
would doubtless unearth more profound correspondences.

Consider, for instance, the following plot, executed by
the pen of a symbolist. Before us we have a boy, sickly, talented, prone to bouts of fever, filled with nebulous fears and
indistinct yearnings, convulsed by ambiguous and dangerous
attractions-cum-repulsions. Living on the family estate, sur-
rounded by ancient tapestries, portraits and ghosts, he occasionally embarks on precarious journeys of discovery which
come to implicate no-longer-youthful yet alluring maidens, his
prematurely-dying mother, another gifted boy (who, needless
to say, dies before reaching his prime), portraits, mirrors, angels,
and so forth.

Now a carriage draws up in the courtyard; the ailing boy
sits in his room, eyes fixed on the door. There is a rustling
outside, and in rushes *maman*, insensible of her magnificent
court finery; dropping her white furs from her bare shoulders, she rushes to the bed and snatches up the child in her

arms. Seized by an astonishment and a delight such as he has never felt before, the boy runs his fingers over *maman*'s delicate face, touches her hair, the cold stones of her jewellery, the silk cascading from her flower-scented shoulders. They weep tenderly together, they kiss, but then his father enters: they sense that the time has come for them to uncouple. The boy hears the words, 'He's running a bad fever,' timidly spoken by *maman*, and his father, taking him roughly by the arm, proceeds to measure his pulse.

And now we see the boy, his face concealed under a mask, a cape about his shoulders, standing at the mirror. The mirror frightens, overpowers him: he appears to *become* the mirror, and the stranger he sees before him fills his soul with dread: it feels as if he no longer apprehends himself, as if he is simply fading away. Several servants hasten into the chamber, the boy stretches his arms out to them, but his voice fails him, his mask hides his tears, and the servants, insensible of the boy's terror, double over with laughter as he collapses unconscious at their feet.

The boy's imagination is awakened by the ghost of a lady that appears in the house from time to time. Entirely indifferent to the circumstances of her life, he sets off down to the gallery one night to see if he can find her picture there. By candlelight he examines the portraits of his long-dead ancestors, lingering chiefly by the renderings of women, but taking note nevertheless of the remarkable number of children's portraits in the gallery – girls with birds on their hands and little dogs at their feet (with flowers and fruit on the table). It occurs to the boy that they might just be standing there in all their finery and waiting, and he worries whether he'll be able to recognize the lady he's looking for.

He is about to head to the end of the gallery when he knocks against something and hears a hot whisper at his ear: 'Her picture isn't here.' It turns out that a second boy is searching for the portrait, as is the lady it depicts, for the portrait has been removed from its usual spot. The boy cannot understand what need the lady could have of the picture, but the other elucidates the matter: she wishes to look upon herself, to which end he has already brought her a mirror, but she herself is not there. The boy is at a loss: 'What do you mean, she's not there?' And the other replies, 'Either you're there, which means you're not here, or you're here, but then you can't be there.' The boys embrace and agree to be friends.

Before long, another – unfinished – picture is displayed in the gallery; the artist working on the portrait of the second boy, clad in an outfit of heliotrope-coloured velvet, had not the time to complete it: he was in no great rush – how could he have known the boy would suddenly give up the ghost?

And the maiden, oh, that entrancing Abelone! She tells the boy about his mother's girlhood, about her sudden marriage, and the boy asks, somewhat indiscreetly, why Abelone herself was never married? She answers, quite simply and freely, that there was no one to marry, and suddenly becomes beautiful. Later, the boy writes her a multitude of letters, realizing only afterwards that these were letters of love. And the narrator refuses to speak of Abelone, for, as he asserts, not everything should be touched by words. But, as becomes clear to attentive readers, women too are better left untouched if you wish to possess them forever.

I have in my collection a Russian rendering of a song that the untouched maiden sings at the close of the novel. I omitted this translation from my anthology merely because I learned of its existence after the book's publication. I don't consider it the best translation, but it is possibly the most precise. I shall refrain from naming the author of the original in retaliation against the fact that the author of the text under scrutiny, too, has been left unnamed.

You, to whom I speak not of my nocturnal
weepings, my sighs,
by whose essence—whose kernel—
I'm lulled, cradlewise.
You, who speak to me not of hours unslept
for my sake:

96

what if we suffered this glorious flame, kept
ever unslaked
in our breast?
Look at those lovers: no sooner they start
professing their yearnings of heart
than by lies are their ears caressed.
You make me alone. Alone are you transmutable.
One moment there's you, the next—some inscrutable
rustle, else a fragrance surging past
me. Ah! I have let them all slip from my arms—yet you,
and you only, shall come into being anew and anew:
having never once held you, it's you I hold fast.

Yadya

Kirill Korzunov arrived at a party thrown by one of his distant acquaintances. As far as he could tell, a mystical or semi-indecent event was in the offing, and there weren't enough 'persons of the male sex' in attendance. He was going through a period of extreme restlessness and personal upheaval, and he readily accepted the invitation, if only to kill off another evening.

When he came in, everybody was already sitting around the table, but there was one seat free, and Korzunov realized that the place had been reserved specially for him. To his right sat an attractive young woman named Yadya Izvitskaya; Yadya introduced him to Innochka Panina, the girl to his left. At first the two bent close to the table to talk so Kirill wouldn't get in the way, seemingly giving him the cold shoulder, but Korzunov began cosying up to the pair, offering them this dish or that and occasionally breaking into their conversation with a witticism. The conversation livened up, and soon Kirill migrated from its fringes right into the thick of things.

As far as he understood, the meal would be followed by a game of 'spin-the-bottle' – the strip version – which had prompted a discussion of striptease. An air of bawdy frivolity wafted gleefully over the table, and the men and women sitting around it looked forward to the game that lay ahead, though not with the sweet terror or swooning thrill of schoolchildren at their first party to feature such a programme, but without trepidation, as if anticipating a dessert concocted by a famous chef at a gastronomic tasting.

Korzunov began to feel a little uneasy. He'd never been a prude and could happily hold or initiate even the most risqué conversations. In fact, he was renowned for tackling any topic without the slightest reticence: whether he was speaking to the old or the very young, he always managed to prevent even a modicum of awkwardness from arising between the various generations, no matter what conventionalities happened to be at work. He could be flippant, witty, playfully irreverent, plain-spoken, self-restrained, sympathetic, confidence-inspiring, inquisitive – but never impudent. He didn't find the idea of striptease off-putting in the slightest – as long as it took place in a professional or, better yet, ritual context. Sacral divestment he understood very well, but to shed one's clothes in public? This seemed shameful to him, and, when done beyond the confines of intimacy, unscrupulous and insolent, too. If he had no objections to witnessing someone else strip (after all, you've got to be tolerant to the otherwise-minded), he'd never have agreed to take part in the impending escapade.

He spoke heatedly about the arcane nature of nudity and the sacredness of divestment, about the warmth of loving coition and the cosmicality of its significance, contrasting it with orgiastic chaos. Yadya and Innochka listened to Kirill with interest but stood firm against the seriousness of his tone, attuned as they were to the evening's revelry and light-hearted spirit. And it was then that Yadya hit on an argument – quite accidentally, it would seem – which, in coinciding with Kirill's views, couldn't fail to convince him that he was in the wrong.

'But what about, well, festivities?' she asked.

'What about them?' said Kirill, bemused.

'Well, you say yourself that during a period of festivities all taboos are temporarily lifted, green-lighting what's impermissible in everyday life and thereby *strengthening* rather than undermining social foundations. Besides, festivities are so rare in our lives, wouldn't you say?'

Flustered, Kirill struggled to come up with a rejoinder, muttering something about personal capacities and boundaries that nobody could overcome. He cited the example of Pushkin, who confessed that writing the whole truth about oneself was a 'physical impossibility': the hand simply refuses to move.

'We'll lend you a hand of our own,' Innochka snickered. 'And no one's asking you to record this episode in your auto-biography, are they? All you have to do is perform the familiar action of undoing your zip. Perhaps you'd like me to take this task upon myself?'

'I'd gladly delegate it to you, Innochka, before happily returning the favour, tat for *tit* – but only on the condition that we've no onlookers.'

'But what if I were to ask you for the same favour?' said Yadya. 'Would you really refuse me?'

'I never refuse a woman.'

'How about two women?' Innochka enquired.

'Whatever – I just can't imagine myself stripping off.'

'First of all, sweetie, don't sidestep the question, and secondly, it's more than that we're after now, right, Yadya?'

'What, is there really such a shortage of fellas around here? We'd better be fighting together for the realization of the slogan "A Proper Partner For Every Woman!"'

'Come off it, Kiryusha, we'll never take part in the battle for the harvest. You can consider yourself a bird in our hands … which, as you know, is worth two in the bush.'

'But then, my dear ladies, your hands would become a cage – a golden cage, perhaps, but still a cage – and as for me, I'd just be a little siskin in captivity.'

'There are worse fates, admit it. And recall, if you will, Pushkin's very last poem, since we've already touched on him tonight.'

'Hold on, let me think … Oh yes:

The siskin, in his cage confined,
Enjoys a bath and pecks his grain:
His forest freedoms swept from mind,
He revels in his brisk refrain.

'There you go! Surely you won't refrain from a quick *peck* – a free *lunch*, even – and (ahem) a brisk *revel*?'

'Sure as hell I won't,' said Kirill, much to his own surprise; his eyes, though, were fixed only on Yadya. 'Still, the group we're in here is a lot bigger than the one we discussed, wouldn't you say?'

'Innochka, looks like we've got to contend with this comrade's inability to function in a collective,' said Yadya. 'I suggest we conduct the examination back at mine.'

'Are we scarpering, then?' asked Kirill, and not without enthusiasm.

'We're sacrificing the festivities for the sake of an experiment in labour,' Innochka proclaimed.

They quietly slipped out of the house, but not before Korzunov had managed to snatch a bottle of champagne from the table without anybody noticing. They didn't have to wait for a taxi, and were soon at the door to Yadya's flat.

Though he was happy to've escaped the stripping shenanigans and the collective insanity, Kirill was nonetheless somewhat apprehensive of the uncharted and, most likely, peculiar experience that awaited him.

'Well,' Yadya whispered, 'I bet you're happy now you're not going to be spinning any bottles, eh?'

'You were saying?' said Kirill, producing the champagne from under his jumper.

'Oooh!' exclaimed both ladies, and both rewarded him with a kiss – one from the left, the other from the right.

'Open it then, don't dawdle!'

'Quietly or with a pop?'

'What, you want our festivities to be firework-free?'

Kirill shook up the champagne with great vigour. The cork exploded from the bottle followed by a jet of foam – and Yadya's chest was struck by both. She laughed:

'Well, that's one way of starting a game of "spin the bottle". Any objections to me removing all non-dry items of clothing? Kiryusha, you're going to have to be true to your word – could you please undo the zip on the back of my dress?'

Korzunov did so without a sound, and the ladies noticed that his fingers were trembling.

'Full marks on assignment number one,' said Yadya, and, so as not to add to Kirill's consternation, pulled off the dress herself.

'A toast to beginnings!' Innochka announced, and, draining her glass, began to grumble about the preferential treatment Kirill was giving to one of the women at the table, and about the inequality that clearly existed between the pair.

Still silent, but now with far steadier fingers, Korzunov unbuttoned what needed unbuttoning, and, noting in relief that his nerves had disappeared, even displayed a modicum of initiative. And yet, monitoring his own state of being, Kirill came to the realization that his disquietude returned whenever he approached Yadya to perform another assignment, yet disappeared entirely when he was in close proximity to Innochka. He'd almost fathomed out what was going on, but the detached self-analysis that accompanied his every action led him to recall his favourite lines from Sasha Chorny:

She kisses me, and I, in turn,
Repay the favour of her kiss,
And watch myself with hawkish eye
To get the measure of my bliss.

… and 'bliss' indeed this was — he realized that fully. He even broke the silence, asking, 'How come you're known as Yadya? Are you Jadwiga? Izvitskaya must be a Polish surname, then?'

'Jadwiga was what my father used to call me for some reason, and my maiden name's Kazarnovskaya. My mother called me Yasha when I was a child, but I'm not a fan of this diminutive: it's quite masculine, though it is, of course, more affectionate-sounding than Yadya. But you've more questions, I see?'

'Are you married?'

'I was,' she answered laconically. 'Izvitsky was my husband's surname, and I didn't fancy reverting to the old one when we divorced.'

'Discrimination again!' Innochka cried, resentment in her voice. 'Why am *I* not being asked about anything?'

'Entirely my fault: allow me to put that right. So your maiden name is …?'

'Panina,' she replied triumphantly. 'And it's the only surname I've ever had!'

There was something comical about this conversation between these now almost-naked interlocutors. Talk about finding the right time and place for making introductions …

Let us not disregard the views Korzunov expressed to the two ladies at the start of the evening: we won't delve into subjects deemed by our hero as being strictly intimate. What favours were bestowed upon him? By whom? But let us hold our tongue. He never said a word about it to anyone himself, and the author of the present account harbours no ambitions whatsoever of emulating the great Leo Tolstoy, who knew *everything* there was to know about his characters. Certain things leaked out, shall we say. The source? God knows.

When Korzunov was saying goodbye to his ladies in the morning, Innochka handed him a note with her telephone number and address, while Yadya whispered in his ear, 'Looks like you're right: this collective has precisely one member too many.'

'A weakness that really must be addressed,' he whispered back, and could barely make out her reply:

'Tomorrow.'

The Portrait
(Eros)

As far as I understand, the theme has been given in the form of a pre-existing and fully elaborated literary subject – that is, not only has the theme been prescribed, it has also been developed.

There's no point in expounding upon this subject: the task at hand, as I see it, consists either of writing a fantasia in any genre, from essay to novel, or of calling to memory anything that bears even a slight resemblance to the tale about the animated painting. Here's one twist we should keep in mind – a pubescent boy before a woman's portrait – and here's another variation: a youth before a mirror.

Having no literary abilities, I shall write about someone I know – someone I've a good feel for, and whom, it would seem, I've got pretty thoroughly figured out. I must warn that I'm not writing about myself, which, apart from anything else, affords me the liberty of uninhibited probing, speculating, fleshing out … and endows me with a great deal of shamelessness, which would be in short supply if I were to talk about myself.

And so we encounter the boy in what is a difficult period for him. He can't stand his own name; he's scared of his own body, of his red, acne-riddled face. He spends countless hours in front of the large mirror in the hallway, shedding countless furtive tears. He thinks his skin is bad: it has this strange gloss to it (that is, it's not dry). He's got himself a little pocket mirror as well: every now and then he takes it out and examines himself. His hair is a shock of flame: 'Who could possibly fall for such an ugly brute?'

'No, it is *finished. No* woman will *ever love* me – not one. What, then, is left for me to do? *Nothing, but to retreat into myself, to live with and for myself.*'

He knows that his peers measure themselves in the toilets with a view to discussing their endowments afterwards, and once he saw a certain something that both flabbergasted and frightened him at the same time. He approaches the mirror once more – armed with a ruler. But of course! He has suspected as much! And he has also heard that the Yids do circumcision. But that must be painful! What's the point of it? How would he look if he'd had it done to him, then? He looks in the mirror. Like this? So does that make him a Yid? And how about like this? Is he now a Russian again? Now a Yid, now a Russian; now a Yid again, now a Russian again, now – But oh God, what's this? How pleasurable these transitions from one nationality (or faith?) to another and back again! What sweet languor – and suddenly, this whirlwind, this mighty earth-moving force, this sensation of almost total oblivion, this volcano and, finally, this lava, gushing madly forth, gently moistening his hand.

Then his friends give him a picture they consider to be pornographic. Abashed, he agrees that it is, yet it becomes a sort of sacred object for him: he entrusts the picture with his nakedness, which, so he assumes, no human being would find anything but intolerable or comical. Before the picture, though, he ventures to expose himself completely.

'Look,' he says, his gaze fixed on the indecent image, 'this is a Russian, and this is a Yid. Oh! Oh! Oh!'

And so the notion of sex came to be forever associated in his mind with something sacred, predominant and simultaneously frightening; something luscious, repulsive and under the control of strangers, aliens – fiends, virtually – who had acquired a mystical power over all humanity on account of their intimate relationship with the genital organs.

He idolized the Jews his entire life – and detested them with a vengeance, accrediting their religion with all manner of virtues and regarding those of Jewish blood as marked by every conceivable vice. In speaking of these vices, he failed to realize that they were the selfsame traits he used to underscore his virtues, or, contrariwise, perhaps he understood this only too well and suspected himself to be of Jewish heritage, even though he knew for certain that he was a pure-blooded Russian – in his words, 'as Russian as Russian can be'. His stories about his own persona often recalled the monologues of Ivan Alexandrovich Khlestakov, but oftener still they were self-deprecating or, conversely, proud, but encrusted with lousiness: 'I'm quite the little shit, aren't I now' – in the tenderest of tones. He could, for instance, assert of himself, 'Yes, I'm as crafty as Cesare Borgia: and I say the devil knows what about my friends. I love this black betrayal, ablaze with the eyes of demons. But how horribly unpleasant it is that my housekeeper should be spreading rumours about my living with a chambermaid – and the yard keepers look at me familiarly as if I were something less than a gentleman.'

And immediately below: 'I thought this up all by myself – my ideas stand on no one else's shoulders but my own. Extraordinary. I am truly an extraordinary man.'

He truly was. First he would clamour for the Yids to be beaten, which, he declared, was the only way to save Russia. Then, begging the Jews for forgiveness, he would implore *them* to assume the mantle of saviours, seeing in them the sole and ultimate hope of his Motherland. Finally, he would go back to claiming that 'the continuing Christian rejection of sex will give rise to an increase in the triumphs of Jewry.'

'This is why,' he would say, 'I began my advocacy of sex at precisely the right time. Christianity must become at least partly phallic.'

Of the absolute phallicism of Judaism he had no doubt.

'There is *power* in *sex*, sex is *power*. And the Jews have *access* to this power, while the Christians are *sundered* from it. And therefore the Jews prevail over the Christians.'

What's more, circumcision was always on his mind – and it was with a great deal of jealousy that he pondered on it. Though he lacked the nerve to go through with it himself, he urged others to take the plunge, finding not only religio-philosophical but also practical grounds for doing so – in particular, he conjectured that circumcision was a sure remedy for childhood masturbation (and here's an echo of his early experiences: a Yid finds himself in better health from childhood onward because he's always been a Yid and can't say, now I'm a Yid, but look, now I'm not any more – which is why few take conversion among Jews seriously). Allow me to quote a lengthy excerpt from the writings of a man who never did graduate from being the boy he always was, forever gazing goggle-eyed into his mirror.

'Precisely how does masturbation begin? *Accidental* stimulation of the penis, whether nocturnal or playful, generates pleasurable sensations, the *membrum virile* being *easily irritated*, its glans *highly sensitive* to the touch. The poor little boy (sometimes of no more than seven or eight years old) has discovered a cheap – free, even – and inexhaustible source of sweeties! How could he not eat his fill? And the vice, in most cases incurable, takes root with terrifying speed and ferocity. It is precisely this *heightened sensitivity* that disappears in a circumcised male (the skin of the glans becomes coarse, thick, lustreless, rough), and accidental stimulation *no longer has the capacity to arouse*. Arousal – the onset of desire – occurs once the seed has *ripened*; it is triggered by internal biological factors, by the ripening of the entire male organism or *corpus*, and not by the whims of the *membrum virile*. Thus, any minor or chaotic pangs of lust are reined in, and the process of copulation returns to its natural course, settles back into its normal rhythms. And what of the process itself? As we might well presume, the male seed is cultivated, enriched, spiritualized – in a word, *educated* – during copulation, just as the period of pregnancy serves to educate and spiritually instruct the foetus. Accordingly, the longer the duration of the sexual act, the greater the degree of perfection attained by the seed: during this time it becomes permeated with the totality of the noumenal world, with 'forebodings', 'pinings', longings, 'innate ideas' and so forth … This is why the moments when the seed, in a state of agitation, alternately

approaches (arousal) and draws away (relaxation) from the ure-
thra, depending on the condition, vigour and level of excite-
ment *membri virilis in actu*, are of utmost importance. After
circumcision is performed, the act becomes so drawn out as to
require intermissions. [Further on, citing someone or other's
surveys and observations, our author informs us that 'it can
often last up to ten minutes and beyond' – the poor, poor
boy!] Eager [he continues], so to speak, to measure this length
of time spiritually, I once took a ten-minute walk (taking care
to note the time on my watch beforehand) from the corner
of Znamenskaya Street and Grodnensky Lane to Kirochnaya
Street, and then up almost the entire length of the latter, from
its junction with Znamenskaya to Liteiny Prospect. I walked
leisurely along, almost strolling, in fact. A stroll like that allows
you ample time to get carried away in all manner of thoughts!
And since the sexual act lasts just as long, it is hardly surprising that it makes your wife as happy as a lark; and she readies
herself for copulation as she would for a religious rite. Why?
Because there is potential here – *and time for that potential to be
exploited* – for both husband and wife to engage in a whole
world of thought …

'The immense vitality of the Jews, their indefatigability in
the battle for survival, their historically tested religiosity (nou-
menality), requires virtually no explanation other than this.'

Once, he (by now an adult) was told by a girl of seventeen
or so:

'The only masculine thing about you … is your trousers …'

He was horrified:

'So, apart from my clothes, am I *all woman*?'

He wasn't exactly spoilt with female love – a source of great
torment for him, though, I believe, only in youth; once he'd
managed to come to terms with this, he even insisted on his
femininity, which, needless to say, didn't win him any more
female love, but *did* reward him, and richly, with female conversations, candid outpourings, confidings, and even gals' secrets.
Despite acknowledging his femininity, he nevertheless declared
his nose to be his predominant organ, being, as he was, sensitive

to smells, or rather to what he called 'odourousness'. Further, both the organ itself and the signals it picked up were endowed in his writings with the entire polyvalent spectrum of meanings that human culture has conferred upon them – and, needless to say, he was very familiar with Gogol.

'A wife,' he would say, 'enters her husband with her smell, completely saturating him with it; she does the same to the house ... And Bismarck, in saying that the Teutons are to the Slavs as husbands are to their wives, meant nothing other than that Germany would eventually be overrun with Russian stink, Russian morass, Russian sludge, Russian booze.'

He would acknowledge his femininity, therefore, but only as long as it was ascribed to national characteristics. And yet, we've heard him aim similar remarks at another target, too, although carrying a different undertone (or rather, aftertaste, or, even better, *niff?*). Here are his exact words:

'Why do the Yids get beaten? Because they're *women*, that's why. Just as Russian men beat their *wives*. The Yids are not *males* but *females*. Their frock coats are women's *dressing gowns*: your fist is just itching to punch the like of them. For it is written, "ye shall be beaten", "ye shall be wounded". There's nothing quantifiable here, only mysticism; and the Yids almost pretend to be angry about it.'

The mysteries of sex tantalized him his whole life, and he found himself both irritated and intrigued by the suspicion that they had been resolved in Judaism and that even the most dimwitted of Yids (he considered rumours regarding the Jews' talent and intellect not simply as extremely exaggerated but as absolutely untrue) knew more about the subject than he did. He took a keen interest in every aspect of copulation, in marriage systems, in prostitution as a phenomenon and prostitutes as individuals, in all kinds of perversion, in the sexual privations and abstentions imposed by monasticism (which he hated as an idea). And every time his thoughts would return to the Jews. The best way to get him excited was to pay him a visit in the company of a Jew. He would become incredibly tender and start asking questions, endless questions, tirelessly, questions so intimate they verged on indecency – and the extraordinary thing was that the answers he received were totally candid and precise. Jews would leave his house entranced and uncomprehending: was *this man* really renowned as a ferocious Judeophobe?

Even out in the street, not a single Jew would escape his attentions. He'd be sure to sink his claws into something and fling out a cantankerous gibe. If he was largely amiable at home, then out of doors he would, in the main, be raising hell and spewing incendiary bile, his tones peevish and surly. Now at home, now out of doors; now a Yid, now not a Yid. One endless wankathon.

And what would've become of this man were it not for his childhood experience of masturbation? Or what if the lad had found out about the Jewish practice of circumcision even half a year later?

I shudder to think!

Kozin
(Symphonie fantastique, Fifth Movement)

J acques Kozin – or Giacomo Goathoof, as he'd been dubbed, for some reason or other, in childhood – knew only too well what lay ahead, knew, too, what he must prepare himself for. And he prepared with a pedantic rigour – but no, forget 'prepared': he *trained* like an athlete before a competition. Every evening after dark, for instance, he would run out into the neighbouring copse, clad in nothing but his shorts, and, clambering up a tree, he'd dangle himself, bat-like, upside down from a branch. Then he'd complicate things a little: freeing one of his legs, he pulled it down to his stomach and worked it out of his shorts before repeating the procedure with the other leg. Having removed his shorts, Kozin hung them neatly on a twig and continued to dangle, birthday-suited, from the branch. He swayed slightly – not through any effort of his own, but because of a light breeze that played upon him just as it played on the leaves of the tree he'd selected for his exercises. The sight of his own body in this unusual perspective – from below – never failed to amuse him, especially the sight of his completely flaccid penis, dangling down towards his *head* rather than his feet and jiggling independently of its owner. His mirth only grew when he recalled these wonderfully playful, remarkably apt lines from Derzhavin:

> *If only girlies sweet and fair*
> *Could fly like birdies through the air*
> *And perch on twigs …*

Glancing first at the twig-peg he'd draped his shorts over, then at his own corresponding outgrowth, Jacques continued to recall the delicious words with pleasure:

> ... I'd long—and how!—
> To be a twig: for then, you see,
> That darling flock would perch on me,
> A thousand girlies on my bough.

Giacomo was almost singing, his entire being suffused with jubilation:

> For they would perch and they would sing,
> All twittering and chirruping,
> And hatching chicks to fill the nest;
> But I would never break nor bend,
> Oh, I'd delight in them no end!
> And of all twigs I'd be most blest.

How delightful it was, this metamorphosis of the 'twig' into a ramiform structure (could a twig really have boughs?), and then into something akin to a mighty oak that would never bend (a slender rowan tree it decidedly wasn't) and stood as the most blessed of all twigs.

This was a good start, and Kozin pressed on, effortlessly and freely. And he fell a-pondering on the oak, mighty of branch and colossal of root, the stout oak that stands upon the Latyr Stone.

And since that oak stands strong and sturdy, would that my cock, my ardent cock stand no less sturdy, no less strong, a lustful vein a-standing against woman's flesh and woman's hollow. Stirred into a frenzy at this thought, Giacomo continued to recall frenetic incantations about youth and fury, and swore that he would never bend nor stir nor falter, and that seven and seventy veins would be a-standing and so too one vein further, seven and seventy joints a-standing against woman's hollow, against woman's cunt and maiden's also, against Russian cunt and black and red and every other.

Words of conjuration followed – mighty words yet hissing, too, fizzing and spluttering and mad-spittle-sputtering.

He must proceed through neither door nor gate – he must worm himself down dark holloways and mouse burrows. He must discharge his mighty strength into her every joint and every jointlet, every bone and every bonelet, into her fervid flesh, her white breasts, her seething core, her zealous heart, that her cunt be set ablaze and so too her body entire! Think awhile how lonesome, how woesome it must be for a raven to perch on a tree, on an oak dead and dry, to perch armless and legless and clawless: I would that my desired one be as lonesome without me, without Jacques the cursèd, Jacques the restless, grief-griever and sorrow-sorrower.

Still further words were needed – to cool down. No getting round that.

Afloat on a fast-flowing stream is a boat great and gleaming: aboard o' that boat, so ye see, is a duo of demons, a She and a He. There thou sittest, unclean he-demon, paying no heed to thy She. Decree that thy she-demon loosen her hair: as she did live with thee, blasted, insufferable fiend – loveless, yea, and repulsed – so may my beloved spurn her man.

He'd not missed anything out, it would seem, and had hung upside down longer than usual. Plucking his shorts from the twig, Goathoof scrambled down the tree trunk and, re-trousering, headed back home with the stride of an athlete. The goal he'd set for himself was, he sensed, closer to being achieved. The incantations were good and enticed him in their magic irresistibility; they were no less to his liking than the great verses of his favourite poets, but his designs were broader than what the conjurations promised. He was building up his strength with the intention of putting it to the test one night in May. Giacomo was confident he was doing everything right, that it'd all work out as planned, that it'd transform his life, and that, no matter how fate might play out, he would bear responsibility for whatever happened to him.

He had a hunch as to where the rite – in which he was readying himself to participate most energetically – would take place, but didn't yet know the shortest way to get there, or by what means of transportation. So he resolved to slink to the site ahead of time and dangle himself from a tree, as he had learnt to do, while waiting for the other participants, whose number would undoubtedly include her, too. Goathoof's plan encompassed only technicalities; as to what he might say and do, he hadn't thought that out in advance and would be relying on improvisation – in any case, providing for all eventualities was impossible. After all, it wasn't just insatiable passion that was driving him to this woman: he himself must've been predisposed to what came so naturally to her, and what she wielded as she saw fit – effortlessly and without servility, like a queen.

Giacomo was occasionally prone to imperiousness and hubris, but what he certainly lacked, and what *she* possessed in abundance, was – as has already been articulated (and brilliantly so, in my opinion) – *youth and fury*. And if you can cultivate fury in your inner being, as Kozin was attempting to do, youth is entirely beyond your control, an innate quality that dwindles in many with the passing of years or disappears altogether, lingering in this world even after the individual herself has exited it only in the rarest of cases. *She* is such an individual! But so too am I! thought Giacomo, beside himself with maniacal fury; but as for youth, he fell far short of that – and couldn't've failed to sense as much, either. Now, fury without youth is pure hooliganism, recalcitrance and sordidness; it spells danger, and in Jacques's case – given his right-mindedness – it spelled his own destruction. Harbouring the most audacious hopes for his undertaking, he was prepared not for success but, above all, for *death*. Or execution. Which is saying not a little, isn't it? Among those bereft of youth, who would proclaim themselves ready for execution if they genuinely knew the meaning of that word?

And yet, Jacques's intentions almost brought him onto an equal footing with those possessed as much of youth as of fury. Indeed, if you cease to see the difference between the road to the scaffold and ascension to the heights of ecstasy, does this not amount precisely to the sort of youthful derring-do that leads to exploits and mighty enterprises?

Beg to differ, we oldsters will say, rendered worldly-wise through bitter experience. *Naïve* derring-do is one thing, *calculated* derring-do quite another. Destiny won't fall for imitations. Then again, who says she won't? Destiny loves a magnificent theatrical gesture. And performance in general. Perform, Giacomo, perform! Your Destiny has taken her seat in the front row. She won't miss a single mise-en-scène in your performance – perhaps she'll even interfere in the twists and turns of your play, but she won't be following your lead, and you'll never have a more exacting spectator than her. Steady your trembling knees and go: *night's darkness is trained on you like a thousand binoculars.* And you've more than a walk in the park ahead of you: you've a mountain to climb. Go then, go! It's time!

And go he did. The journey that lay before him was a long one, and he needed to size up the locale, pick a tree, think out his positioning, survey the bushes and glades – so that afterwards he could find his bearings in the darkness. And thus he set out from home on the thirtieth of April, on the eve of the day known in the Soviet Union as the magnificently oxymoronic 'festival of labour' – which, come to think of it, perfectly reflected the essence of both labour and festivities in that country at the time; by the same token, the shit sold in the shops was described, entirely accurately if also euphemistically, as 'alimentary products'.

How useful it is to be able to avail yourself of a pithy formula so as to avoid being long-winded, getting too deep into the weeds, delving into details, if, of course, it's not the details that create the meaning! Don't assume this to be an attack on expressive means: metaphors are often of greater significance than bare meaning, or rather, it's only *in the metaphor* that meaning resides, just as epithets can be more substantial than the objects they designate. This is no criticism of literary devices: on the contrary, it has been said in anticipation and in praise. Folk tales, for instance, invariably omit as insignificant all description of road and journey, replacing it with the formula *whether long or short, whether near or far*. Don't forget, though, that *a tale is sooner told than a deed is done*.

Long story short, Kozin expended considerable energies in arranging a festal and somewhat carnivalesque night for himself, if such terms can be used to describe the ritual that he'd determined to attend not in disguise, as normally happens at masquerades, but in his birthday suit, suspecting it to be the only acceptable form of attire for the rite's participants.

On the stroke of midnight came the sounds of hissing and whistling: participants flying in from every direction simultaneously. To Goathoof's surprise, there were almost as many men as women, and he couldn't decide whether this disconcerted or reassured him. For some reason he'd envisaged there being a majority of ladies, but now, as he watched the guests arrive, it became clear to him that, had everything turned out as he'd imagined, he wouldn't be leaving this place with his skin intact: the fair sex in attendance at this revel evinced a heightened degree of demandingness. Even oaks, no matter how sturdy, break eventually, as per the laws of material mechanics – to say nothing of the fact that, after some looking and comparing, he found himself more akin to Derzhavin's overweeningly ambitious twig than to the unyielding thyrsus of folklore.

Jacques felt the branch he hung from shake – a new female arrival had latched on and was now dangling next to him. The sight of her inverted face framed by her tousled hair was a peculiar one, and he didn't realize immediately that it was *her* – long desired, unimaginably beautiful, for whose sake he had embarked upon all this – and that out of all the trees here she'd chosen the one he himself had taken a fancy to.

'You?' she whispered, betraying no surprise. 'I knew you'd come.' Then, putting a finger to her lips: '*Défense de parler*: do as I say, else you'll end up here forever.'

But far from everyone was silent. Many were shrieking so frenetically as to render themselves unintelligible: commingling with other outcries, their words morphed into heart-rending hysterical squeals. Nonetheless, Kozin managed to amuse himself as he watched a dishevelled brunette flying from one tree to the next, screeching, 'Bulgakov? Bulgakov? Bulgakov, where are you? Mikhail Afanasich, answer me! Margarita's here. I'm Margarita! Don't hide from me, I beg you! I'm Margarita!'

'Margarita, Margarita,' mumbled a porker of impossible dimensions, 'what's Margarita got to do with it? His one was called Elena Sergeyevna, no? Get yourself over here, though, and I'll give it to you no worse than Mikhail Afanasich would've.'

The brunette did so, and they hit it right off, and Jacques's sensibilities were anything but offended, despite the energetic juddering of their fat elephantine bodies.

'Let's fly!' she whispered.

'But I don't know how,' was his mouthed reply.

She only smiled and repeated, 'Let's fly!'

Ready for anything, he meekly took her hand and tore away from the branch … but understood what had happened only when he saw her face from a more familiar angle – that is, uninverted – against the light of the moon. So effortless was their glide through the air that it seemed as if the *scenery* was moving, an advance of trees, lakes, clouds, while *they* were motionless, ahover.

'By tradition, initiates here are subjected to a period of ritual testing,' she informed him, 'but the testing is overseen by whoever's introduced them into the society. Whereas it seems you arrived here unchaperoned?'

'I'm alone,' Kozin admitted.

'For the life of me I can't think how you managed that, but it gets you out of having to undergo some rather painful procedures and means you can start taking advantage of your privileges straightaway.'

Only now did it finally dawn on Jacques that this wasn't simply a hand-in-hand stroll under the moonlight: they were actually flying, in the nude, without any stormy Chagallian exaltation, as calmly as if they were ambling down a crowded park alley in the broad light of day.

'I want to show you what would've happened to you now,' she said, 'if you'd got here in the traditional way, for example, if I'd presented you to the society as a neophyte.'

They flew toward the firelight, toward the tumult and the sound of women's screams. Giacomo saw an enormous revolving wheel – a rack of sorts, thirteen men fastened down to its circumference. The wheel was slowly revolving, and not one of these heroes was left deprived of female (multitudinously female!) attention.

'And that,' she began, 'that's known as – '

'I know, I know – it's a Devil's Wheel.'

'Nonsense: a Wheel of Pleasure is what it is!' Her eyes flashed. 'Fancy it? No? Gets a lot of people going, you know.'

'Yes, for a little while it might,' said Giacomo. 'Then again, look at those poor bastards over there: they're completely worn out but still can't get any peace.'

'And they're the ones you identify with,' she cheerfully continued. 'Just as well, too: in all fairness, that's where your rightful place is.'

He scoffed: 'In all *fairness*?'

'All right then, in all lawfulness,' she said conciliatorily.

'And, just out of interest, what law would that be?' asked Kozin, who'd read a variety of books in the vein of *Malleus Maleficarum*.

'I'm no pettifogger, but you have to know that we've our own *Corpus Juris Canonici* here. Enough about that, though. While you're wriggling out of being tested and aren't yet familiar with your privileges, I'd do well not to forget about my duties as a voluntary hostess, about my rights as a long-time member of this society, and – well, about my own desires. Am I any worse than those women crowding around the wheel? Don't go thinking you'll have it any easier than the thirteen sufferers over there. Do you like this glade? You do? Then that's where your initiation shall take place. I don't really have to ask, but I will anyway: do I have your consent?'

Fixedly he eyed her, eyed her with all his body, for in that moment he was Argus, all the pores in his skin becoming organs of sight and fastening themselves upon her simultaneously, and, perhaps for the first time in his current state of disquietude, he realized that he was not alone in his nakedness, but that she, too, had been fully unclothed from the very beginning of their encounter, and that she was incomparably beautiful – beautiful from the tips of her hair to the tips of her toenails. Remarking the apparent scrutiny in his gaze, she rose *en pointe*, so to speak, as if she were about to do a midair *fouetté*, and turned several times.

'Well?' she said.

No answer was required. They began their dance on the wing, but both felt the need for earth, for the cool touch of young May grasses, and they literally collapsed onto the glade, which began quivering frenziedly under them, thrashing about with all its knolls and tussocks, pawing their fervid flesh, lustily licking droplets of sweat off their backs and chests, leaving green grass stains on their buttocks and bellies ...

A week later, or just under that, on the fifth of May, Kozin's friends announced a search for him: Jacques was nowhere to be found.

The Portrait
(Big Brother)

Well then, my good sirs and ladies! Rummaging through the shit of yesteryear, petrified and stenchless, I keep wondering: when, precisely, were the foundations of this whole affair laid? and where – beyond God's will, of course – would you have me seek out the origins of what unfolded? I understand only too well that people will likely want to accuse me of arbitrariness and ascribe extreme individualism and subjectivism to me, as has happened already, and not infrequently. But I don't care a damn for all your pigeonholes. I'm no stranger to them, and all this seems strange only at first: eventually these little labels make you feel warm and cosy, as if you've donned your favourite bathrobe and settled down on the sofa with that wondrous Russian novel – you'll have guessed which one, of course, it's one of a kind – while on the radio a magnificent tenor belts out a cavatina (which, without doubt, you know too): 'All hail, thou dwelling pure and lo-o-owly / Home of an angel fair and ho-o-oly ...' I have often imagined myself as an Ilya Iliych and always considered him (not unjustifiably so, I swear!) the single positive protagonist in Russian literature and reality – assuming, of course, that literary protagonists bear even the slightest resemblance to real life.

Give me your hand, gentle reader – But there it is, already extended! Oh! What a delightful little hand! A lady reader, I see? So much the better, so much the better! You won't be frightened, will you now, of the secluded little spots that I intend to show you? Nor, I'm certain, will you be alarmed by the possible *équivoques* that shall arise – inevitably so, in fact – over the course of our excursion. Whoever declares a lady reader's curiosity to be illaudable shall answer to me – I give this warning in all seriousness. Stay with me, my precious one: I'll let no harm come to you, and shall endeavour to quench your thirst for knowledge – a thirst which, you must know, I think in no wise indecent, even if what you learn is nothing but 'gossip', as certain sanctimonious persons are wont to call true histories about real-life people, especially if those people are possessed of celebrity. I'm not in the least put off by their long faces, are you, my sweet? I see, I see – they simply don't exist for you; already your fingers drum impatiently upon the table. How I should like to observe the changes in the expression of your dear face as I tell my story, but – alas! – I am compelled to walk a little ahead of you, the better to show you the way. Denied the joy of gazing upon you face to face, I shall abandon myself to the delight of storytelling, for to present my history to *you*, my dear woman – whoever you might be – is happiness indeed.

At life's beginning, Madame, I remember school. At the very entrance we were greeted by portraits of our state's founders, our leaders. In the middle hung a portrait of our very first supremo, the wise Ivan Vladimirovich Michurin, his face seamed by kindly wrinkles. We all thought reverently of him, and not a single one among us was undesirous of paying at least one visit to his Mausoleum, particularly in autumn, enticed by the firm ripeness of the fruit on the Winter Beurre pear trees that lined the Mausoleum building.

Next to the study of Michurin hung an identically sized portrait of the leader who elaborated his theory and took it triumphantly forward – the unreservedly beloved Trofim Denisovich Lysenko, who, as we all know, was the best friend of children, and is depicted in many a photograph in the company of Young Pioneers, standing against a background of seedlings planted with his own hands. This humble, approachable man was not only the orchestrator of all the victories of our people, and not only our profoundest thinker – one endowed, no less, with an understanding of all the minutiae of the universe, and the ability to rectify the least of nature's blunders, so that cosmic harmony might reign everlastingly; no, he also entered every household as its most sacred, most luminous, most indispensable element. Before the eyes of T. D. Lysenko unfurled not only the life of the nation as a whole, but the life of each individual family, the lives of every bachelor and every spinster. Limitless was his love for, and his interest in, any living creature on our earth. We felt upon us the gaze of his watchful and radiant eyes, and grew accustomed to being under their perpetual scrutiny.

You will enquire, Madame, why I am telling you this – it is, after all, history. And there's the rub, my gracious lady: historians would falsify anything and everything, according to the day's demands, and not even such heroes as Gleb Vladimirovich Nosovsky and Anatoly Timofeyevich Fomenko were able to quell the turbid tide of lies and insinuations. Few will recollect, for instance, that the Mausoleum formerly bore the name of I. V. Michurin, and not at all that of V. I. Lenin. This changed when the communists secured a majority in parliament and clandestinely replaced the embalmed body of our leader with a dummy representing the founder of their party. Within a single day, all the Winter Beurre trees in the Square were felled, and the entire space planted with solemn and cold blue spruces.

No less ignominious was this party's treatment of T. D. Lysenko. First, party members began to comment derisively of his portraits that 'Big Brother is watching you' – a phrase they expressly memorized in English, for which purpose they sent out for native speakers from Boston (their remunerations, it is said, were nothing if not handsome). Next, they started ascribing Lysenko's achievements in the history of the nation to Stalin, a heretofore-unknown communist functionary. This occurred as a result of a minor misunderstanding.

One day, Trofim Denisovich was sharing reminiscences of his boyhood days with some old-timers, and mentioned that he was at seminary with one 'good Georgian'; his surname, he said, was lost to him, but he clearly recalled his sobriquet – Przhevalsky. 'He fought indefatigably,' said Trofim Denisovich, 'against racists and nationalists of all stripes – even anti-Semitism, the plague of all high-souled people, never afflicted him. Granted, he wasn't overfond of Chechens, yet he was always ashamed of this.'

The individual recalled by T. D. Lysenko was soon tracked down in Georgia: his surname was Ioseliani, and he lived in Kutaisi. By an irony of fate, the man sent after him happened to be a Chechen and, as such, he deemed Trofim Denisovich's reminiscences to be sufficient grounds for sending Ioseliani off to gaol. A year into his incarceration, Soso – as his friends called him – made a daring escape from Kutaisi Prison, whereupon he crossed the Georgian border and fled to Siberia; basking in the Siberians' emotional warmth, he settled there for ever. From time to time, fervent articles he penned in defence of minority peoples – particularly Chechens residing in Siberia – would appear in the local press.

Precisely this affair was seized on by the communists when concocting the legend about their – coincidentally also Georgian – expert on the national question. His surname was Dzhugashvili, a fact generally unforgotten, yet the propagandists found it more convenient to call him in Russian by the name of Stalin – the very name under which Ioseliani's articles on the questions of interethnic relations were published in communist journals, and which was thus foisted on the people. (The pseudonym *Iosif Stalin* was, I assume, chosen on account of its phonetic similarity with the surname Ioseliani.)

When I was a schoolboy, we never heard tell of this man, for history was written by clean hands at the time: Trofim Denisovich saw to this personally, inflicting severe punishment upon any who so much as entertained thought of falsification. 'How can you look our children in the eyes?' the leader would ask of the falsificators, meeting them prior to the carrying out of the sentence. He cared deeply about children and, come a holiday, he'd inevitably plant some Young Pioneer girl or other on his lap.

My school friend Troshka's mother used to tell me how, one May First, she'd sat on the leader's lap in her Pioneer youth. Her face radiated joy as she spoke, and she gazed rapturously at her son. She had no husband, she'd dedicated her whole life to Troshka, and yet her existence was forever warmed and brightened by this memory from her childhood. She spoke of her invitation to the celebratory banquet, of being called to join Trofim Denisovich at the table, of his kindliness and affection; yet, overtaken by spasms in her throat, she never once reached the end of her tale. Our leader had bestowed something else upon her – something which, choking as she was on tears of joy, she found beyond her power to recount.

But I should like to speak further about portraits. Before the communists seized power (and that is precisely how we should regard their winning of a majority of seats in parliament), the role of culture in the life of the country was entirely different, and portraits of writers would feature in May Day demonstrations alongside those of state leaders. Next to the school's portrait of I. V. Michurin – across from that of T. D. Lysenko – hung a study of Ivan Nechuy-Levitsky, while the portrait of Lysenko was flanked by a photograph of B. L. Pasternak, once proclaimed by our leader in a private letter to Ivinskaya as 'the best and most talented poet of our age' (how the communists exploited these words we know only too well).

If I recall, I myself once carried a portrait of Mikhail Bulgakov at a demonstration, little suspecting what place this most likeable of writers would be accorded by our current leadership, who utterly distorted the meaning of his creative work. Claims began to circulate that a friendship had existed between himself and Stalin – a man of whom, I suspect, Mikhail Afansievich had never even heard; meanwhile, some expeditious journalist, one of today's brownnoses, dashed off *Batum*, a playlet about the youth of the 'ardent revolutionary', and attributed its authorship to Bulgakov. Who among us, having turned out for May Day processions as children, having brandished portraits of this classic of our literature, would ever believe such unimaginable absurdity, such insolent fabrication, such scandalous calumny? Print this false concoction, gentlemen, print it in the last volume of Bulgakov's collected works, in the 'Unfinished' section – and in due course, the name of whoever defiled our literary glory will be unearthed and made public!

But another few words about who it was that we, here in this country of ours, were wont to revere: it's imperative to call this to mind, and to record it, lest it be lost for those born today, under the communists, and who have been inculcated with a version of our history that isn't even believable. In our youth, we were taught to think that the individual personality played a role of paramount importance in every epoch. Hence the importance of the literary-critical research carried out in our country to determine the authorship of masterpieces deemed to be erroneously attributed. I remember the joy we felt when literary theorists, joining forces with historians and mathematicians, proposed an entirely new method for research and developed a computer programme which took mere minutes to reconstruct the splendid features of the never-before-glimpsed author of the *Kama Sutra*. T. D. Lysenko himself stood beside the electronic machine at the moment of the portrait's emergence, and was hence one of the first to lay eyes on the still nameless yet almost certainly bona-fide author of the immortal tract, so lovingly studied in the middle schools of the day.

It's shameful to state that today's Left have questioned in the Duma the advisability of teaching this work to children. The spiritual life of the young generation is of little concern to them! The communists have even gone so far as to claim that the *Kama Sutra* never had an author, so odious do they find the very notion of individual personality!

But let us not speak of the here and now: this, after all, is a reminiscence, not a debate. I generally cannot abide debates and consider them a deplorable consequence of the leftist-enforced 'freedom of speech', brought in to replace the standard procedure of communicating scientific information to the populace. Imbeciles! Who'd be interested to hear your opinion on a matter in which you've no competence? The experts are talking – so listen up! No, they need to 'exchange views', you see – and only because (in the words of Zyuganov) Lenin, supported by Stalin in his fight against Bogdanov, declared at one of the Social Democratic congresses that freedom of expression was an essential precondition for party discipline.

But let us put all this aside! All this is fleeting, it shall pass; so let us talk awhile of things eternal, of Oscar Wilde, for instance, whose images, too, adorned the celebratory processions and whose portrait, it is said, stood atop T. D. Lysenko's desk in his Kremlin office. Yet something peculiar was happening with the works of this wonderful writer. As everyone doubtless remembers, the translation of his strident confession *De Profundis* was published in Russia even before the release of the English original. I cannot say where the translator got hold of the source text, or how he managed to circumvent the ban on publication imposed by Wilde's puritan heirs, but our edition of the book was promptly followed by an American one, the introduction to which stated that the back-translation into English was done from a Russian-language edition. I mention this only because it should be clear to anybody how highly esteemed the great Englishman was in our country. It is yet more remarkable that one work of his formerly remained untranslated into Russian, and not even a British edition of *The Picture of Dorian Gray* was to be found in any library. Vague hints abounded that it shared similarities with Balzac's *La Peau de chagrin,* which is why everyone read Balzac, but the Frenchman wasn't to everybody's taste, and many contemplated why it was that our acquaintance with the universal idol stayed incomplete. Today, the translation having finally been published through the efforts of the communists, whose every deed contravenes the will of T. D. Lysenko, our amazement – my generation's, that is – knows absolutely no bounds.

The novel, so leftists assert, was deliberately withheld from the reading public, and not only was freedom of expression infringed, but the transmission of scientific information, the right to which was enshrined in the Lysenko Constitution, also failed to occur in full measure. I can't make heads or tails of this! What exactly was being concealed, why, and from whom? Communist acquaintances with whom I'm on handshaking terms just shrug mysteriously, and, if we happen to be talking at my place, they shoot occasional glances up at a portrait of T. D. Lysenko that has hung in my home since I was a child.

Surely they cannot be hinting at some sort of link between the subject matter of the English novel and Trofim Denisovich's biography? It's true enough that of the many famous portraits of Lysenko, one was preferred above all others – the most ubiquitous one, whose peculiar, radiant gaze led opponents of our leader to quip that 'Big Brother is watching you'; but this portrait was chosen by the citizenry themselves, and nobody can claim that it, in particular, was foisted upon them. As for assertions that Trofim Denisovich appeared not to age for many years, he was, to be sure, rejuvenated through sporting activities and constant interaction with the younger generations – but what's supernatural about that? Malignant tongues accuse our leader of a vampirism of sorts: it was not for nothing, they allege, that he sat Young Pioneers on his knees, using their life force and energies to replenish his own. But we shall not entertain this malicious hypothesis – shall we, Madame? – in view of its patent absurdity: his appearance *did*, in point of fact, alter irrevocably over the years (as photographs bear witness), whereas the famous portrait, executed by the great hyperrealist Laktionov, did not change in the slightest and remains unchanged to this day.

And yet – here we can but agree – the portrait retained, and continues to retain, an element of the puissance that undoubtedly distinguished Laktionov's model. Perhaps the hyperrealistic method discovered by the artist allowed him not only to render the leader's spiritual qualities but to undertake, as it were, a living portrayal of his soul in its everyday labours (the leader's favourite lines of verse were these: 'The soul must labour / Day and night, day and night'); or perhaps Trofim Denisovich's spiritual qualities were such that his image – independently of himself – began to emanate a most powerful and imperious energy that intervened beneficently into the lives of all, directing them, steering them towards things wholesome and reasonable and meaningful.

I beseech you to believe me, Madame – I know what I'm saying, for I have experienced first-hand the power radiated by the portrait, a permanent fixture in my bedroom from earliest childhood, as I have already mentioned; observing me at every age, monitoring each and every change I underwent, the portrait was not only *witness* to my actions, to my very thoughts, but, it would seem, *determined* them to a considerable degree.

Your hand grows moist, my dear lady; you have understood, I see, that I am making the transition from my long preamble to the story proper. This is hardly easy for me to do, because I intend to speak – guilelessly, unequivocally, without hiding behind a character persona – about intimate experiences; you and I, Madame, are not, alas! in bed together, which considerably complicates my task of constructing a direct and confidential narrative, addressed to a member of the opposite sex. I'll confess: I should like to be liked by you, and in such cases any man (much like any woman, for that matter!) resorts – *n'est-ce pas?* – to embellishment and prevarication. This I shall endeavour not to do, or else to do it only to a most trifling degree; rather, I promise not to resort to lies at all, but shall, on rare occasions, avail myself of non-disclosure, and then only if my hand refuses to reveal the ultimate truth in spite of my most sincere intention of being candid to the very last.

Standing before our nearest and dearest, we feel no shame at our nakedness; nor are we ashamed to stand naked before God, aware that our every movement is visible to Him. And yet, whereas, for instance, being apprehended by our parents in an act of fervent nose-picking is sure to result in embarrassment for us in childhood, we grow so accustomed to the gaze of the Lord that, left alone with ourselves, we can indulge in the aforementioned pastime (and perhaps, too, in yet more objectionable ones) even in our maturity. And so it was with the portrait of T. D. Lysenko. Living in a room with this portrait, you inevitably came to sense the immutable presence of this individual and his benign involvement in your life. Your actions were thereby evaluated, as it were, against their potential assessment by this moral yardstick, and, just as an act of churchly repentance accounts for transgressions against conventional morality, but does not even touch upon manifold disapproved-of (by yourself included) and culturally unsanctioned methods of cleansing one's nasal passages and other suchlike deeds, so too must your intimate displays in the presence of the portrait never be noticed by either party. Be that as it may, the gaze of the portrait is not – how to put this, now? – is not tantamount to the eyes of an iconographic visage, nor to the attention of the omnipresent Lord; it is, after all, a *human* gaze. This being the case, you must correlate yourself in a very particular fashion with the presence in your room of a creature which, if highly conventional, is nonetheless analogous to you in every respect (I am comparing, of course, only biological parameters).

Catching the soul-penetrating gaze of T. D. upon me, I often pondered on the following: in exposing one's private sphere to a stranger, no matter how warm-hearted and benevolent, intimate and wise, just how far can one permissibly go? Now, though, the question is decided in my mind: I know precisely what's good for me and to what extent my feeling of being protected in this world depends on my fundamentally personal contact with the portrait, guardian to me since I was scarcely out my swaddling clouts. But in my rebellious boyhood I often resisted its sway and sought seclusion, spending hours on end locked away in the toilet (excuse me, Madame) or soaking in the bath. Even in the bathroom, however, no sooner did I stand at a particular angle before the mirror than I fancied I could glimpse the presence of a highly engrossed stranger-onlooker.

Things came to such a pitch that I even concocted a plan to alleviate the disquiet that I – as an individualistic adolescent – was feeling on account of this incursion into my private existence.

(Well, well! It's just dawned on me that back then my mode of thinking barely differed from today's communistic 'Big Brother is watching you'; perhaps I never uttered these words simply because I didn't know them! Then again, youthful leftism is hardly a source of surprise for anyone, and besides, I was – needless to say – far removed from the political subtext inherent in that saying.)

I realized, then, that I could hide the portrait of T. D. – without taking it off the wall, so as not to arouse my parents' attention – under some other picture. For this I would need to procure an image of identical size; every time I wanted to indulge in such acts as would be shameful to justify to T. D.'s face, I would simply slide this image under the glass, using it as a screen – a temporary one, merely a temporary one! – for the revered countenance. The idea utterly took hold of me, so much so that I set off to the library, intent on committing a theft. You see, Madame, while perusing for the umpteenth time an excellent history of Italian painting, published in Rome, I took a fancy to a picture which, in respect of its format, corresponded precisely with my needs. When nobody was looking, I cut the page from the book with a razor blade. Naive boy that I was! I had neglected to take into account the fact that the reading room of the library was adorned with the exactly the same portrait as hung in my room, only larger in size. But I was so preoccupied with my black undertaking that I noticed nothing, and, in spite of my behaviour, T. D.'s goodwill towards me doubtless remained strong – I'd have sensed any change immediately. Many years passed before I realized, resurrecting this shameful episode in my memory, that my deed had never been a secret to my protector.

In all likelihood, I shall not be able to explain what, beyond suitability of format, motivated my choice of reproduction; in fact, if I'd had it in mind to explain myself immediately after the event, I could not have done so then either. Indeed, I don't even quite remember the name of the author of this undoubted masterpiece – an artist, I believe, of very modest reputation in this country. It was something along the lines of Giacomo Bellini or, as I sometimes recall it, Giovanni Bardolini (difficult to evoke it precisely: 'Bardolini' may be a type of wine; there's a town of that name on Lago di Garda in Italy, though this town, after all, could be the birthplace not only of the wine but of the artist as well). No matter: the name is of little importance. The painting itself was, to my current taste, something of an oddity. For some reason, incidentally, the reproduction is no longer in my possession. It's possible that I destroyed it when the pangs of conscience became too much to bear. Yet I remember it down to the tiniest detail and would not fail to recognize it on any wall or page, even from a distance at which every painting is reduced to an assemblage of diffuse blots of colour – almost like the work of an abstractionist. But I've never encountered the picture – whether described or reproduced – in a single catalogue, nor, despite scouring numerous libraries, have I been able to find the copy of the history of Italian painting from which I cut out that page.

What, then, was the picture I used to prevent the 'stranger–onlooker' from beholding my shame (or, conversely, my shame-lessness), and to screen my (brazen lack of) conscience from his gaze? No easier to describe it in words than a Brahms Intermezzo or a piece by Schoenberg. Verbal attempts to evoke the condition in which Chopin, *inspired in flight, transforms the probable into the right* are beautiful yet wholly inadequate. And so it is with any work of art inextricable from the pure specificity of its form (as should well be the case – wouldn't you agree, Madame?). Just try translating a verbal creation into words of your own, for starters. And remind yourself of Leo Tolstoy's entirely unparadoxical refusal to encapsulate the idea of *Anna Karenina*: the brilliant old man responded that, in order to do so, he would have to reproduce the entire text of the novel, down to the very last comma. But I find myself in a no-win sit-uation: while I've no reproduction at hand to show you, words, though slow to arrive, do eventually come to me. These words shall satisfy neither of us, Madame; but consider what follows, if you will, not so much an account of the picture itself as a verbal expression – albeit an ill-executed one – of my experiences.

The creature depicted on the canvas oozes mystery, and the picture as a whole is, I would say, suffused with fury, or, more precisely, with furious tenderness, or, if you pre-fer, with tender fury. In my opinion, the mysterious quality of Leonardo's Gioconda is highly exaggerated – merely a transparent nod to something unburdensome and airy, perhaps even ironic and mocking, as compared to the tenebrous abyss lurking in Bardolini's work. The canvas – which, alas, I have never seen in the original – is literally aquiver with personal turmoil, so much so that it seems to have moved beyond the limits of art, although we can speak *in these terms* only of a unique masterpiece. What's more, it's not any cryptogram created by the artist that represents the enigma of the painting, but his astonishment before his own model; the creator, it is clear to see, is *begging* his viewers to take part in the unriddling of what he himself proved powerless to decipher – powerless not even as an artist but simply as a human being.

In guise at once androgynous and marble-white,
He might be someone's joy—as dreamt in former years.
His verses blaze like dahlias in solar light—
They blaze, but with the chill of yet unsuffered tears.

I don't know why these lines have insinuated themselves into my mind, but they've made a non-figurative sortie onto this page and I cannot withstand the pressure they're exerting; I assume they're pertinent in some way to the essence of what I seek to expound, and make no attempt to rein them in. Or perhaps it's only on account of a single word that I've made the association between poem and image: *androgynous.* For the sex of the creature on the canvas was indeterminate, though as an adolescent – that is, precisely when I was adjusting the reproduction into the frame – I had been almost completely sure that I was hanging up a portrait of a beautiful woman and thereby adorning my room with a work of pure art, or, as Marx freaks might put it, a work of 'art for art's sake'.

The model stands semi-exposed, certain regions of her body smothered, as it were, with a transparent fabric – a ruse not unlike those employed in today's pinups, whereby skimpily garbed temptresses are plunged in water and emerge simultaneously clothed and nude, the degrees of dress and undress allowing the viewer's aroused imagination to fill out the missing elements in either and both spectacles. What was concealed becomes revealed, yet only *partially* – and not out of prudery but for precisely the opposite reason: to under-score the creature's foundational essence, which, nevertheless, remains unriddled – and hence all the more alluring.

As for the model's pose, she's either breaking into a solo dance or else inviting the viewer to dance with her; the index and middle fingers of her right hand, extended outward and twisted smoothly at the wrist, are strangely entwined; with her left, meanwhile, she holds up the transparent fabric, float-ing about her in myriad folds and gatherings. One hip, slightly raised, thrusts outward. Knees disagreeably pointed. Eyes brown, almond-shaped, their depths exuding a certain oriental listlessness, or perhaps simply a slow languor. Brow prominent, rounded; hair pale, arranged in large curls. Lips indescrib-ably sensual – yet pursed in such a fashion that the face radi-ates coldness, as if frozen in a moment where, having heard something unexpected and not knowing what to answer, you assume an air of inscrutability, of momentary aloofness, and your eyes film over with affected nonchalance and abstracted-ness, the kind of imponderability which, superimposed here on the model's aforementioned languor – seemingly innate in her nature – generates an incomparable aura that can be expressed only by artistic means.

Oh, how well I know this nonchalant lethargy, this absent-minded iciness, this languor, this unnatural affectation; how familiar to me this vortex of unfathomable mystery, sucking you in, and, driving you away, this inhuman lack of feeling and reciprocation. I trust, Madame, that you shall be generous enough to forgive me for this last outburst!

Such was the picture I slid into the frame, atop the image of T. D., when my parents were not in a position to witness the deed. I believed it would serve as a screen between myself and my benevolent – yet, as I understood things then, 'intolerably' ubiquitous – guardian. At first this was a novelty to me; I felt a certain discomfiture and anxiety and merely scrutinized my chosen masterpiece, in no doubt of its artistic merits, for hours on end. Yet I was gripped by the relentless fancy that I could sense T. D.'s gaze emanating from underneath the picture: the rays beamed forth by his eyes penetrated my improvised screen and illumined Bardolini's work in a peculiar fashion, interfering with its composition and colour scheme, reconfiguring its structural elements, and altering the Italian's very conceit. To his surprise, the great seventeenth-century artist had acquired several twentieth-century co-authors, one of their number – in addition to T. D. and Laktionov – being, of course, yours truly: in the changeable light of the two eye-beams, my imagination was firing on all cylinders. To be frank, although I've described the painting to the best of my ability, and was not untruthful in claiming that I could recognize it from any distance, I cannot be confident that my verbal portrait is in the least germane to the original, rather than to the composite product of a collective undertaking.

At any rate, I had, even if belatedly, accomplished my original purpose – or so it seemed, at least – of concealing myself, ensconcing myself behind a screen. But, as my lady reader will have already divined, my intentions were changing in accordance with the demands of this new portrait, for we too were engaged, the model and I, in studied mutual contemplation. Her involvement in these events demands that I call her by name, if only as a matter of convention. In point of fact, I can do so effortlessly, having styled her Bianca from the very moment I espied her; why, I do not recall – perhaps I gleaned the name subliminally from the Italian text on the page facing the reproduction and impressed it upon my memory, forever associating it with the portrait.

Oh, Bianca, Bianca! How she gazed at me! As I have already said, it soon became apparent that the screen was no hindrance for the rays beaming forth from T. D.'s eyes; yet they now coalesced to such a degree with Bianca's emanation that I no longer sought to elude them. As for the temptress herself, I had no wish to shy away from *her*! At that time I was already fantasizing about the opposite sex, and images of naked couplings (with quite accidental partners) flashed through my imagination one after the other – until, that is, I thought up a happy ploy involving Bianca, who immediately ousted the accidental conjoinings from my fantasy. I attempted to seduce her, and, being inexperienced in the art of seduction, did everything that might rather have been done by *her*, if only she had the desire to transport me into absolute ecstasy. Madame shall not insist, I trust, on a more detailed testimony, if only because, at the time, but little was required to bring me into such a condition – and it was but little that I did, setting myself ablaze and falling into my own trap on every occasion. But I made progress with Bianca! My performances started to exert an unmistakable effect upon her – this I could not fail to see.

To begin with, I remarked that, not long after I began my act, the crossed fingers of Bianca's right hand would change position – the index migrating underneath the middle – before rubbing one another in turn. At the same time I detected a change in Bianca's facial expression: a ghost of a smile alighted on her lips, serving not so much to soften her features, as to sharpen them. And no sensation, so far as I recall, has transfixed me more profoundly than what I felt when Bianca's eyes – superimposing themselves, it would seem, upon the eyes of the portrait beneath – bathed me in a supernatural luminescence. And yet I'd ascertained more than once that, providing the paintings were placed into the same frame, the two faces did not align. This was, of course, a conjoining not of two pairs of eyes, but of two gazes, their object one and the same: myself. My eyelids grew heavy and closed against my will; presently I heard a rustling in the room and distinctly felt the touch against my breast of two slender crossed fingers. I became aware of a certain unrest in the air around me, of thermal streams colliding close by, and I imagined – but no! I *knew* – that it was Bianca bending over me, enticed into reciprocation – to my tenderness? – no: to my wanton desire. For neither she nor I could be called tender; our collective condition would be better termed *self-perpetuating fury*.

Were these hallucinatory episodes? To this day I cannot say with certainty, but even if they were, they can scarcely be regarded as visual illusions for, try as I might, I never succeeded in prising my eyelids open, and I *felt* – felt, rather than saw – Bianca awaiting the opportune moment, straddling me, deftly piloting my body. I barely felt her weight upon me, and did not apprehend her flesh, perceiving nothing but the stirring of unquiet air, the ebb and flow of currents now cool, now hot; and yet this was a fleshly experience – I swear to you, Madame, it was real in every respect. It was to her – to her, and to no other – that I lost my virginity, whatever psychologists or, Devil take them all, psychoanalysts might have to say about it. I only remember my nails digging into the sofa as I struggled to stifle the cry that rose in my throat at the moment of the final convulsion. Then I rested for several minutes with my eyes closed, and when I was finally able to see anything at all, I could discern no change in Bianca and took the portrait out of the frame, leaving the room exposed to T. D.'s gaze.

On one occasion (I beseech you to understand, Madame, that to continue with the telling of this tale requires an ever more arduous effort on my part), I happened to have need of a slightly shorter period of time to recover from a session of such exertions as I have just described; I opened my eyes and at once fixed them upon the portrait. You cannot know what I saw! ... I divulge this exclusively to you, empress of my soul, my beauty, to you alone! But how, how can I put it into words? Encapsulated in a single pithy sentence, my discovery was this: 'Her name was not Bianca.' Oh, but I'm afraid I have not made myself sufficiently clear. What if we rephrase? 'She was not Bianca: she was Bianco.' That clarifies things a little, does it not? Well, one last attempt at transparency: between the legs of my goddess nestled a mature, full-grown male organ ...

When I came to, Madame, I found myself in a hospital ward; and the first words I heard there – I heard them even before seeing who it was that spoke them – were words I would never forget, despite not grasping their meaning in that moment: they were the Latin terms *somnambulus* and *febris cerebralis*.

As soon as I returned home from the hospital, I glanced up at the painting – but Bianca, or Bianco, or however you might like to style the creature, had vanished. I shuddered: so that meant my parents must have – But this thought melted away as soon as my eyes met T. D.'s. And never again did I consider hiding myself away from his effulgent gaze – and not even because his gaze was all-penetrating and irresistible, but because I realized once and for all that we are equally exposed both to Evil and to Good, and that our understanding of the words, *Father, this is my body*, must embody (if you'll pardon the pun) the entire spectrum of their meaning, including the literal.

'Big Brother is watching you' – yes, but so what?

'Where are you, Job?'
    'Here I am …'

I could not find the Italian reproduction and have not seen it since, despite numerous attempts to track it down …

I kiss your hand, my lady.

The Artist

There once resided on the Via del Tritone in Rome a distinguished French nobleman named Henri de la Maisonneuve. Some thirty years had passed since he settled in Italy, only seldom returning to his native Orléans. The reason for this was something of a mystery, and Messire de la Maisonneuve took great pains to ensure that it remained so. The mystery was this: when the Frenchman visited the cities of Florence, Milan and Siena for the first time, so entranced was he by Italian painting that he resolved to learn the secrets possessed by the masters of what he supposed to be the greatest art of all, and, attempting to further this end while remaining incognito, he began to take lessons from celebrated Florentine painters. A number of years passed before Henri permitted himself to put the fruits of his labours on display in his house under the name of Giovanni Giacomo Bordolini.

Visitors and friends of the house opined that Henri had made a highly respectable acquisition, all the more so given the master's declaration that he had commissioned the paintings for a negligible price on account of the artist's poverty and obscurity. Many of them began to wish that their friend would recommend them to the artist so that they too might make similarly successful purchases and beautify their chambers with his portraits and landscapes. In his gentility did the master of the house pledge to make the recommendation, when occasion should arise, for, in his own words, the artist was a mighty zealous wanderer and carouser who, upon receiving but a mite in payment, would straightway cast all prudence to the winds, and presently his fortune, though modest in our understanding, suffices nevertheless to guarantee a gay, well-to-do existence for a year or two.

The guests, persuaded by such reasoning, might have dismissed the artist entirely from mind, were it not for de la Maisonneuve's intermittent proposals to his friends that they take a look at and, if they so desire, purchase at a reasonable price a landscape or a portrait of a certain lady or other executed by the brush of the enigmatic Bordolini. Owing to the latter's ever more comprehensive mastery of his art did Henri's enraptured acquaintances invariably manifest eagerness to pay the demanded recompense without so much as an attempt to bargain, delighting in Henri's evasive recounting of the latest *rencontre* with the master. No one ever succeeded, however, in commissioning a portrait of themselves; by the same token, there was no portrait of Henri in the house.

Ineffable was the joy of Messire de la Maisonneuve: without undue exertion and for so long had he been able to preserve his nobleman's honour, suffering not the slightest aspersion, which might easily sully his name should his artisan undertakings be discovered. Furthermore, he was similarly contented with his successes in the domain of his art, for word of the mysterious Bordolini's masterpieces spread to sundry cities in Italy, and, so it was alleged, even reached France, where a number of canvasses were resold at great profit to the enlightened nobility of that country.

One thing alone served to taint the reputation of Henri, who was renowned for his exemplary comportment, for his courtesy, and for the decency of his manner: a vile rumour must have been propagated by his enviers, to the effect that his house was being frequented by loose women. It was this very circumstance that Messire feared when, taking every possible precaution, including the alteration both of mien and attire, he began to request the company of comely Roman townswomen in his house, not forgetting to blindfold them so that afterward they might not be able to identify the dwelling where the amiable signor in the mask would first ply them with meat and wine most exquisite, then delicately assist them to undress, and, under the sneering gaze of avaricious Roman women willing to go to any lengths to fill their purses, exercise his brush until the break of dawn.

Naturally, Messire was saddened by these rumours, but it was far from easy to suppress them and, though it was unclear whence the tittle-tattle came, for not a single one of the women who had been in his house could find her way back there by daylight, and his domestics maintained their silence, yet the malignant tongues found grounds for wagging. It is true, however, that there occurred a certain strange happening which may have cracked the veneer of mystery with which the French magnate had so craftily covered his existence. Yet Henri himself refused to entertain the possibility of a threat therefrom, although there was every indication that the redoubts constructed by him with such extraordinary diligence were under siege.

While strolling along his street one day, de la Maisonneuve observed a lady openly beckoning him from the window of a passing carriage. Hat in hand, Henri approached the carriage and bowed to the signora, whose acquaintance, as it transpired, he had already made in the highest society of the city. She invited him into the carriage and, bidding him sit at her side, said:

'I have a proposition for you, Messire de la Maisonneuve.'

'I am all attention, madam.'

'I should like to commission you to paint my portrait.'

'Me, madam? Have I heard you rightly?'

'Yes, sir, you, for not a moment did I believe the cock-and-bull stories about the wild and wayward Bordolini (by the by, what a ludicrous name – evidently, you came upon it when your grasp of the Italian tongue was still feeble).'

A flush of shame and humiliation coloured the cheeks of the Frenchman, and he lowered his head, not knowing what to reply and marvelling greatly at the astuteness of the young signora and at her impudent audacity.

'You are discourteous, sir,' persisted the lady, 'to tarry for so long with your answer. What are your conditions?'

'I have only one, signora. I work at home and …'

'Yes?'

'And in secret …'

'That need not be said. I shall come to you tonight. Don't worry: by cover of darkness no one will tell me from a trollop.'

'But won't you be afraid to come alone at night?'

Her eyes flashed and, producing a dagger from her cloak, she proudly intoned:

'I'll always be capable of taking care of myself.'

They were silent for a while, and then she spoke again:

'I see that you are flustered because you do not know how I am to be called. Both in family appellation and in Christian we are almost namesakes: I am Arianna del Castelnuovo. Only my name is a little more extravagant – your new house stands opposite my castle. But henceforward ours will be the relationship of artist and model, so let us discard our titles and simply be Henri and Arianna.'

'How simply and solemnly you said that, my dear Arianna,' replied Henri, almost overwhelmed by the happy knowledge that there was a person, this enchanting signora, in whom he could confide entirely and who had taken it upon herself to enter into his mystery – and not with the intention of betraying him, but with the intention of becoming his accomplice. 'I'll be expecting you after the sun sets. What I mean to say is, after the sun sets, my sun will rise.'

'Pompous French gallantry,' laughed Arianna after him. 'Expect me at the rising of the moon.'

And, faithful to her promise, she arrived with the young moon.

Leaving her wine almost untouched, she asked him where his atelier was, selected herself the colours of the silks for the background, and undressed. The astonishment of the experienced connoisseur of female beauty upon seeing her nakedness set against the dark red drapery was such that he almost dropped his brush. In truth, it would have been meet if he had acquiesced to the brush's exhortations to set it aside. For it was a wild and wayward brush that night all the same. It may be that Arianna recognized the artist's impotence, and curtly, as if addressing a domestic, she commanded:

'Enough. Bring the wine.'

Henri hastily threw a white cloth over the canvas and went to fetch the glasses. When he returned, he found his visitant naked as before.

She took the glass and drank the wine in slow sips, her eyes never leaving the artist. Her lips, stained by the wine, did glisten moistly; and between them, also stained slightly, glittered her teeth. She regarded him and called to him – called to him soundlessly and yet distinctly. Henri did not make her wait.

As if offering recompense to his visitant and to himself for his artistic impotence, he entered her three times. All the while she did not change the position of her body – only a shadow of a half-smile alighted on her lips, which drove Henri mad: and he was possessed either by fury or by exaltation when, desisting not from his exertions, he attempted to divine the meaning of the expression on her face, with its scarcely moving, half-opened lips. And each time he entered her, he felt as if his fiery heart were being penetrated by an ice-cold rapier, and for a moment he would be frozen through and through, which, it must be said, did not deter him from his engagement, but, quite conversely, inflamed him all the more, just as rage compels a man to go further than he intends.

And, as it was in the atelier, after the third time she gave her order:

'Enough!'

And immediately she began to dress, refused his offer of escort, and said but five words of farewell:

'I shall find you myself.'

As soon as he had locked the door after Arianna, de la Maisonneuve passed into the bedchamber, so that he might find solace in slumber, if only for an hour. He fell asleep the instant his head touched the pillow, but three times more did he enter Arianna in his dreams, and each time he was run through by a great chill, as if his heart were aquiver on the point of a blade. His dreams were interrupted at the juncture where the recent events of the night, too, had come to an end, at the words, 'Enough, I shall find you myself.' But there had been time enough for him to entertain a certain thought, and because his tongue expressed this thought aloud of its own accord, Henri was able to decipher the pronounced word and to remember it. The word was 'succubus'.

'Succubus!' cried Messire de la Maisonneuve at the top of his lungs, and, drawing away the hand that was already reaching for the jordan, refrained from passing urine. 'I know what to do,' he said to himself, and, sending for his manservant, he ordered him to go out and gather some fresh nettles. When the nettles were delivered, Henri put them into a phial and urinated in it. The nettle leaves immediately wilted, yellowed, shrivelled, as if the plant had been brought into contact with a flame.

'Verily, it is a succubus,' said Henri, conviction in his voice, and lit a fire in the hearth. When the fire was kindled, he cautiously placed the phial into the hearth and drew his hand away at once, for the phial exploded with a terrible crack, surpassed in terror only by the cry of pain which emanated simultaneously from the hearth.

This ancient technique was intended to serve as a safeguard against further incursions the succubus might essay: in the region where de la Maisonneuve was born this particular method was well known, and, moreover, there were many more succubi – and incubi – in his homeland than he had heard word of in Rome. His worries were allayed. But as the day gave way to evening, he perceived that there was encroaching upon him not so much a sensation of disquiet as a burning impatience: Henri was waiting for his Arianna. He waited for her until dawn – Arianna did not come. She appeared only when he was lost in slumber, and three times did he enter her, before the words, 'Enough, I shall find you', were uttered. And he awoke, recalling that the sensation engendered by fleshly union with Arianna is akin to entering an icy cavern. And he plunged into sleep once more, and Arianna awaited him there: and thenceforth he would realize union with her as many as twelve times in a single night.

Every morning Henri approached his great Venetian looking-glass, inspected the bags under his eyes, his overhanging belly, his anxious swollen eyes, took note of the new strands of grey in his beard, shook his head, and for a long while stood engrossed in thought. He had already understood that death was near, but he did not want to surrender proximity to Arianna at any price, however torturous it was, however given to dream, however divorced from his waking hours – and even if Arianna herself were not a woman but a nightly hallucination, even if she were a succubus!

Such were Henri's nights, and, it must be said, he awaited her arrival after sunset now as before, putting fruit and glasses for wine out onto the table. During the day he endeavoured to make pastel sketches in order that he might express what he had succeeded in understanding in this woman. The number of these sketches eventually ran into the dozens, but the artist was not satisfied with a single one. In the last sketch, the image of the enchanting Arianna bore the unmistakable aspect of a dæmon, but, although the drawing was not devoid of genuine feeling, Henri saw that it was contaminated with the germ of falsity.

Messire de la Maisonneuve left the house to take some fresh air. Not far from the house he spied two elderly Jews – one large, the other scrawny. They were gesticulating comically, ardently discoursing in their own dialect. One of them was known to Henri: he was an authority on the Talmud and on Kabbalah in general, and especially on the *Zohar*, which he knew almost by heart, for he pored over it daily, answering the questions of his brethren when they required counsel on one quandary or another. Henri remembered that his name was nigh impossible to articulate, but that, to facilitate address, he suffered himself to be called 'Vittorio' in Italian.

Henri beckoned the Jew, and he, taking leave of his interlocutor, did hastily approach, reverently saluting the French magnate. The artist said he had business to discuss with him, for he had heard word that Jews have a good knack for warding off succubi, and his friend happens to be suffering from their attentions. The Jew regarded Henri with sad eyes, sighed heavily, flung up his arms, and muttered:

'Oh, Lilith, Lilith!' Then he sighed again and added hotly, 'I know there is a widespread conviction among Christians that such ills can be remedied with a Jew's spleen – is it not for this, then, that Your Serene Highness has need of an old Jew?'

Henri was flustered, and with the greatest of courtesy he invited Vittorio into his house, where they might converse over a good wine. Vittorio consented, advising Henri that conversation with enlightened individuals was a passion of his and that he valued greatly the respect with which such a distinguished magnate spoke to his brethren, who, in consequence of a strange prejudgement, were being forced to endure all manner of oppression, humiliation and persecution all across Europe. And he followed the artist inside.

Henri led the Jew into his rooms, where the astute old man immediately remarked the artist's last sketch.

'This one?' he asked. 'This one's a succubus, you say? You speak in jest, sir, do you not? I've known that signora ever since she was born, and I daresay she's an honest, upright signora. She never did us Jews any harm, and not one usurer whose services she employed heard a single slur out of her. And I've lost count of the number of times she's come to me to seek out my advice. And she's never been anything but grateful and good-humoured. What's true is true – she's whimsical and wilful – but tell me, sir, who of sound mind could refuse to serve such a signora?'

He snapped his fingers and chuckled:

'And there you were, making noises about Lilith. Oh, I don't know, if she's Lilith, I must be Methuselah.'

'But is not a dæmon capable of assuming any number of guises?' countered Henri.

'If I were speaking with one of my brothers, I would tell him, "Young man, that's enough foolishness out of you." But I shall tell you otherwise: look closely at her features, Your Illustrious Highness, for in them there is not the slightest vulgarity – only virtue. Have you ever laid eyes on a dæmon who could infiltrate the body of a man with not so much as a suggestion of vulgarity about him? And I shall answer for you: no, you have not laid eyes on such a dæmon. Therefore do not worry your mind with questions of succubi; I can see already that yours are the sufferings of a man in love, and not those of a man being tempted by the Devil. This is nothing other than an amorous attraction, young man. Oh, I do beseech apology: Your Illustrious Highness!'

In answer Henri silently pointed to his beard, which now was greying considerably.

'Oh, come now,' said the old man, and brandished his own, which was grey through and through. 'If I may be so bold,' he added, 'I shall give you one piece of advice, for I see that you are skilled in drawing. Abandon your efforts to depict the signora while your desire for her remains alive in you. Direct your gaze inward. Make a portrait of yourself. And while you're working on it, your impressions of the signora will somehow settle down as well. And I know not what else ...'

Henri saw the Jew out with a sense of the profoundest gratitude, which he expressed in terms most cordial – to the great pleasure of the old man.

There goes a sage, he thought, a veritable sage.

And he gathered up his brushes and placed a glass before the easel. Looking into the glass, he transferred onto the canvas all that he was able to fathom in himself. And he worked without intermission for several nights, until at last he understood what was lacking in the portrait, and he knew already that his was the power to bring the work to an end. And with confident strokes he superimposed onto the dark background the bright form of Arianna, and could not help but marvel at how well everything was coming together. He was about to put Bordolini's signature in the corner of the canvas when he heard a rustling behind him. He turned around, saw Arianna before him, opened his arms to embrace her – and dropped dead.

PART THREE

Notice

Such was the manuscript in the envelope.

You think I'm repeating myself? It's true, the words have been said – but not by me. I am aware that this is going to make things difficult for me, and I seriously doubt whether I'll be able to retain the reader's trust, not even if I give a detailed explanation of the situation.

The truth of the matter is that the previous part of the manuscript, together with its first part, were authored by the same hand, and the hand – the hand is not mine! After he'd written the beginning of the account and sent it to me so that I could familiarize myself with it, N., as he liked to call himself, came up with a continuation as well, which consisted of a commentary composed in my name. As for the note permitting me to do what I wished with the manuscript, this was in fact enclosed with the text.

In this way I am offered a dual authorship, both of the part supposedly written by N., whose identity I have to discover, and also – which is the most curious thing of all – of the commentary that I am *alleged* to have composed. I must make it clear at once that this generous gift is one I couldn't possibly accept! Having taken the decision to go public with the contents of the parcel I received, I began to wonder what form the notice preceding the text should take, and I must confess that I was at an utter loss.

Really, think about it: just imagine that I'm writing a foreword to a book that opens with *my own* foreword (the fact that the alleged authorship of the introductory note is spurious doesn't change a thing)! After all, if I wish to preserve the work's sanctity (and I consider editing that contravenes the will of the creator to be profoundly immoral), it is essential that I supplement it with an avant-propos, but if this were to be preceded by the present note, the note would seem not only far-fetched and pretentious but also *invraisemblable*, fictitious from beginning to end, artificial to a degree far greater than any fiction, leaving aside the fact that I would lose the reader's trust once and for all, which won't be easy to re-establish as it is, given what has already been read.

Nonetheless, since I have taken it upon myself to publish the manuscript sent to me, I cannot leave it without commentary and clarification, the necessity of which is highlighted in Part Two by the author himself, divided (or multiplied?) by two. But because I have to contend with this will to multiply or to divide as well, I am forced to assign different names to the authors of the two parts, although I know for certain that they are one and the same and that I will occasionally have to answer to myself as a result, since fragments of the narrative are ostensibly written in my name.

First and Second

nd so, let one author be known as the First, and the
other as the Second. Curiously enough, this corre-
sponds to the two names of the real individual about
whom I intend to speak presently. In his literary activities he
employed the somewhat strange pseudonym of M. Glubakov,
insisting on the *a* in the middle of the word even though many
pointed to the ridiculousness of such a surname and suggested
he substitute it for more natural-sounding ones. His real name,
however, is Nikolai Kazanov, and not Khazaner, as some of his
ill-wishers liked to call him. Which of them – M. Glubakov or
N. Kazanov – was dubbed N. by the First and Second Authors,
I cannot say with complete certainty.

I did, of course, recognize the author immediately, without even looking at the first page, and feel obliged to say a
few words about him. He was the first professional littérateur
I became acquainted with as a young man; in fact, he wasn't so
much the first littérateur – by the time I made his acquaintance
I was already friends with several unpublished young poets and
ceaselessly versified myself – Glubakov wasn't so much the first
littérateur as the first member of the Union of Soviet Writers
with whom I unashamedly maintained relations, paying no
mind to those among my friends and compeers who condemned any association with engaged literature. Glubakov had
a marvellous knack for getting love stories printed in Soviet
journals and the biggest state publishing houses of the country
despite entirely emancipating their narratives from questions
of ideology or industrial production. My poet-friends smiled

derisively, but their secret respect was clear to see. Yet I was never a particular admirer of his art: rather, I liked him for what he was, more as Kazanov than as Glubakov – for his utterly undemanding independence, or, put another way, for that particular kind of firmness which, fully self-aware, affords infinite patience and – *softness.* An unfortunate choice of words, perhaps, but that's the best I can do.

It was my duty to do justice to his name, and this, I hope, has been achieved – in his own terms (see Part One). As concerns A. – but no! – I'll refrain from calling her Adele: let this be her name in the works of Glubakov-Kazanov alone. Nor do I wish to deal with the actions of a literary heroine; I am not inclined to delve into the particulars of invention and fantasy, if only because I knew and loved the prototype herself. She is with us no longer, and the circumstances of her death are correctly set out in the First Author's preamble, where the source of information about her demise is no less accurately specified. Friends and acquaintances called her Ritochka, and I – I called her Margot. Both authors are misleading in their accounts of our relationship, for it is common knowledge that I was Margot's first husband, and my love for her was eternal and undiminished.

I don't know why the First and Second authors insist on persevering with the use of the sobriquet 'Adele' and its variants, despite making mention of several real names over the course of the narrative: I have reason to believe that both Glubakov and Kazanov were fond of the true name of this woman, but that she herself found it somehow inadequate – as far as I can judge, she was drawn to the sound of the word 'Marina', though she didn't allow herself to be so called. 'Margot', its first syllable corresponding to that of her favourite name, compelled her to respond: nevertheless, I always felt that she did this somewhat detachedly, if not with a degree of irritation.

Still, I do have one theory about the origin of the sobriquet 'Adele', a theory which, admittedly, sometimes seems fantastical even to me. It concerns the fact that it was none other than yours truly who from time to time addressed Margot with the words, 'O Delia, my darling', and, as the reader will see, she herself occasionally employed this form of address. Now, it may well be that this very 'O-Delia' became the Adele of Glubakov-Kazanov, though for the life of me I cannot explain how or where these authors could have come across this intimate, playful sobriquet.

I wonder whether the reader has noticed that the author – multiplied or divided as he is – begins each part with an apology, even while simultaneously making clear his discomfiture at having to beg pardon, though whose, he cannot say. For some reason, the vague sense of guilt that neither the First nor the Second Author quite manages to formulate has assailed me as well: Is the feeling contagious? Is the obligation to settle scores with a deceased woman the cause of these pangs of conscience? Or is it, perhaps – horribile dictu – is it that this is required by the subject?

Be that as it may, it is now my turn, which is, I have to say, a little strange, because I consider myself, to a certain extent at least, to be the guardian of Margot's memory, and since her archives are in my possession, along with written authorization to dispose of them as I wish, I plan to turn the manuscript I received into a supplementary section of a book about a woman who is nothing less than extraordinary; and the book shall be dominated by the authentic voice of its heroine, while the various fictions with pretensions to 'artistic merit' and 'novelistic convention' shall be relegated to the lowly status of occasionally bumbling, often absurd commentary. If you found out even the most trifling details of the life of, say, Lou Andreas-Salomé, would you not then regard Wedekind's 'Lulu' plays or, for that matter, Alban Berg's opera of the same name, as marginal notes to the private episodes in her biography, whatever the artistic value of these works?

Should I apologize for making the letters of Margot public on these pages? Long gone, I believe, is the epoch when ladies were prepared to pay colossal sums to safeguard the secrets of their correspondences, and it is now deemed valorous to set about the business of publication as early as possible – even within the correspondents' lifetimes. Moreover, I am not sure that Margarita's epistolary endeavours were ever actually sent by post, nor do they give the impression of being drafts, and it is unlikely that she made copies of her letters: at any rate, the one that appears to be addressed to me was never even put into an envelope. I read it many years after it had been written, and I believe that, for all their vitriol, for all the tremulousness of their content, almost all of her letters were, in a sense, literary exercises. In this respect, they are at least as deserving of publication, if not more so, than the efforts of Glubakov (or Kazanov).

The letters are not dated, and I have not attempted to establish any sense of chronology, just as I have made no effort to ascertain which letter was addressed to whom. I cannot deny that in places they made for difficult reading and left me with a multitude of painful impressions. Belated jealousy this wasn't: needless to say, I understand the literary nature of Margot's epistles better than anyone else! But I came face to face once again with her intensely idiosyncratic personality, her courage, and her ruthlessly self-critical, almost unbelievable, honesty. I also imagine that if one of her addressees has read, or were to read, the lines intended for him or, conversely, the words written about him, but not for him, he would be highly perturbed and, most likely, indignant at my publication. I hope it is clear that I do not wish to cause anyone offence: I am simply constructing a memorial according to my own understanding of how it should be done, and my greatest desire is for everybody who knew Margot to agree that this isn't the worst way to go about it. If the worst does come to the worst, though, I trust that the reader will let God be my judge, and that should be enough, at least as far as I'm concerned. But this isn't about me, after all – is it now?

Commentary

Before moving on to Margot's epistolary legacy, which, as I have promised, shall transform the novelistic flourishes of Glubakov-Kazanov into a simple commentary to inconsequential (or, come to think of it, perhaps significant) episodes of her biography, allow me, without passing judgement on the quality of the First and Second Authors' literary work, to draw attention to one particular (and, in my opinion, disgraceful) escapade. This concerns the nineteenth-century stylization which, according to the Second Author, is based upon a rhymed source. Mystification, nothing more! Hardly difficult for me to riposte to this tomfoolery or, if you like, to this thrown-down gauntlet: I'm very well acquainted with the source text, though I don't quite understand the point of manipulating and interfering with it in this way. I shall simply quote its opening lines; you don't have to be an expert to recognize the author — any lover, let alone 'connoisseur', of Russian literature will have no difficulty in identifying him.

> *A throng of recollections, like a swarm*
> *Of gnats, has recently enveloped me.*
> *I could review the fleet and wingèd form*
> *Of all the mottled memories I see,*
> *Yet of a single one shall I inform*
> *The reader; contrary tho' this might be*
> *To sense, this one event has held great sway*
> *Upon me—let it now school you, I pray …*

To find the rest of the text, the reader has only to consult a volume of the works of Alexei Konstantinovich Tolstoy and look up *The Portrait*, a narrative poem. And that's all I have to say about the matter …

Now, as regards Evgeny Vitkovsky's response, cited by the Second Author: I contacted the poet, whom I hold in great esteem, but he categorically denied authorship, claiming he has never engaged in any games of this kind and that he does not consider Rainer Maria Rilke's *The Notebooks of Malte Laurids Brigge* to be a potential source for the Russian text, and all the more so because the paraphrase of certain episodes of the novel, written in his name, distorts the essence of this marvellous work. As for the text of the given translation, it is indeed in his collection. This last detail caused me no little surprise, for, you see, I myself authored the translation, yet by my reckoning nobody should have been aware of its existence. Or rather, Glubakov may well have known about it from Margot, though she did give her word not to show it to a soul, and in situations of this sort you couldn't have hoped for anyone more reliable. That the translation came into Vitkovsky's possession, then, acquires a wholly mystical dimension in my eyes; then again, the same applies to many texts plucked literally out of thin air by this indefatigable translator.

For the sake of integrity, and to afford the reader as comprehensive an insight into the matter as possible, I shall quote 'Abelone's Song' in the language of the original. Margot knew and loved this poem. In point of fact, it is precisely for this reason that I set about translating it: somehow existing versions never really satisfied her. I had no intention of publishing my work, but there's little I can do about it now that the translation is no longer confined to my files, having found its way into at least two other collections as well, which means that sooner or later it'll come to light whether I like it or not.

In any case, here is Rilke's poem – in the original:

Du, der ich's nicht sage, dass ich bei Nacht
weinend liege,
deren Wesen mich müde macht

wie eine Wiege.
Du, die mir nicht sagt, wenn sie wacht
meinetwillen:
wie, wenn wir diese Pracht
ohne zu stillen
in uns ertrügen?
Sieh dir die Liebenden an,
wenn erst das Bekennen begann,
wie bald sie lügen.
Du machst mich allein. Dich einzig kann ich vertauschen.
Eine Weile bist du's, dann wieder ist es das Rauschen,
oder es ist ein Duft ohne Rest.
Ach, in den Armen hab ich sie alle verloren,
du nur, du wirst immer wieder geboren:
weil ich niemals dich anhielt, halt ich dich fest.

Both parts contain an assortment of allusions and literary games, inviting the reader to engage in intertextual analysis. I do not approve of this literary technique, just as I cannot endorse the various theories concerning some sort of 'metaliterature', under the influence of which, it would appear, the opus published on these pages was composed. But simply to *react* to these hints and intimations would not be sufficient – I am also obliged to *expound* them for the reader, although, in doing so, I stand to tarnish my reputation: anyone who has undertaken to read this book in the first place will undoubtedly guess or immediately realize what it is the First and Second Authors are hinting at. Many will decide that I'm forcing an open door, but I have no other choice. Nevertheless, I shall endeavour to keep my comments to a minimum.

For instance, when they speak of Yadya-Ariadna's 'infernality' or the 'diabolical nature' of the portrait by the artist Cosini-Corsini-Cazène, characters often invoke the names Biondetto-Biondetta, with no explanation whatsoever given for their doing so. It's almost embarrassing for me to have to spell out that this is a nod to Jacques Cazotte's *Le Diable amoureux*, a far from obscure novella whose protagonist is seduced by a demon who, assuming now male, now female – but equally alluring – guises, goes by precisely the names in question. Nor, of course, can even the least attentive of readers fail to take note of the choice of surnames, all of which recall, to some degree or other, the last name of the French author, though no less so than they do that of another – an Italian – whom, however, I shall not identify in view of the total transparency (and crudity!) of the reference – *honni soit*!

And here's another allusion. It is imperative for the authors to hint in some way at the 'Letter to the Amazon' without mentioning it directly, for which purpose our heroine in one of her erotic poses is dubbed an 'Amazon'. But this is utter twaddle: though the Amazons did do their fair share of riding, as we all know, they also kept their virginity intact and so could never have found themselves in Adele's position.

Just as inaccurate is the comparison to the *maja* into which our heroine – I forget which of her guises she happens to be in at that point – metamorphoses. The desire of the *maja vestida* is *as yet* ungratified; that of the *maja desnuda*, meanwhile, is *already* ungratified. What, then, was being implied, when nothing needed to be said other than that our heroine had moved from a sitting to a reclining position? That's all there is to it! Still, we mustn't be overly nitpicky. 'Metaliterature' though this might be, it's certainly no stranger to metaphor, nor to metonymy, which contemporary postmodernists, caught up in the throes of a creative frenzy, have dubbed 'metametaphorics' – how ghastly!

The Letters

1. Little one

My little one!

Just like Vertinsky: 'Listen, little one, can I love you gently?' Just like him, yes, but that's not what I wanted to say. No: but write me a letter, my little one, and I'll take it to bed with me. And in it I would find meaning, perhaps even meaning that you yourself did not discern, that was beyond your intentions, perhaps even that which is not there at all – whatever; I like going to bed with meaning; I like turning it this way and that, swaddling it in my notes and comments, in my similes and metaphors; and I like arranging punctuation marks in my own way – especially the dash (they say this is a characteristic of feminine punctuation, which I concede readily and without shame).

You will say that in view of my aspirations I'd be better off bedding you and not the letter. Let's keep the trite and the trivial to a minimum, shall we, little one? – but no, can't get by without that: of course you'll end up spouting some triviality or other – it would almost be a shame if you avoided doing it somehow – just not now though, all right? First let our mouths talk, and only afterward our souls, for it is *in bed* that the 'negotiation of souls' really takes place. Naturally I can tell spirit from matter, but I'm convinced even so that it is only through interlinking bodies that souls can caress one another: *we owe our bodies thanks, because they thus, did us, to us at first convey, yielded their sense's force, to us, nor are dross to us, but allay.* Yes, yes, we'll have our share of the higher things, and our souls shall gaze lovingly at each other, but now let us busy ourselves with semantics, with euphony, and perhaps with glossolalia as well – ultimately, that is, with the generation of meaning. Call me Roxane if you must, only I'm not about to overlook my Cyrano, I won't miss out on him; and even if a Christian were to come between us, it wouldn't be for more than a day. Well, speak then, speak!

When I listen to you – or, better yet, when I read you! – my entire being unfurls – all my darkness, all my femininity becomes unshackled – I can feel it! I look into myself; and to the world – and to you, little one, to you too – I am blind in that moment. Oh blissful blindness – blissful clairvoyance! In that moment I'm alone, there's nobody with me – which is why I do not call for you but only call upon you: write me a letter – and I shall sleep with it!

I don't need to apprehend you, I want to anticipate, to fore-know you – figuring you out doesn't seem the most difficult of tasks, but I like the way in which, like a flautist from a flute, you manage to tease out, work loose from me, from my deepest, darkest recesses, a store of secret strength. This strength, though inside me, is incomparably bigger than me, like a flame I per-ceive as moisture, if you'll excuse the oxymoron, and I bathe in this moisture, feminine, all too feminine to tolerate the close presence of a man. Don't peep now, Actaeon, or you'll be torn apart, torn with such force that shreds of you will be propelled beyond our orbit into the Great Nowhere of the Universe, getting clogged up in its cloacae – the explosion will be of cosmic proportions! Nothing more dangerous, nothing more delightful than the essence of femininity. But this essence, dark and denuded as it is, is not for men. Pray, take heed of it, but let *me* delight in it, too, for you, and at present only you, can loose it from my depths.

Wait, my little one, wait just a little while longer. You can say everything that needs to be said in letter form! Well, go ahead and say it!

If I hadn't written you, I couldn't have possibly found out about everything I've said here. But now I can let you in on it too! Do you know what you'll write me about? Then again, what does it matter? The meaning must be sought elsewhere: there's never any to be found in 'what about'. I doubt whether even 'how' is particularly meaningful. I'm convinced that meaning nestles somewhere 'betwixt' and 'between'. Even now, as I write to you, meaning swells menacingly between us, and only a portion of that meaning comes from your as yet unwritten – and will you ever write it? – letter. It is 'betwixt' and 'between' that any hollow, slit or gaping hole comes to acquire its substance, its signification. Don't be afraid – you needn't think I'm playing about with erotic symbols: it's not my fault all these things have a sexual connotation, though, come to think of it, I did unwittingly summon up this throng of pseudo-innuendoes when I began to speak – too seriously, perhaps – of the quintessence of femininity.

Can you feel just how *loaded* everything I've said here is?

Goodbye.

2. Madman!

Madman!

You brought a broom into my house! Oh! Oh! Oh! What did you mean by it? That the place is always a mess? (Ah, I know, I know!) That I'm a witch? (Not only I know that!) That you've guessed who I am? But I've spoken openly about it before, and not only spoken – I've *warned* you about it on more than one occasion! And by the by, I need no broom to fly me to the Sabbath: I fly without contrivance – a broom for me is nothing more than a symbol for the odious activity of keeping house. You might as well have made me a gift of washing powder, you cretin!

And I can guess where you came from. Put you up to it, did she? Yes, and what now? Everything's as clear as day as far as I'm concerned: I shall not change; but you – are you resolved to bring change about? Madman! Madman! And those flowers you significantly presented me with last time. What, have you been brushing up on your floriography? Yellow, eh? Was it rupture you were hinting at? Or did you just happen to pick precisely those flowers that arouse nothing but irritation in me?

You're not fit to fill the void, even if one were to appear in my life. I can get by without men, I can get by without anything. You know nothing, and you shall never penetrate into my pain. And you shall never have the power – the capacity – to hurt me. I hope that pains you. I know that I can hurt you – and I do. I, a witch! Now that's a discovery and a half! You should have guessed as much from the very beginning – and you did, of course: no use pretending you realized it only now and that in the beginning I wasn't what I finally came to be! The wax of immortality has the tendency to melt, my dear friend. And our immortality was short-lived. But why all this suffering? To outlive your own immortality is not the greatest of misfortunes!

Hurt you though I do, I still want to have a monopoly on that endeavour. I mean that I've no wish for you to torment yourself with utterly senseless suspicions and entirely unfounded misgivings: you haven't a single physical shortcoming; it is merely that you suffer from a lack of freedom, which keeps me under lock and key as well – and there, and only there, is the rub. *My* freedom suffers within me if the man by my side has none of his own to speak of. That is all.

Je t'embrasse, my dear. Stand unbridled and serene. As for me, I fancy I might try out your broom after all, seeing as you've gone and given it to me, no matter what it was you were insinuating. And you have a go and guess what I'm going to use it for: flying or tidying up the house?

3. Dear …

Dear Vasiliy Vasilievich,

I remember only too well that you once promised to box the ears of anyone who dared to pay you a compliment. Naturally, I've grown accustomed to taking everything you say *cum grano salis*; even so, I shall begin this letter – a letter that might be regarded as a kind of declaration of love – by asserting that I literally cannot stand you, you fussy, peevish, piddling excuse for a man! The only masculine thing about you is your trousers. But, judging from your own words, you've heard this all before and know it for yourself. And now I must add that it is your trousers that I love more than anything else. You'll understand, of course, that I'm not talking about any old men's trousers – in all cases save for yours, I'd openly prefer the contents to the packaging. In your case, however, I love the trousers *themselves* – yours, and no one else's. Time and time again you've dissociated yourself from many of your pronouncements, but this one, I'm sure, you shall not disown:

'I wear literature like I wear my trousers. It's just as familiar and generally "your own". You take care of your trousers, you cherish them, "you're always in them" (I'm constantly writing). So why stand on ceremony with them?!'

And elsewhere:

'I feel no constraints in literature, because literature is just the trousers that I wear. That there are other littérateurs and that literature has an objective existence does not bother me in the slightest.'

And it's your literature that I love. I almost couldn't care any less about your ideas. They hold more appeal for the man through whom I first became acquainted with your works (I don't know whether you'll be pleased to learn – you'll be amused at least, no doubt – that his surname is Beilis). You were often whingeing (or was it bragging?) that no one could understand you as well as the Yids. But how would it be for you if understanding were to be forthcoming from the Russian side of things? For I, just like you, am 'as Russian as can be', which, in contrast to you, was never a source of pride for me, nor yet a cause for self-belittlement.

Can you be proud of Pushkin, for example, when you're not fit so much as to stand in his shadow? – And to whom are you to proclaim your pride: to the compatriots of Shakespeare or to the tribesmen of great African sorcerers? You can adore Tchaikovsky, but what about Brahms? But nor will I hang my head in shame should anyone call my people 'uncouth and rude'. Though I wholeheartedly understand you when you say, 'I myself am forever berating the Russians. In fact, I do nothing but berate them. "I am a most unbearable Shchedrin." But why do I hate anyone who does the same? Virtually the only people I do hate are those who hate and particularly those who despise the Russians. Yet without a doubt [and here our sentiments diverge, Vasiliy Vasilievich], I despise the Russians myself – to the point of loathing. It's abnormal.'

Jews arouse no particular interest in me: I neither like them nor hate them. Now Beilis I do like, and Levinson too – but hardly because they're Jews; Trotsky I detest – but his Jewish blood doesn't come into the equation.

Now put me to the test. I shall remind you of two ideas of yours that I believe to be the most significant; I truly set greater store by them than by anything else. I could say that I thought them up myself, and that would be almost true, but in fact I conceived of them wordlessly, becoming *consciously* aware of their existence only once I discovered them in your books. And so, I quote.

Idea number one:

> 'Where, then, can truth be found?'
>
> 'In the plenitude of all ideas. Simultaneously. Choose one over the rest at your peril. In *vacillation*.'
>
> '*Vacillation*? Is it truly a principle?'
>
> 'It is – the most fundamental of them all. The only one that is secure. The one that brings everything into bloom, into life. The onset of *stability* would bring with it the petrifaction – the icing over of the universe … God, too, was of "a hundred minds". About how to make "a single day". And He made every hour, even every ten minutes different from the rest.'

Idea number two, yet more precious to me than the first:

> 'Peoples of the world, I shall reveal to you a thunderous truth that not a single one of your prophets has ever articulated …'
>
> 'Well? Well? … Hh-hh …'
>
> 'The truth is this: personal life transcends all else.'

'He-he-he! … Ha-ha-ha! … Ha-ha! …'

'I mean what I say! No one has said this before me; I am the first … Simply to be sat at home, picking your nose, say and watching the sunset …'

'Ha, ha, ha …'

'But yes: this is more *fundamental* than religion. All religions shall cease to be, but this shall remain: simply to be curled up in your chair, staring into the distance …'

There it is! nail on the head! First of all, thank you for the gift for all seasons: 'personal life transcends all else' – yes! yes! yes! Secondly, I love your trousers precisely because they're the great equalizer. Your work flattens hierarchies of meaning, recognizing no difference between the murmur of the forest, the music of Beethoven, masturbation, the novels of Dostoyevsky, nose-picking, and every other human endeavour you could care to bring to mind – in its *personal* incarnation. How literarily you expound this principle in your ostensibly non-literary writings! Shklovsky alone spoke of the high degree of literariness in your books, but he merely called attention to it, explaining nothing. And yet, you discovered an entirely new method of constructing literary works. I'm not talking about the genre so crudely misconstrued by your innumerable imitators. They think that to become your pupil and follower you need only cover the page with chaotic jottings that hint at clandestine, shady doings, and add in a footnote that they were written in the bathhouse on a pack of Belomor cigs. And what they failed to get to grips with was your most important law – the law of *vacillation*.

Your books, after all, not only dazzle with their by turns astute, original, scandalous ideas – they're also full of barefaced and provocative nonsense. And how often they twist the facts, bend the truth, conjecture erroneously! But it's impossible to tear yourself away from them, they enchant and mesmerize, though at times they can also be torturous – not because they grapple with life's 'big questions' à la Dostoevsky, but because trifles are placed on an equal footing with moments of revelation; the whole thing acquires a content-moulding function, thematic lines are musically extended, compositional rhymes become apparent – the architectonics is extraordinarily complex and rich. But how pleasant it is to trace the development of particular motifs, composed in a variety of different registers, and follow them as they interweave and unravel and merge and plunge underground and soar up to the heavens. And your voice – your voice is pretty well disagreeable, unoperatic, often squealing, but at times it becomes so heartrendingly confidential and intimate that in spite of yourself you let it into your personal life, into the study, into the library, into the bedroom – and shall I say where else? Oh, but you don't need me to tell you!

Wholly yours.

P.S. Beilis used to tell me he'd give anything to spend ten minutes with you on your walk – you remember the one: from the corner of Znamenskaya Street and Grodnensky Lane, along Kirochnaya Street and up to Liteiny Prospect. Oh, if only you could take me with you as well! How does this idea of this – how shall I put it? – group sex sound to you? And with Jewish participation to top it all off?! We'd ask Beilis to leave his knife at home. Don't be angry, for God's sake. I remember, of course, that 'no man is worthy of praise; every man is worthy only of compassion'.

4. O, Delia …

O, Delia, my darling!

I've long been meaning to talk with you, but so instantaneously do you grasp the meaning of words that have not yet been said, that are merely being primed for articulation, that I scarcely have the time to finish my own thoughts. You understand, of course, knowing me as only you do, that I like to formulate my thoughts fully – and not for my interlocutor's sake but for my own – and the clearer my expression, the more receptive to my words said interlocutor becomes. Your responsiveness in our interactions is sublime, almost magical, but – don't be angry, now – it is precisely this that bothers me: I sense no resistance, only acquiescence and concurrence.

You remember how fearful we were at the very start of our relationship, how, trembling with sweet terror, we imagined our connection to have something of the preternatural about it, even though we had both read and heard enough to know better. By the time we'd met I was already sufficiently experienced with men; as far as our own sex is concerned, I believe that, in order to attain a thorough understanding of almost every aspect of her sisters' feelings and behaviour, it is enough for a woman simply to know herself. For you, however, all this was new: I turned out to be both *prima* and *primus* in your life.

In this respect I feel that I'm the senior and more responsible half of our whole. As I see it, the coming together of two women can prove to be exceptionally harmonious, conducive as it is to the perpetuation of a particular kind of love, a love that is an extension of the desire you have for yourself (in other words, the most powerful desire there is!) – and at the same time not entirely for yourself but for another you (for *you*, O Delia, my darling!). And yet how fragile the love that receives a strong affirmative response. Or perhaps it's not the feeling that is extinguished but the lovers: Romeo and Juliet must die so that love may remain. Or else it's the lovers' sundering, their unslaked passion, that immortalizes for the world the hypnotic force that drew them together. As someone once said (can you remind me who it was?), 'lovers are children', but – and here we come to the crux of the matter – 'children don't have children'.

As you know, Nature, having bestowed upon me certain feminine virtues, proceeded to deprive me of the most important one of all – the ability to give birth. Lovers don't have children, I've never had nor shall ever have children, ergo – can you complete the syllogism? Hence, I suppose, the strength – and the purity of my infatuations. Neither shall I be able to give anybody a child, nor shall anybody give a child to me. And in our case this is an a priori impossibility. But *you*, O Delia, *you*, so far as I know, have been denied nothing by Nature, and I can already see the day when all your being shall scream, 'I want a child!' Most likely you'll want the child to look like me, assuming you're still in love with me at that point. A dismal prospect! You'll start looking around, thinking you're in need of nothing more than a substitute, nothing more than ersatz – well, what can you do: as yet no one's come up with a better way of going about things. And the day shall come when you'll show me your candidate for the job – a trivial job for him, but how repugnant for you – and you'll say, I need him only for this, you must believe me! And look, you'll say, he has your face – the same eyes, the same long lashes, the same line of the nose, even his earlobes have the same shape as yours, can you see? Our child, and it will be ours, *yours and mine*, you'll say, my dear Delia, our child will look like you – in other words, like me.

Yes, I see, my dearest, I can see it all now, though today, of course, you'll want to call such reasoning into question. Not at all, not even in the slightest respect shall your ersatz resemble me. And the child, a child I could love and fuss over, coming to your house only to be greeted by the hateful gaze of your husband, shall never be *ours*. The past, in which I'll remain, shall torture you and weigh you down, and your sufferings shall unquestionably become intolerable for me as well. I know you'll not find it easy to believe all this now, but for God's sake isn't it better to part at once, with the storm only beginning to brew, and not wait for the deluge itself?

Yours, ever yours, and henceforth forever yours.

P.S. Beilis once told me about how an analogous situation would be dealt with in certain African cultures. There, a sterile woman, or one who is past child-bearing age, has the right to 'woman-marriage'. She brings a consort into her husband's house and gives her over to him. The child born from this union is regarded as belonging to the sterile woman, and the mother of the child as her wife. But we're a long way off matching the achievements of African culture – and will we ever match them? Oh, go on, give us a smile.

5. Unaddressed

I leave this unaddressed, even though I've christened you with a pet name of my own invention – a name I shall never reveal to anyone else. Were I to begin the letter with it, the end result would turn out quite different from what it ought to be.

I could easily write to you in less ceremonious fashion after what befell us – befell, rather than merely happened between us. 'Between', and not 'to', for everything unfolded in the very space that divided us, having brought us together for the first time. In my thoughts I am on more familiar terms with you, but, seeing as our biographies have been in no way transformed by external events and it is only our destinies that have suffered, please accept my ceremonial manner and behave towards me in the same way.

As our host was introducing us, your gaze lifted me off the floor, and a kind of receiver for your thoughts turned itself on inside me. How little correlation between what you were thinking and what you were saying! When, for instance, you spoke thus – 'Delighted to make your acquaintance. I've heard so much about you!' – *thus* ran your panicked thoughts: 'What's this? Never have I laid eyes on such a creature.' And while you courteously enquired about my work, your entire being was pulsating to the beat of a simple refrain: 'I want her, I want her now.'

What? You're going to deny it? Don't even think about it.

Listen instead to a confession of my own upheaval. I was saying – but you remember, of course, what I was saying. And I suspect that, just like me, your ears were also attuned to that which was not spoken aloud. But in case you failed to make out this tumultuous din, I shall articulate it clearly and concisely for you: in response to your call I sent forth a pulse of my own desire, and never before have I done so with such intensity.

That, essentially, is that; there shall be nothing more. I implore you, don't try to see me, don't phone, don't write. What happened was so complete and comprehensive (conclusive) that any development would be death or – worse – madness.

Farewell.

6. Dearest artist

Dearest artist, I know you're unhappy with the portrait, that you've been tearing up sketches everybody likes and feverishly repainting completed sections of the canvas – in a word, that you've been behaving yourself like the perfectionist you're renowned for being and whom I recognized as such in my attempt to penetrate into your vision.

How shall I be rendered on the canvas? This concerns me not at all. Nor should you be concerned by the likely prospect of presenting the model (myself) with the completed work in fear of (my) female resentment. Vain worries, all!

You may render me in whatever way you see fit. I could be naked, swaddled in furs, mopping and mowing, decadent, sinister, sarcastic; I could be a witch, an androgyne, psychologically substantial, heavy or empty. You have my permission to transfigure me into blotches of colour on the canvas – I'm flattered by any use of my persona as material for art.

Your average model wants to recognize herself in the picture she's been sitting for, and her friends invariably enjoy a good natter about whether or not it has successfully captured the 'fundamental essence' of her character. As for me, I couldn't care less! Not in the least do I insist on your creating a portrait as such: let it simply be an *image*, a piece of art, a tattered fragment; and if a fragment is indeed the result, so much the better – it shall be asteam, aquiver with life.

You'll see it through, I know you will. And I know this too: someday, believe you me, the fruits of your labour shall be called a masterpiece.

I must ask you not to regard this letter as an attempt to give you thinly veiled advice or as some kind of insinuation. I simply wished to affirm, as far as I am able, my belief in your pre-eminence as regards that sphere of human endeavour to which I myself would have liked to contribute in some small way and which, denied the talent to do so by Fate, I am happy to be playing a part in, if not through my own efforts, then through you.

7. Beloved

My beloved, and, I should like to say, my one and only – were I not able to conjure up the image of you wincing even at the very first epithet. I understand that, being familiar with my biography, you must find it very difficult, if not impossible, to accept these words as true. But remember nonetheless that I spoke them.

My pretext for writing you? – a happy one! I'm going to Rome, and you can appreciate, of course, what this means to me. Never before, and especially not when we were together, could I even so much as entertain the thought of such a possibility, but now I've gleefully plucked up my staff and set out for far-off Rome.

You enjoyed admonishing me with lines you often used to mutter: '*It's not Rome the city that's eternal, but man's place in the Universe.*' But I'm sure that Rome is precisely that – *my* place in the Universe. In the Eternal City death itself is a less than terrifying prospect, and perhaps – yes, yes, I'll say it – perhaps even a desirable one. I say this without bombast, without solemnity, but I do not say it in jest. To see Rome – and to die. I toyed with this idea back when I was banned from travelling abroad, and nor do I think *any differently* now, when I open my little handbag to see the tickets lying inside.

It really would be something to be able to preside over your own life, in the sense that you could – without resorting to suicide – will it to end once you've decided that you've had your innings and that the remainder of your days would amount to little more than wholly superfluous inertia and illusoriness. Once your greatest wish comes true, everything else is surely nothing more than phantasmal, while the moment I'm explaining to you – that moment is an explosion of light that simultaneously dazzles and illuminates, affording you, unseeing, a view over all four corners of the world (as in Gogol's 'A Terrible Vengeance'). Incidentally, Gogol, too, if I recall, considered Rome his proper place, and, in my opinion, died by virtue of his own desire to die, upon sensing that he had run his course. And died in Rome, befittingly enough.

Don't get any ideas: this is no premonition, and I haven't forgotten that you can't stand what you used to call my 'soothsaying', my witch's antics; I'm not trying to prophesy,

I'm merely fantasizing about how good it would be – and my innards leap with pleasure at the thought! How fittingly this letter would read then: a valediction! But this is no fare-well – whether in this life or the next, our paths cannot fail to cross again. Tell me you'll forgive me, only don't tell me goodbye.

Well, God speed me on my way!

Notes

I deliberated for a long time whether I should pass some sort of comment on these letters so as to shed light on the character of their author or on the motives for the correspondence. In all honesty, I don't know, and nor am I sure whether I could do this in the appropriate manner. I hope, nevertheless, that the image of Margot will not slip away entirely from the attentive reader. I have to confess that certain details in the above-quoted texts unexpectedly compelled me to see her in her entirety and to mourn quietly over her demise once more.

I wont insist no & wouldnt dare to either that she look here I found her hair in a book we read together yes this is her hair & in front of this mirror she brushed her hair & dressed & undressed & how I loved to watch her at her evening toilette with her eagle eye scrutinizing the movement of her own hands pencilling her eyelashes Ive always been touched by precisely this attentiveness this endless concentration this complete disavowal of everything else in the world nothing matters now but the eyelashes & she never noticed me watching her or no of course she did but she never allowed herself to linger over the fact because being aware of anything other than cosmetics would corrupt the seriousness of the moment & only when she had brought the affair to a complete close would she give me a good jab in the side for spying on her but on the very same page where her hair lies & where it will stay a note is pencilled in a marginal gloss written by her & how precise it is how profound

the energy of her words & the quickness of her wit & what
about that withering smirk which would drive the most self-
confident men wild & her broom there she stands holding it
she sometimes liked to greet her guests with said broom
pointedly in hand what do you know about that Kazanov
what can you say for yourself Glubakov & who could get
one up on her who could even so much as depict her neither
brush nor lens could capture her now here it is on the table
the photograph which I used to say showed her with her
wrist joints achatter with some wordsigh playing at her lips
youd be more likely to guess the sound faintly suggested by
her mouth than to explain that unexpected wrinkle on her
forehead nowhere to be seen in any other image of her only
she herself would be able to explain it everyone listened to
her & she knew they were listening but never sang her own
praises never pushed a soul away & no pleasure greater than
telling her a story shed catch the meaning on the wing & she
had an ear for poetry beyond question I detected the convul-
sions of sensuality which ran the length of her body when
she liked a piece of music or a painting everything through
the senses but she could explain it all as well & everyone
rushed to ask her what does she think about the show the
film the book they craved conversation with her sought out
her friendship she had enemies but she never betrayed a soul
rumour had her linked to many men & she left many men
but no one ever had her down as a traitor shed slight & snub &
stupefy but without a hint of duplicity without a trace of
guile or venom without strain or stress she was light wished
lightness upon everybody & I often thought she could fly no
need of beating wings or stretched out arms for that but just
as shed take a step forward smile say hello so she could lift
herself up off the ground & into the air & no one would bat
an eyelid simply feast their eyes upon her in spite of themselves & maybe thats why shed never flaunt her skill didnt
want to be the cause of any hollow transports of delight thats
why shed produce the broom to redirect attention to an
object of course shed accept worship & sometimes shed

concentrate her efforts on winning it but her taste & her
discretion never let her down she would smile & her lightness never abandoned her & her company was light & only
N. in the writings of Glubakov-Kazanov could unimagina-
tively tie down the heroine named Adele or however else
with heavyhanded eccentricities in the spirit of Dostoevsky
whom of course she loved but hated too precisely for these
psychosodomitic perversions which were so utterly alien to
her though in her literary efforts she explored them as possible avenues of style no more than that generally she doubted
whether Dostoevsky had revealed anything in the Russian
national character though in her opinion he had marred it
with his passion for torment she too could be a tormentor
the Glubakov-Kazanov manuscript is concerned with exactly
that but is the torment she caused not akin to the sensation
engendered by the plenitude of life because the strength of
feeling she brought about is so great that even the harm she
did is tantamount to catharsis & ask anybody who was with
her & lost her even before her demise would they agree to
start life over without having met her & Ill say this too no
one who lost out on her really lost her & after her death even
N. in his gloomridden account of her passing uses the words
lightly & freely everyone dreams of lightness & freedom but in
her this was bred in the bone & could never be taken away
did she ever suffer I can only hazard a guess I was never witness to it myself but you cant do without suffering can you &
is there such a thing as freedom gained without suffering &
without excruciating meditation there is no answer to that
question & in memory of her I wont toil away at this weari-
some task & Ill easily shirk a straight answer if you want to
pore over the solution to this riddle make sure you dont
thuffer like Glubakov-Kazanov & the not inglorious Karenin
before him how well she died by the fountain wishing for
her return & she will return I believe she will as she believed
it is it possible to imagine her demise being an abominable
one akin to the one chosen by the wife of the *thufferer* &
which would befit the gloom of Glubakovs poetics happily

the prototype did not permit it despite being named Ada whereas it did not become Margot & was not capable of it here is the limit of authorial caprice it is forbidden though who forbade it the hand its own sovereign ruler but no her fate cannot be infringed upon even posthumously & she herself to dictate the play with us no longer but her will is not to be violated or transgressed not even on a sheet of paper filling the sheet with your characters & being account-able only to yourself but perhaps thats the thing not only to yourself & God will suffer no sin & everyone who knew her will most likely consider the power wielded over her in a textual space created wilfully & without license not merely as a betrayal but as a crime or even as a simple physical impossibility you might really want to do it but you just cant bring yourself to raise your hand against her & you wonder how such a thought couldve possibly occurred to you how you couldve possibly conceived it anyone who charges at her with an inkdipped quill shall surely die by the quill I know what Im talking about yes die but in truth he died & unlike her perished forever at the very moment when he enter-tained the thought crashed & burned long before the end & disappeared without trace eradicated himself as an author wanted to dynamite the monument & blew himself up into the bargain though if memory serves that was exactly what he had in mind he meant for the explosion to go off in the vicinity & nowhere else so people would always associate his blownup remains with her name no better (worse?) ploy could he concoct no one can learn from his example only you to love you to embrace you to mourn over & this too is death you always did slip away from the arms that made to embrace you & only he who never once held you will hold you forever Rainers right & it was she was it not whom he wished forever to hold fast that thought up the name Rainer for René how silly this vengeful Lulu sounds shes Ljolja as she was nicknamed in childhood but this isnt about her after all though it really does seem to be at times right Sigmund? rest in peace & you rest too you who armed lovers with whips did she not help you who composed romances set to her words the words of *die bösen Lieder*? play on Adele where once a feast was spread a coffin lies for theres rapture on the battleground & where the black abyss is found but she alone enraptures us absolutely or does she O how tormentingly happy you make me did you know that in your freedom mistaken by many for detachment though no one ever accused you of coldness of dispassion unlikely anyone would dare indifference it wasnt merely perhaps the cosmos breathing the cosmos breathes on her breast let him who can embrace the cosmos be the one to cast the first stone at her a cosmic stone a meteorite music of the spheres & no romance a cruel romance thats what N. produced ungainly & sentimental enough to make you tear up a little while he was thinking construction architectonics strummed guitar husky vocals oh so maudlin thats not it neither condescension nor contempt required & every man is worthy only of compassion & she knew it but expected no compassion herself & never showed any neither victim nor executioner nor mourner nor offender didnt want to be anyones enemy but could be nonetheless & if someone did consider her a foe you couldnt wish a better foe upon him cant quite say her soul was tender but it was decent & guiltless no matter what its mistress did & what a firstrate experimenter she was the positions she invented the connections she made the men the women she connected with which was no guarantee of future rights to her for any of them & theyd come to her lips dry from jealousy mumbling incantations proclaiming their desire to serve her on an equal footing with others she knew these lies off by heart & if they crawled over to her happy to be executed willing to wring their own necks she never gave assent for she rightly read *carmen* for *cruciamentum* knew a *handsaw* from a *hernshaw* always made her choice decisively should she stand back & let the *coffin pass* or stand back & let the *parson cough* her impeccable taste perfect vision allearness helped her on every occasion to resolve the irresolvable while she herself was unapprehended by anyones creativity neither brush nor word could enframe her & endow her with completeness portraits deceived & faltered words proved too nebulous & not a single photograph could capture her features with an *objective* precision her essence eluded any method of expression or fixation & the more complex the design of the 'simulative' system selected to eternalize her the greater the quantity of meanings imbued in the symbols the more insincere & bombastic the expression became a plurality of meanings barely took shape before being overtaken by inauthenticity while she only laughed & I think everyone who suffered one way or another at her hand was made to suffer by precisely this inauthenticity by false images of her which anyone who knew her had in abundance it can be assumed but no forget assumed it can be said with complete conviction that a certain number of the attempts to epitomize her were not devoid of artistic value but she herself remained invariably above & beyond all these attempts it was clear that the potential of the model was greater in itself than all these creative endeavours although naturally the portraits should they be read or seen out of the context of reality might produce a serious or better yet a spectacular impression as for me I settled on *one* of her photographs where you will remember her joints are achatter no doubt others had their own favourites but suspected all the same that they were ephemerae pages soaring past filled with wondrous poetry cant even make out the lines all you get is a faceful of wind the anguish of a happiness speeding away forevermore but has anyone ever realized its not *her* theyre being tormented by but this rara avis so nebulous materializing momentarily only to disappear again *flung into the deep of space should we destined to expire pine for sweet devotions grace and to constancy aspire* only she knew how to have no regrets about anything only she was betrothed to that extraordinary kind of freedom others can only dream sweetly about she never took off the crown she wore so lightly & was made for her head alone how regally she could pay no mind to the old wives wittering of Fate how on occasion she ignored the mouselike scuttling of life & perhaps turned a deaf ear to it because she was fluent in this obscure tongue from birth & meaning was nothing more than a needless hassle for her when she knew that phonetics is the seraphs handmaiden & I put down my pen because whats this Im doing am I not forcing sense from that selfsame phonetics passing my brush over vacuum conjuring spirits or are they conjuring me whos calling & am I alive & where am I & the portrait O devil take it the infernal portrait!

APPENDIX:
THE PORTRAIT (1873)

Alexei Konstantinovich Tolstoy

1

A throng of recollections, like a swarm
Of gnats, has recently enveloped me.
I could review the fleet and wingèd form
Of all the mottled memories I see,
Yet of a single one shall I inform
The reader; contrary tho' this might be
To sense, this one event has held great sway
Upon me—let it now school *you*, I pray …

2

Now all events are wont to leave a trace:
The shackles of his past, be it serene
Or sad, no man escapes scot-free, nor race
Of men; we're all fast-clenched. It must have been—
But I can scarcely reckon. It took place,
I think, ere even I had reached my teens,
When I was twelve, or little more than ten.
We've seen a metamorphosis since then!

3

A *century*'s gone by, you'd think: all's greatly
Altered, the world's been turned upon its head …
'Tis very simple, I've been thinking lately,
So simple that—but I'll resume my thread,
For that's another tale! Our house stood stately
By Anichkov Bridge; it need not be said—
And nor would any one think this untrue—
That its façades were of a yellow hue.

4

I've noticed that the patriotic heart
Finds pleasure in this yellow colouration;
We Russians are just hankering to tart
Our buildings up with ochre—a fixation
That highly-ranked officials, for their part,
Regard as loyalty and dedication;
We ochre, without pausing once to think,
Fire-tower, temple, spital-house and clink.

5

Unswerving lines embody, for our nation—
Inheritors of Batu and Mamai—
The very essence of sophistication,
And thus we've learned to subjugate the eye:
'Twixt square and steppe we see a correlation,
And itch with great desire to espy
The distant Tula straight from Arzamas,
While seeking beauty in the trite and crass.

6

Contrast our tastes a century ago—
We favoured curves, eccentric, complicated,
And garlanded pilasters, just for show,
Preferred façades medallion-decorated,
And roofs bedecked with cherubs in a row …
Our forebears' style we've newly recreated,
And borrowed, tho' it's gloriously daft,
Selected features from their lavish craft.

7

But in my youth, our tastes were less unruly:
The barrack style was deemed to be *bon ton*,
With a quartet of columns marshalled duly
Beneath the regulation Greek *fronton*
Of each façade. And I'll express this coolly:
In France, it was *le grand Napoléon*
Who, in his age of bellicose plebeians,
Began all this, while here 'twas Arakcheians.

8

Indoors, contrariwise, our house maintained
An old-school, eighteenth-century complexion,
And two or three apartments might have gained
An expert's awe, and drawn an interjection
Of amazement. The anteroom retained
Its bronzen lamps, and I'd a predilection—
Altho' unversed in art—for our large halls'
Rich ceilings, and the mouldings on the walls.

9

My parents … With a schedule like my mother's,
I seldom saw her; Father?—busy man.
And since I had no sisters and no brothers—
Just ever-grumbling aunties—I began
To roam the house, uncompanied by others.
Each room I filled with fancy's flights. I'd plan
Great deeds—each worthy of a novel's pages—
When but a chit, from th' earliest of ages.

10

Reality—now *that* I could not bear;
From boyhood on I've found it nauseating.
Life's humdrum stream, about me flowing e'er—
Prosaic pace! not rising nor abating;
Life's so-called sober, serious affairs—
All this I'm prone, instinctively, to hating.
But if I'm incorrect in this position,
That's just the nature of my disposition.

11

Diverse and sundry plants stood in our rooms:
Wallflowers, with their golden-orange hue,
And hyacinths—azure and crimson blooms,
And white, and pallid yellow, and light blue.
And I drank blissfully of their perfumes,
In search of worlds fantastical and new;
On each distinct aroma seemed to float
A low, enchanting music's far-off note.

12

On other days, upstarting from a spell
Of rev'rie, I'd remark a withered flower—
A crumpled bloom betwixt my fingers! Well,
I never could recall its plucking's hour,
But splendid visions, conjured by its smell,
Enthralled me. My imagination's power
Transformed our house into a magic world—
But life, meanwhile, unchangingly unfurled.

13

Reality—a seasonless procession!
Same settings, same décors, the same array
Of teachers, visiting in swift succession …
My dancing-master, brimming with ballet,
Would gambol in for our Thursdaily session;
His shrill violin in hand, he'd flit and play.
And I was taught by my domestic tutor
The tricks of Latin's third-declension neuter.

14

Teutonic to his very toes, well-read,
Well-ordered, staid, he'd reprimand me tartly
Whenever I spilt ink or broke my lead
(In fairness, he reproved *himself* most smartly).
But the profundities of what he said,
I must confess, I understood but partly,
Not least when he endeavoured to reveal
The shades of meaning in the term *Ideal*.

15

He relished Strabo, Pliny highly rated,
With Horace was disgustingly au fait;
All flowerings of art he keenly fêted—
A penchant we so seldom see to-day.
The principle of S-shaped lines, he stated,
Was beauty's precondition; to convey
His system by example—prove it finely—
My tutor'd sip and sup most serpentinely.

16

He always was decorous thro' and thro',
With form his principal preoccupation:
'*Das Formlose*—zis simply vill not do,'
He'd oft repeat, beset by indignation
If anyone should wilfully eschew,
Or fail to hone (a lesser irritation),
Exactitude in form. And he'd portray
Form's beauty in a histrionic way.

17

'Observe!' he'd say: 'by way of illustration,
I now shall imitate an antique pose—
Nay, sev'ral! Zeus, in Homer's fine narration,
Is *thus* described; here's Eros, head to toes,
As per Praxiteles's interpretation,
And here is Milo's Venus; but to close,
I'll presently assume Apollo's shape'—
And promptly gained the likeness of an ape.

18

O Reader, it's not difficult to see
That with all this I couldn't be contented;
Moreover, Nature had bestowed on me
A sense of beauty all my own. Presented
With the humdrum, our phantasies run free—
What isn't there shall always be invented;
The term I couldn't grasp, yet I could feel
The power of a different, fresh Ideal.

19

Altho' I sought its presence, craved it greatly,
Our home was little suited to this quest.
My pedagogue was anything but stately;
My ancient aunts with beauty were unblest.
That I dismissed these models as innately
Unbecoming, you surely will have guessed;
But there it was, true beauty, in the Hall—
My fancy found it, hung upon a wall.

20

'Twas this: a portrait of a youthsome girl,
Most lithely poised, its colours dulled away—
Or p'rhaps the light that filtered through the swirl
Of window-curtains made it *seem* that way.
Upon her shoulder fell a powdered curl,
Her breast, meantime, adorned with a bouquet;
She clutched her pinafore's taffeta trimming,
With myriads of roses over-brimming …

21

'An empty beauty, ruled by trite convention!
Mere decadence!' So others will maintain,
Yet every fold enraptured my attention;
Meanwhile, one subtle feature teased my brain,
A riddle that invited comprehension:
Altho' her eyes were filled with sorrow's pain,
I thought her lips—all rascally and wily—
Were quirking upward, edges curling wryly.

22

Th' expression of her face, to my surprize,
Was predisposed to constant variation;
I spied these metamorphoses of guise
Sev'ral times a viewing—fluctuation
In the elusive colour of her eyes,
Her lips' mysterious configuration—
And saw her gaze alternately express
Reproof, entreaty, coquetry, tendresse.

23

Her fate's a mystery: perhaps—O pity!—
'Twas on the guillotine she met her end,
A French marquise? Or was her native city
Our splendid Petersburg, and did she spend
The evens playing ombre, cordial, witty,
And, thriving under Catherine, then attend
Potyomkin's glittering, resplendent ball,
Her beauty, sun-like, charming one and all?

24

I never voiced these questions; all the same,
I had good reason for such strict discretion:
Back then, I couldn't quash my furtive shame,
But now I'll make an effortless confession,
Discarding it for good—I was aflame
With passion for the picture, an obsession
Which, alas, left my Latin high and dry:
Love's first hello is Wisdom's last goodbye!

25

Unhappy with my academic flailing,
My tutor sighed; his brow began to cloud.
Ach *nein*—I abso*lutely* was not ailing:
'*Wer will, der kann*,' he soberly avowed,
''Tis sloth!' And he persisted with his railing,
And windily proclaimed that we're endowed
With reason so we may control our will—
And leash our errant selves with growing skill.

26

A devotee of Kant, if I recall,
He had forgot his idol's proclamation
That carnal forms of things *an sich* lack all
Free will and any self-determination;
I think our wants, which hold us in their thrall,
Are the result of prior ordination:
I willed myself to will what I willed not;
My will, unwilling, wouldn't budge a jot.

27

'Parse *zis*!' I parsed … her facial fluctuations.
He gave me zeroes, reprimanded, frowned;
I grew accustomed to his castigations—
For diligence I've never been renowned,
And with regard to beauty's conjugations,
It wasn't till much later that I found
Their meaning. Classicism, you can see,
Does not, alas, come easily to me!

28

No realist am I, withal; and yet,
By Stasyulevich may I be forgiven!
I've been besmirched by more than one gazette
For this, but by resentment I'm undriven:
Would that the negligence of their toilette
Be well disguised by leaves of fig, unriven,
And that old Zeus, whose power has no fetters,
Bestow them with the gift of Russian letters!

29

Yes, I'm a champion of classic schooling—
But merchants, greasers, ticket-boys on trains
Should not be forced, by arbitrary ruling
(That era now has passed), to cram their brains
With Virgil, say, or Homer: fruitless fooling!
To maximize our economic gains,
We should, on every possible occasion,
Create more schools of the 'Real'* persuasion.
    [*pronounced 'ray-al' (Ger.)]

30

But I'll declare this too: no glass retorts,
No engine-steam shall edify our nation—
For this, we can but discipline our thoughts,
Engaging in gymnastic cogitation;
My namesake very prudently supports
Our institutes of classic education,
Whose plough is turning up the virgin ground
So learning can be broadcast all around.

31

A question of degree … But I'm digressing—
My thread is dropt! Permit me to reprise:
I felt the urge—habitual and pressing—
To probe the picture's shifting forms (unwise,
Imprudent boy!), and wondered, while undressing
Before bed, what air her metamorphic eyes
Might don next morn—attempting to divine
Precisely how her gaze would welcome mine.

32

Her eyes' eccentric beauty tempted me—
An icy streamlet for a desert-rover.
I'd take my dose of Latin and ennui;
Released at two, I glorified Jehovah!
We then took luncheon, served at half past three,
But by this time, the day was all but over;
In January, the light is quick to die—
By four it's gone, and cheerless dusk is nigh.

33

Each day at two, foretasting liberation,
I dusted off my collar, smoothed my hair
And washed my hands; replete with animation,
I shut my books, leapt high into the air,
And headed picture-ward … for observation.
'Twas on the sly, of course, I wended there,
'Whole-heartedly indifferent' to the way
My charming girl might gaze on me to-day.

34

A semi-darkness veiled the empty Hall,
But th' ingle's quick, unsteady flicker, flung
Across the frescoed ceiling, lit the wall
On which my dear beloved canvas hung.
A barrel-organ, whence, if I recall
Correctly, Mozart's cavatinas sprung,
Was playing in the street. Against its swirl
Of sound, I gazed, unblinking, at the girl.

35

This tune, or so I fancied, held the keys
To her perplexing traits. Desire wended
Through my soul, progressing by degrees,
And rapturous delight with sorrow blended.
A slave to youth's tempestuous decrees,
This vague desire I scarcely comprehended;
My lips half-whispered something, or half-sang,
Until at length the bell for luncheon rang.

36

I'd spoon my soup with a reluctant sigh,
My psyche filled with brooding ruminations,
While all regarded me with mocking eye;
As a result of these preoccupations,
I daily grew more reticent and shy,
And, gawking vacantly at my relations
(My face, no doubt, inane!), I oft incurred,
Thro' my dis-ease, a reprimanding word.

37

But as regards my greatest apprehension,
The very *thought* sufficed to turn me red,
Constricting my young breast with nervous tension:
If any one should take it in his head
To speak—or even make a passing *mention*—
Of the picture, I'd quake with anxious dread,
And would far sooner die by rifle-fire
Than broadcast my iniquitous desire.

38

And to this day I still recall the sort
Of ruse that I inventively created
To shift the conversation and thus thwart
Embarrassments, when any such awaited;
And all allusions made to Catherine's court,
Robes rondes or powder, lace or panniers, grated
On my ear, while anxiety was sowed
E'en by Derzhavin, master of the ode.

39

Were *you* young, Reader, if I may be so bold?
Not all have tasted of this poison-platter.
Love's youthful hunger, agony untold—
All this, for many, is but empty chatter;
In Russia, love is thwarted by the cold,
And the demands of employ, for that matter:
Here in our land, the naked-born are few—
Most are birthed in full regalia (épées, too!).

40

But if, having observed our country's ways,
You're nonetheless a curious exception,
And smoulder with the passion of those days
When vigorous and new was our perception,
You'll grasp, perhaps, how its refulgent rays
Illumined my aloneness; some conception
You shall hold of its daily-growing fire—
You'll know the way I nurtured my desire.

41

This is a time of brazen speculation:
Our psyche spins, with endless questions fraught;
The merest swish of skirts, and titillation
Comes upon us, as does torment of a sort;
Our soul's bewildered, dizzy perturbation
Permits us not to quell the swash of thought.
We, rudderless upon its waves, explore
Th' horizon, seeking some uncharted shore.

42

Upon those distant, shimm'ring days I glance,
When of our souls we lacked all comprehension!
—To ope a lexicon, and swiftly chance
Upon some word that sparks exquisite tension!
O nervous thrill, begot by happenstance!
Sweet-scented bloom! no fruit is thy extension!
First sign of worry that would soon begin:
Mad dream of virtue with a hint of sin!

43

I hearkened to my inner tumult, peering
Through wafty curtains of a dreamlike murk …
In this milieu, detached and domineering,
She seemed receptive to my love. A quirk
Of sudden fancy: in my eyes, unsneering
Now was her expression, 'twas gone, her smirk;
And soon in her new mien I could discern
Encouragement, compassion and concern.

44

'Enough despond: be strong, our time is nigh!'
(I read this in her gaze.) 'Let's not be fretters:
For we've sufficient power, you and I,
To cast aside the burden of our fetters;
This canvas is my gaol, while you must try,
According to your elders and your betters,
To "not be such a child". They hound you so,
And yet you're *ripe*—I saw that long ago!

45

'For you were *meant* to come to my assistance.
My friend! 'tis for your help that I appeal!
I'll trust you with the truth of my existence:
I'm more than paint, I cogitate, I feel!
It shan't be hard, if you've enough persistence,
To gain me, tangible and fleshly-real,
The fond companion that your dreams have spun—
Just finish what you've already begun!'

46

… Miasmic palls descended: I was dazed.
For how was I to act upon her pleas,
And rescue her, on whom so long I'd gazed?
Where would I gain the needed expertise?
By murky riddles are the sick thus crazed
While in the throes of feverish disease.
'I'll save her,' I repeated. 'She'll be mine …
But *how*? If only she could send some sign!'

47

At th' sacramental hour—at twilight's fall,
The barrel-organ playing in the street—
I stole, observed by none, into the Hall,
That I might meditate upon my feat,
But vainly racked my brains; against the *wall*
I could have dashed them in my passion's heat,
When, all at once, my young imagination's
Vigour put speedy end to my frustrations.

48

The girl, flecked by the dancing ingle-light,
Seemed animate: she trembled, and her gentle
Gaze appeared upon me to alight,
Eyes glistening, imploring, temperamental;
She lowered her long lashes, and her sight
Now came to settle on an ornamental
Clock. 'Look thither!' her gaze commanded me.
I looked—the hour was precisely three.

49

And then I understood: she'd never dare,
Amidst diurnal clamour, to adorn
Her form with flesh and sinew. No: 'tis *there*,
In nightly shade, that miracles are born!
Why fix the clock with an unswerving stare?
To counsel me: at three that coming morn,
With every body slumbering benignly,
I must creep down and meet her clandestinely.

50

No doubt remains, I speculate aright!
I'll liberate her, if I so desire,
For there's no limit to my ardour's might!
O yes—I'll clothe in bodily attire
What for so long has ghosted thro' my sight!
And at this thought I felt an icy fire—
'Twas sweet yet eldritch, ghastly yet divine,
A chill sensation dancing up my spine.

51

I donned my primmest, most decorous faces,
Revised my verbs without a single sigh,
Attentively reviewed all Latin's cases
(With prepositions they were governed by),
And, to remain in the adults' good graces—
For sleeping dogs are better left to lie!—
I stepped with poise, attempting, all that day,
To hold the least suspicion well at bay.

52

That evening we were entertaining guests;
I had to show my face, as per convention,
But by their dreary talk was I oppressed,
Was bored to death by every last contention.
Yet presently, 'twas time to take my rest:
To bed, to bed—an end to my detention!
I said good-night, and sped upstairs with glee;
My pedagogue, of course, went after me.

53

I lay me down, as if in enervation;
Before the looking glass I heard him tread,
His forehead furrowed in deliberation,
And saw his German 'bacco glinting red
As he inhaled in solemn cogitation.
But finally he clambered into bed—
And drifted off contentedly, no doubt,
While *I* was stricken by a fever's bout.

54

But time advanced. Our visitors, perforce,
Must homeward now: the carriage-drivers started
To bustle in the yard; I heard a horse
Let out a snort, and lay there, fervid-hearted,
As rivulets of light began to course
The ceiling and the carriages departed.
The hour of my tryst—lest you forget,
O Reader!—was extremely distant yet.

55

I'll fall now in the ladies' estimation—
How to excuse my conduct I don't know;
I'll lose their sympathy and approbation,
Yet shall surrender to their mercy tho',
Of course, it will besmirch my reputation.
I cannot say why I should blunder so,
But as I waited for the stroke of three,
I fell asleep—a dream enveloped me.

56

That base, unseemly dream is now a blur—
From memory today 'tis all but faded;
Yet what could I be dreaming of but *her*,
By whom my inmost core had been invaded?
Ennui-afflicted, needing me astir,
My shameful torpor gravely she upbraided;
Guilt weighed so heavily upon my heart
That I awakened with a violent start.

57

My fingers quivering with agitation,
I struck a match, remorseful and aghast,
And watched the shadows' ghostly fluctuation
(My pedagogue, thank God, was sleeping fast);
To my astonishment and jubilation,
The designated time had not yet passed:
There were—'tis no eternity, I know!—
Another five whole minutes still to go.

58

To make amends, I hastily got dressed;
A burning taper in my hand, I sped
From my apartment, scarcely breathing, lest
Anyone should hear.—Silently I tread;
How raucous are the pulse-beats in my breast,
How dizzying the lightness in my head,
As through a lengthy suite of rooms I pass,
Not daring gaze at any looking-glass!

59

I *know* this house, its every niche and nook—
But now, enveloped in the silent pall
Of night, it wears a strange, uncanny look.
These steps of mine don't sound like me at all,
While overhead, eccentric shadows hook
Their claws into the ceiling, scale a wall
And, never still, descend. I pay no heed
To them, and ever onwards I proceed.

60

The omened door already looms ahead—
And now a single step shall clinch my fate!
Yet something unexpected stops me dead—
A whisper. Disbelieve what I relate,
O Reader, if you must; I *swear*, it said,
"Tis better to retreat, 'tis not too late!
But if you choose to enter through that door,
You shall emerge an innocent no more.'

61

Is this the voice of an angelic guide,
Or else the whisper of some furtive fear?
I stand conflicted: lust and dread collide,
Desire's stoked by guilt … But no! all's clear:
I made a pledge by which I shall abide!
I vowed to her that I would reappear!
Though trials impend in yonder empty Hall,
Yet, honour-bound, I'll keep my word withal!

62

—And so, with wrist aquiver, I rotated
The handle of the lock. The door now sprung
Inaudibly ajar; half-dark awaited—
But there was pallid radiance among
The gloom, a bluish glintering created
By a crystal chandelier that softly swung
Upon its chains, and conjured up the sight
Of trembling leaf-borne dew in lunar light.

63

Then, heralding some mystic visitation,
A fresh aroma wafted through the room:
Was it a trick of my imagination,
Or was I drinking in the sweet perfume
Of roses? I felt a chill of trepidation,
An icy shiver 'midst an inner brume;
But having overcome my body's quav'ring,
Towards the portrait I advanced, unwav'ring.

64

As if in moonlight bathed, 'twas all aglow;
I spied the slightest folds in her attire,
Her face's every feature was on show,
Her eyes replete with sorrow and desire
(The lids were rising, languorous and slow);
If filmed with tears, they also were afire,
And radiated some restrainèd power
As I had never glimpsed in daylight's hour.

65

Afraid no more, I fell beneath the sway
Of luscious torment. Ardent yearning blurred
With languor, intermixed in such a way—
So fathomless, so chasmic—that no word
In human language ever could convey
This feeling. From afar, I thought I heard
Some muffled call; foretasting holy bliss,
I felt the looming of a black Abyss.

66

My thoughts, meantime, ran thus: they were no lie,
Your promises of love! This morn you'll gain
A fleshly form.—I'm here!—I wait!—But why
Must you delay? I've come for you again,
Do you not see? I sought to catch her eye—
And passion shuddered through my every vein,
While raging jealousy (of *whom*? God knows)
Revealed itself amidst my mental throes.

67

You stand stock-still! I didn't comprehend,
Perhaps, the implication of your glances?
Too young, am I? Unworthy, in the end,
Of trust? You're loath, I see, to risk your chances?
I'm *childish*, then! Or did you—God forfend—
Surrender to another man's advances?
Who was it stole your love? And by what right?
Disclose yourself! I'll handle you! I'll fight!

68

I writhed, in waking dream, under the sting—
The *torment* of an inner conflagration ...
O god of love! You're youthful as the spring,
And yet your ways are ancient as creation!
But then, the cadence of a triple *ding*—
Preceded by a hiss, and slight vibration
Of the walls—broke the silence with its sound,
Compelling me to swivel and look round.

69

What sudden transformation! The air ateem
With echoes of that final chime, night's pall
Was lifted, extinguished was the lunar gleam,
The lustres burst alight; the antique Hall,
Ashine, aglitter, was ready, it would seem,
To host some dazzling gala or grand ball—
I saw distinctly, 'neath the lustres' blaze,
The new-born splendour of its bygone days.

70

It was old-fashioned yet refreshed, possessed
Anew of former beauties. Oh, mad-bounding
Pulsings!—I bore a smithy in my breast,
And in my ears, a stormy blood was pounding,
Akin to spring-time's clamour and unrest
In youthful groves, with twitterings resounding,
Or humble-bees a-droning o'er buckwheat
Meadows amid July's oppressive heat.

71

Is this a dream? And am I still abed?
But no, I'm here! for 'twas my fingers skirted
Across the picture's frame. And now a sled
Scraped up the street, all silent and deserted,
While plaster trickled down from overhead ...
I heard the panels creak, and then, diverted
By a sudden silken stirring, raised my eyes—
And caught my breath in worshipful surprise.

72

She'd almost left the limits of the frame,
If still in wonted posture, lithe and gainly.
Her breast, illumined by the lustres' flame,
Was heaving—indeed, I saw it plainly,
Its steady fall and rise. But all the same,
She fought for *absolute* release, yet vainly;
I sensed her every molecule implore,
O, *will* my liberation! Will it *more*!

73

Soul trained on her, I strove to concentrate
With every fibre of my frame, and willed
Her free. My fervid gaze did animate
Her form; with vital force was she instilled—
As steppe-land feather-grasses undulate
In summer's gentle breezes, so her frilled
Attire streamed: I heard it swish, and saw,
Distinctly, the shudders of her pinafore.

74

'O will it hard!' the dewy eyes beseeched.
With fervour springing from my inmost core,
I longed for her release. My longings reached
Beyond the frame! The girl, now ever more
Unhindered in her movements, swiftly breached
The confines of the work: her pinafore
Dropt open and disgorged a flower-fall—
A flood of roses gushed into the Hall.

75

Uncrumpling her attire, and stepping clean
Beyond the frame and onto the parquet,
She looked much like a damsel of sixteen
Who, desirous to drink the scents of May,
Abandons the veranda for the green.
But, truly, was it *she*? I could not say,
Struck dumb with joy yet terror-fraught;
We gazed upon each other, saying naught.

76

If I were colonel, had I donned the vest
Of an hussar, I'd surely have collected
All my senses, and artfully exprest
My ardour, plying her with well-directed,
Admiring remarks. I was, alas, unblest
With swagger and, embarrassed and dejected,
Knew not if I must halt, or else, in fact,
Advance—yet duty goaded me to act.

77

So I, remembering my dance tuition,
Advanced two paces, readying to bow.
Unforcedly, as thro' its own volition,
One foot drew close against the other now;
Arms hanging loose, consistent with tradition,
I bent before her like some pliant bough.
The instant I unfolded my poor torso,
She archly courtsied just as low, or more so.

78

In retrospect, 'tis all too clear to see
That this was nothing but a big confusion:
A dance! she'd thought, and played the invitee,
My old-school bow provoking her conclusion;
Alas, my bashfulness prevented me
From disabusing her of this illusion;
And thus, a beaded sweat upon my brow,
I offered her my hand, all flustered now.

79

There issued forth a music's distant ringing,
Faint phrases of a *menuet antique*
Evocative of water sedges singing
In th' shallows of a susurrating creek,
Or spring-saluting billy-witches, winging
Circles high above a linden's peak
As evenfall approaches, their thrumming tunes
Recalling strains of cellos and bassoons.

80

My fingers scarcely touching hers at all,
Maintaining a decorous separation,
We tip-toed slowly forth, and looped the Hall
Together—an unspeaking, grave rotation;
But after two brief turns, I felt her stall
Abruptly, in apparent expectation,
And from her fresh, vivacious lips there fell
A lilting laugh—a trill of Philomel.

81

By this comportment I was much offended.
'My friend! Don't be indignant, now,' she cried—
As to the floor my gaze, still proud, descended—
'And, pray, my flippant manner do not chide!
You're droll! Believe me (no offence intended),
In all my days, I've none like you espied!
Was it for *this* you blazed with passion's fire?
A dance with me is *all* that you desire?'

82

How best to answer?—I was all at sea,
And anguished. What *does* she want? I wondered;
She's discontented, and displeased with me—
But *why*? So where, precisely, have I blundered?
She *made* me dance! And I, her devotee,
Began to cry. I'm 'droll', am I? I thundered
Inwardly, searching for some sharp retort;
I'm ready to detest you now, I thought.

83

My blood grew turbulent with indignation—
But then, my ire was assuaged by *this*:
She granted me, against all expectation,
The fire of a fleet and teasing kiss.
'Don't cry!' she said, and then, to my elation,
'I love you!' Flooded by unfathomed bliss,
And stupefied, I tenderly was pressed,
All faint, against her alabaster breast.

84

My thoughts grew dim: a petering away
Of consciousness, of lucid cogitation.
I felt the clasp of tender arms, the play
Of girlish shoulders—heavenly sensation!
My circumstance occasioned not dismay
But sweet delight in me. Life's expiration?
I deemed it *nice*, and slowly, pleasure-drunk,
I lost myself, aswoon or slumber-sunk ...

85

... I lolled on a divan. (I had awoken
In the Hall, tho' I forget how I regained
Possession of my senses.) Day had broken;
Relations bustled all around; I strained
To breathe—but in my hand, a telling token!
Within my mind, a great confusion reigned;
I burned and quivered, racked by fever's throes—
But all the while, I held a withered rose ...

86

Within my chest, a mad, frenetic dance
Began—the night's events I recollected,
And at the picture stole a furtive glance.
About her lips, a phantom I detected—
A smile's ghost. But she'd resumed her stance:
Her lissome form, which I'd so oft inspected,
Was still, her fingers clutching, as before,
The taff'ta trimming of her pinafore.

87

My kinfolk pondered: why was I so poorly?
'Tis measles, said Mama. My aunts preferred
A different diagnosis: scarlet, *surely*!
My pedagogue? In Latin he conferred
With our physician; their debate, obscurely,
Contained two terms that frequently recurred:
The first—it was *somnambulus*, I reckoned—
And *febris cerebralis* was the second ...

TRANSLATOR'S AFTERWORD

… there really is no avoiding a number of explanatory remarks;
it's true, these words have already been said, and just as well:

Quotation

One of the most immediately striking features of *Death of a Prototype* is what I would venture to call a 'quotation mania'. As evidenced by the very first exchanges in the second chapter of Part One, the novel's characters have a seemingly insatiable predilection for quoting at length from literary classics, and from Russian nineteenth- and twentieth-century verse in particular. It might appear to English-language readers that these extended verbatim quotations represent deliberate violations of *vraisemblance* on the part of a postmodernist author (who, after all, could possibly have such a perfect memory for poetry?), but this particular aspect of the novel is, in fact, perfectly 'true to life'. To employ a term coined by media theorist Walter Ong, Russian culture has always been characterized by a greater degree of 'residual orality' than its Western counterparts, and the tradition of verse memorization and declamation has thus proven highly tenacious: the Korzunovs of the real world genuinely could recall and recite Pushkin's 'very last poem' at the drop of a hat.[1]

But quotation and related devices – citation, allusion, paraphrase, appropriation and so on – are by no means confined

---

[1] '[O]ral societies must invest great energy in saying over and over again what has been learned arduously over the ages. […] Indeed, the residual orality of a given chirographic culture can be calculated to a degree from the mnemonic load it leaves on the mind, that is, from the amount of memorization the culture's educational procedures require.' Walter Ong, *Orality and Literacy: The Technologizing of the Word* (New York: Routledge, 2002), p. 41.

to the characters' conversations: the aforementioned mania runs far deeper than that. Straining ever outwards, *Prototype* is thick with references. Some are explicit, others covert; some are of local importance, others crucial to the novel's macro-architecture. Alexei Tolstoy's narrative poem *The Portrait* is, of course, the foundation stone of the entire edifice, the sine qua non of the grand intertextual game that plays itself out chapter by chapter. Its appropriation by Victor Beilis is an almost Menardian act: the poem and its prosified version are verbally very similar, at times virtually identical, but, integrated into a novel series of twentieth-century literary and cultural contexts, the latter attains a richness that the former could not possibly possess.[2] The youthful protagonist of the 'Big Brother' chapter naively attempts to neutralize the power of T.D.'s portrait by concealing it under that of the Italian signor(a) – but the result, much to his shock, is accretion rather than attrition; when the Italian picture is laid over the Russian, the two images conspire to produce something unexpected and new. So too in *Prototype* as a whole: overlays of incongruous sources generate what might be dubbed *constructive interference*.

The tropes and themes of Tolstoy's poem – a gothically tinged, psychologically astute portrait of the maelstrom of adolescent sexual awakening – are filtered in Part Two through the apparently unrelated prisms of fin-de-siècle existentialism ('Abelone'), political satire ('Big Brother') and religious mysticism ('Eros'). While the 'Abelone' chapter is later revealed to be a (highly truncated and somewhat distortive) paraphrase of Rainer Maria Rilke's *Malte*, it is never made fully explicit that 'Eros' draws on the idiosyncratic philosophy of turn-of-the-century Russian thinker Vasily Rozanov (see 'Explanatory Glosses and References' for further details). If Tolstoy's portrait of the 'youthsome girl' (pp. 29 and 188) is, on some level at least, a *self-portrait* of the narrator's younger incarnation, a boy who imbues the image with his own fears and desires (his feelings of

---

[2] See Jorge Luis Borges's 'Pierre Menard, Author of the Quixote,' in *Labyrinths* (London: Penguin, 2000), p. 69.

claustrophobia and entrapment, for example, spawn the belief that the girl is literally imprisoned behind the picture frame), the portrait in 'Eros' becomes an outright autobiography of a self-loathing adult male who 'never did graduate from being the boy he always was'. Meanwhile, the notion of a male self-portrait realized via (the process of depicting) a female model surfaces in other chapters. Advised to 'direct [his] gaze inward' and 'make a portrait of [himself]' (p. 147), the seventeenth-century artist Henri de la Maisonneuve ends up conjuring an image that his twentieth-century analogue, Yakov Novodomsky, recognizes as the 'wall-creature' Henriette. Beilis develops this gender-bending motif by making use of another unnamed – and no less important – source. This is Marina Tsvetayeva's *An Adventure*, a play featuring one Henri-Henriette, an 'ambiguous being [...] who can function as either man or woman and be alternately a brawling hussar, a seductive and erudite beauty or a virtuoso musician'.[3] I return to these metamorphoses of gender below.

Variation

If the novel's sources are alienatingly heterogeneous, the construction of its narrative is no less alienating in its near-total resistance to forward momentum. The short, largely self-contained chapters comprise a set of contrapuntal variations; there is a rich development of *theme* – episodes are linked by means of resonances, parallels, 'compositional rhymes' – but almost none of *plot* as ordinarily understood. Readers conditioned by conventional novelistic form may expect some kind of global teleological thrust as well as a degree of stylistic consistency, but these expectations are repeatedly frustrated: *Prototype* straddles the gap between novel and short-story collection. (In this sense, if not in others, it recalls the work of David Mitchell and, in particular, the century-spanning

---

3   Simon Karlinsky, *Marina Tsvetayeva: The Woman, Her World, and Her Poetry* (Cambridge: Cambridge University Press, 1985), p. 90.

echoes of *Cloud Atlas.*) But although several chapters in the novel – 'Big Brother', 'Kozin', 'The Artist' (both versions) – do indeed resemble stand-alone stories, and could, if excised from their native context, be read as such, the work as a whole cannot be neatly dissected into its constituent parts, for it folds endlessly back on itself.

While self-contained, *Prototype*'s chapters are *not* hermetically sealed: they are simultaneously independent and interdependent. The 'K-characters' (Koretsky, Kiryushin, Kazarnovsky ...) and the 'A-characters' (Adele, Ada, Yadya ...) are, of course, analogues of one another, and variants, respectively, of the same male and female archetypes. It becomes gradually apparent, too, that the dinner-party sequences in Part One are all reworkings of a single scenario, depicted with subtle shifts of emphasis each time. However, far from being confined to parallel, cleanly demarcated universes, the characters exist within what appears to be a *unified story space*: Kazarnovsky does not simply 'displace' Kiryushin, for example, but actually interacts with him – somewhat like a musical theme being superimposed, in modified form, upon itself. This manoeuvre allows Beilis to demonstrate, in the course of a single brief scene, the highly paradoxical nature of the influence exerted by the portrait upon the males who encounter it, and who (to quote from a different chapter) find themselves 'convulsed [...] by dangerous *attractions-cum-repulsions*' (p. 93, emphasis mine): 'Yasha chose his seat so as to avoid looking at the picture that had been encroaching so powerfully upon his existence; Mstislav, in contrast, chose his the better to see it' (p. 47).

Instead of advancing the plot in a teleological manner, Beilis repeatedly counterpoints the original theme against itself; it is for this reason that *Prototype* exhibits none of the inexorable onward thrust of a conventional novel. This is true, too, of the macrostructural level. In terms of the number of episodes that it comprises, if not in terms of its absolute length, Part Two is a more compressed 'restating' of Part One, albeit with certain crucial modifications and elaborations (the most obvious being the filtering of 'The Portrait' through the aforementioned generic and thematic prisms). But the parts do not simply parallel each other. The Notice to Part Two calls into question various elements of Part One, while the Notice to Part Three problematizes the very ontological status of both preceding parts, as well as the nature of their interrelationship ('the previous part of the manuscript, together with its first part, were authored by the same hand' (p. 151)). Nowhere is *Prototype*'s self-reflexivity, its tendency to fold back on itself, more evident than on the macrolevel.

Transformation

These structural metamorphoses mirror Beilis's preoccupation with changeability and flux. It is not for nothing that Ovid is invoked before any other author. The parameters of the novel's fictional world are no less polymorphous and changeable than its protagonists: as Rozanov avows, '[t]he onset of *stability* would bring with it the petrifaction – the icing over of the universe' (p. 166).

Take the time period, for example. Allusions to samizdat (as well as a footnote informing the reader that 'in those days' Nabokov was still banned 'on one-sixth of the world's landmass') imply a pre-perestroika setting, but an offhand reference to email in the first Notice would seem to date the writing of that introductory text, at least, to no earlier than the late 1990s. The author of the Notice emails N. to advise him of Adele's sudden death in Rome, and Adele herself refers in a letter to her impending trip (p. 173), meaning that this letter, too, must have been written in the '90s. In any case, she could not have travelled to Italy – or to any other Western country, for that matter – prior to the start of perestroika: by her own admission, she had been 'banned from travelling abroad' (p. 173), along with the vast majority of her compatriots. The internal chronology and time span of the novel's events, therefore, are left more or less indeterminate.[4]

The age of the portrait itself is uncertain, and changes from chapter to chapter. It is initially described as being 'attributed to the mid-eighteenth-century artist Antonio Bartolini' and as demonstrating the latter's 'predilection for mannerism' (p. 25) – a movement that reached its apogee some two hundred years previously. Elsewhere, however, it is said to be the work of 'Giovanni Giacomo Bordolini, a second-rate mannerist' (p. 65) – and, who, as such, might have been active between the sixteenth and the early seventeenth century – while the narrator of the 'Big Brother' chapter believes it to have been authored by Giovanni Bardolini (or Giacomo Bellini), 'the great seventeenth-century artist' (p. 135). Matters are made yet more complicated by the reference to an 'even gold' background (p. 83), which is suggestive either of (pre-)Renaissance devotional painting … or else of fin-de-siècle decadence (and indeed, we read that the portrait betrays 'a hint of the decadent mysticism characteristic of the beginning of the twentieth century' (p. 25)).

Of even greater thematic importance is the androgyny of the figure depicted on the canvas. In Tolstoy's poem, the object of the narrator's passions is unequivocally female; in Beilis's novel, conversely, the figure exhibits varying levels of femaleness and maleness: (s)he is now a slight-breasted signora, now a creature of 'indeterminate' sex, now an effeminate adolescent boy, and now a middle-aged man (with the 'bright form' of a young woman in the background). While the portrait is

---

[4]   The fact that it is often impossible even to ascertain with any real certainty whether a particular episode is set in the pre- or post-perestroika era reflects the belief – articulated by Rozanov but shared by Adele and, it would appear, by the novel's other characters as well – that 'personal life transcends all else' (p. 166), and that there is no higher aspiration than the desire simply to 'be sat at home, picking your nose [and] watching the sunset' (p. 167). This, incidentally, is a highly political apoliticism: there is no greater affront to a totalitarian regime than an implicit refusal to accept the totality of its reach.

described in a series of ekphrases interspersed throughout the novel, the outward characteristics of its flesh-and-blood protagonists remain unknown. Nevertheless, we can surmise from the 'Edward' chapter that Adele-Ada-Yadya, too, is of androgynous appearance; Koretksy, meanwhile, fancies that Adele 'had, if only fleetingly, belonged to the opposite sex herself' (p. 81), and, elsewhere, Yadya reveals that, as a child, she was addressed as Yasha – the diminutive of the male name Yakov.

Not at all coincidentally, this is also the first name of the artist Novodomsky. The oblique pairing of Yasha and Yadya echoes the more obvious Henri-Henriette dyad, touched on above; these couplings of names reinforce the notion of a fluid and wavering line between femaleness and maleness. Interestingly, this gender-bending comes to be tied up with questions of authorship and artistic production. *Prototype* appears to rely on and exploit the familiar topos of male artist and female model, whereby masculinity is equated with creativity, but this topos is quite possibly inverted on the novel's macrostructural level. The second Notice suggests that the (co-)author of (elements of) the text may actually be Adele; if so, we might regard the manuscript(s) as (in part) the disguised and fragmented self-portrait of a *woman*.

Simulation

The just-mentioned ekphrases of the portrait offer readers a handful of (ever-shifting) details about its appearance while simultaneously inviting them to flesh out the rest in their imaginations. These ekphrases are effective in their very *non-exhaustiveness*, no attempt being made to capture the totality of the image – whose state of perpetual metamorphosis makes it impossible to simulate in its entirety. It is precisely the lacunae in the descriptions that endow them with their suggestive power. If *Prototype* were a film or graphic novel, the portrait could never be shown in full, for this would destroy the effect; the verbal medium of the text is a *limitation* in the best possible sense.

Beilis self-consciously thematizes the 'translation' or the transference of meaning between different semiotic media in other ways, too. The various authors in the novel — writers and painters alike — are united in their preoccupation with the process of *modelling*, that is, of using a particular representational system to encapsulate certain aspects of the world. Now, models are, by definition, abstractions or schematizations: they preserve salient features while necessarily discarding other elements as incidental. 'Total' representation of the real — or, for that matter, of already-existing representations — is therefore impossible. This impossibility is explicitly underscored by the narrator of the 'Big Brother' chapter: 'Verbal attempts to evoke the condition in which Chopin, *inspired in flight, transforms the probable into the right* are beautiful yet wholly inadequate. And so it is with any work of art inextricable from the pure specificity of its form' (p. 132).

Also inadequate, if perhaps no less beautiful, are all attempts — whether verbal or visual — to express the reality of Adele-Ada-Yadya. Henri painfully comes to realize as much upon seeing that his sketches of this woman, 'though not devoid of genuine feeling', have nonetheless been 'contaminated with the germ of falsity' (p. 145). The sketches are simulations in both senses of the term: despite his sincere efforts to model reality as he understands it, Henri inadvertently produces a series of counterfeits. Indeed, any *totalizing* attempt to capture in words or on canvas what Adele calls the 'fundamental essence' of her character results in a kind of semiotic imprisonment that the *human* prototype nonetheless ultimately eludes:

> she herself was unapprehended by anyones creativity neither brush nor word could enframe her & endow her with completeness portraits deceived & faltered words proved too nebulous & not a single photograph could capture her features with an *objective* precision her essence eluded any method of expression or fixation & the more complex the design of the 'simulative' system selected to eternalize her the greater the quantity of meanings imbued in the symbols the more insincere & bombastic

the expression became a plurality of meanings barely took
shape before being overtaken by inauthenticity (p. 180)

De la Maisonneuve, Novodomsky and Kazanov undoubtedly
succeed in capturing certain elements of the woman's nature;
furthermore, it is emphasized that their respective works exhibit
a considerable degree of imaginative power. However, in their
frenzied desire to 'hold' Adele – significantly, the urge to encapsulate her artistically is presented by Beilis as being of a piece
with the longing for sexual possession – they end up arresting
the 'extraordinary freedom that breathed in this woman's soul'
(p. 74), and which had drawn them irresistibly towards her in
the first place. As Adele herself suggests in her letter to the 'dearest artist', the only authentic way to evoke this freedom is to
renounce any ambitions of representational totality: instead, the
reader or viewer ought to be presented with 'a tattered fragment
[…] asteam, aquiver with life' (p. 172). And it is precisely such
fragments that comprise the textual fabric of *Death of a Prototype*.

Translation

On some level, this anglicization of the novel represents the
next stage in a game embarked upon by Victor Beilis when he
translated Alexei Tolstoy's poem into prose. To paraphrase a sentence from the 'Big Brother' chapter, the nineteenth-century
poet would no doubt have been surprised to learn that in the
early twenty-first he was to acquire a duo of co-authors, one of
them, of course, being yours truly. Beilis's translation is between
literary modes, while mine is between linguistic media, and
these prosified and anglicized versions of *The Portrait* both
'interfere' with the character of Tolstoy's original. Take, for
instance, the vivid contrast in style. While Tolstoy handles with
ease the current Russian of his time, the archaic style of Beilis's
prose rendering suffers from a certain affectation;[5] and the sense

---

[5] See 'Pierre Menard, Author of the Quixote', in *Labyrinths* (Penguin,
2000), p. 69, and also p. 93 of the present work.

of affectedness can only be compounded in my own interpretation, which is *forced to masquerade as English nineteenth-century Romantic prose ... masquerading as English Romantic verse ... masquerading as Russian prose ... masquerading as verse!*

As the novel itself demonstrates, translation – whether interlingual, intersemiotic or intergeneric – is never neutral, never transparent. The translator's task is to simulate a message expressed in one medium by means of another, but, as with any model, the message cannot be preserved in its entirety: certain elements must be set aside. This is especially true if message and medium are as tightly intertwined as they are here. Although certain losses cannot be prevented, they can be compensated for in other ways. Thus, with the author's blessing, I have inserted into the text several unsignposted quotations from Chaucer, Shakespeare, Donne and others. Sometimes, these serve as surrogates for allusions which, though theoretically translatable, would be utterly incomprehensible in Englished form by virtue of their sheer fragmentedness and obscurity. In several instances, however, they are not surrogates at all but deliberate additions designed to entice non-Russianist English-language readers into Beilis's intertextual game. Does such a manoeuvre 'interfere' with the original? No doubt; but I would argue that it does so *constructively*, and in a manner that remains faithful to the original's spirit, if not to its letter.

I shall conclude on a personal note. However this translation may be assessed, I hope that, as with Henri's sketches of Arianna, the 'genuine feeling' behind every English word is plain to see. I embarked on this project in December 2006, but other commitments quickly forced me to put it aside, half-finished; I returned to it only in the summer of 2014, but in the intervening years it was quietly metamorphosing in some half-dark chamber of my brain, its pull faint but unmistakable. It has inhabited my consciousness for so long that it is with a strange bittersweetness that I finally put down my pen. On one hand, the difficulties of translating such a complex and stylistically diverse work have, on occasion, driven me to the verge of despair. Having to master strict iambic pentameter was particularly demanding, and for a while, afflicted by some bizarre variety of the Tetris effect, I was automatically scanning the rhythm of *everything* I read or heard – infernal *Portrait*, indeed! On the other, the concerns of the book have merged so profoundly with my own thinking over the last almost-decade that, as I release its anglicization into the world, I am filled with a sense of protectiveness and personal responsibility.

I hope, above all, that I have done the *Prototype* justice.

EXPLANATORY GLOSSES
AND REFERENCES

These notes elucidate allusions to Russian literature and culture only, to provide (as it were) a 'level playing field'. Everything else, dear Reader, has been left for you to decipher on your own.

Unless otherwise stated, translations of excerpts from other works are Leo Shtutin's.

4   *Union of Soviet Writers*   The creative union, founded in 1932, of professional writers in the USSR. An instrument of ideological control over literature; non-membership meant little opportunity to publish.

7   *one of Pushkin's prose fragments*   The fragment in question is 'The Guests Were Arriving at the Dacha' (1828).

8   *They say that Jupiter, soused with nectar*   This translation of the *Metamorphoses* is by Stanley Lombardo (Indianapolis/Cambridge: Hackett, 2010).

9   *When Tiresias was asked if this boy would live* Ibid.

10   *I'm not impartial to a pregnant man*   A line from 'The Childing', by David Burliuk (1882–1967), painter, poet and founder of Russian futurism.

17   *Play on, my sweet Adele*   The first six lines of Pushkin's poem 'To Adele' (1824). Koretsky then takes the poem in a direction of his own.

18   *As Pushkin 'read his Noels'*   This is an allusion to a self-reference in Chapter 10 of *Eugene Onegin*; the 'Noels' were traditional French yuletide satires, of which Pushkin wrote several, but only one remains extant.

18   *Dmitry Aleksandrovich Prigov and Timur Kibirov*   Prigov (1940–2007), writer, poet and conceptual artist whose works were circulated via samizdat during the Soviet

era. Kibirov (born 1955), translator and conceptualist poet.

18   *the braid of Venichka Erofeyev's beloved* Venedikt Erofeyev (1933–1990), dissident, prose writer and author of the cult novel (or 'prose poem') *Moscow Petushki* (published 1973), which features a pseudo-autobiographical protagonist called Venichka.

21   *Tatyana Tolstaya* Writer and television personality from the Tolstoy family, born 1951.

21   *Andrei Lebedev* Classical scholar, born 1951.

22   *Pasternaktsvetayevamandelstam?* Boris Pasternak (1890–1960), poet, novelist and literary translator. Marina Tsvetayeva (1892–1941), poet. Osip Mandelshtam (1891–1938), Acmeist poet and essayist. Spoken in one breath like this, their names become a kind of password, a demonstration of one's belonging to the intellectual elect.

22   *'our everything', that is, the very 'sun of Russian poetry'* That is, Pushkin. These epithets were coined, respectively, by poet and critic Apollon Grigoriev (1822–1864) and critic Vissarion Belinsky (1811–1848).

23   *this was, of course, Rubinstein* Lev Rubinstein (born 1947), literary critic, essayist and conceptualist famed for his minimalist 'index-card' poems.

25   *the World of Art* An art movement that originated in St. Petersburg in the late 1890s. It tended towards aestheticism and symbolism.

25   *Somov* Konstantin Somov (1869–1939), an artist associated with *Mir iskusstva*.

32   *Dear friend, why do I have to laugh?* This passage is translated from the German by Helen Tracy Lowe-Porter.

33   *Are you Jadwiga?* Yadya is the diminutive of Jadwiga. Jadwiga, the first monarch of the medieval Kingdom of Poland, was married to the Lithuanian Grand Duke Jogaila. In the context of this chapter, the historical

identities of these figures are of less significance than the fact that their names feature in a famous Pasternak poem called 'Let's Scatter Our Words' (1917).

33   *D'you think the name Jogaila would suit me?*   See note above.

33   *the great god of details*   The characters are engaging in a kind of 'literary tennis' here: Yadya picks up on Korzunov's implicit reference to the Pasternak poem and 'rallies' with a reference of her own.

33   *I think I could even style him Agathon*   The 'tennis rally' continues. Innochka brings Korzunov down a notch by calling him 'Agathon' – a reference to a divination scene in *Eugene Onegin* where Tatyana attempts to discover the name of her husband-to-be. In Pushkin's era, Agathon was regarded as a rustic, lower-class name, and in this exchange, therefore, it contrasts with the noble name of Jogaila.

33   *in the company of a Lithuanian Grand Duke*   That is, Jogaila.

42   *Gentle youth and lover tender, / Mine forever, have no shame*   From Pushkin's 'Arabic Imitation', tr. James Falen (with a minor amendment by Leo Shtutin), in *Selected Lyric Poetry* (Northwestern University Press, 2009).

49   *For I tear my words from the depths of my being*   This passage is translated from the French by Bernard Frechtman.

62   *eavesdrop on a shard of music / And dub it, jokingly, their own*   Lines from 'The Poet', the fourth poem in Anna Akhmatova's cycle *Secrets of the Trade*.

62   *verses fluently dictated / Alight upon the snow-blank page*:   From 'Creation', the first poem in the same cycle.

63   *You shall forget Henriette, too*   A line from Tsvetayeva's play *An Adventure* (1918–19), based on the memoirs of Casanova and featuring a character known as Henri-Henriette.

64   *Worthy of the brush of Ayvazovsky!*   Ivan Ayvazovsky
      (1817–1900), Russian Romantic painter, predomin-
      antly of seascapes.

64   *To the Pushkin*   The Pushkin State Museum of Fine
      Arts, Moscow's largest museum of European art.

66   *Central House of Artists*   An exhibition space with a
      restaurant open only to members of the Artists Union
      that also served as a club of sorts.

84   *a bouquet of yellow flowers*   An allusion to Bulgakov's
      Master and Margarita (written 1928–1940, published
      1967), and in particular to the titular characters' first
      encounter (Margarita is holding a bunch of 'repulsive'
      yellow flowers).

85   *'Godlike Princess of the Kirgiz-Kaisak Horde'*   An
      apostrophe to Catherine the Great from the poem
      'Felitsa' (1782) by Gavrila Derzhavin (1743–1816).
      Renowned for his odes, Derzhavin was Russia's great-
      est eighteenth-century poet.

86   *… the woman we are destined to enjoy, / Having first
      endured her torments*   Lines from 'The Sixth Sense'
      (1921, tr. Martha Weitzel Hickey), a poem by Nikolai
      Gumilyov (1886–1921), the co-founder of the
      Acmeist movement.

86   *throwing away the selfsame flowers she had in the
      museum*   Just like Margarita, who throws hers into
      the gutter on learning that the Master dislikes them.

90   *It could be that whisper was begotten before tongue*   Lines
      from an untitled poem (1934) by Mandelstam.

93   *Evgeny Vitkovsky*   Poet and translator, born 1950.

99   *a 'physical impossibility': the hand simply refuses to
      move*   From a letter by Pushkin to his close friend,
      Prince Pyotr Vyazemsky (1792–1878), dated
      November 1825.

99   *take part in the battle for the harvest*   A piece of official
      Soviet bureaucratese; here, used as an ironic response
      to Kiryushin's parodic slogan 'A Proper Partner for
      Every Woman'.

Misha Berlioz. The programmatic *Symphonie fantastique* climaxes with a witches' sabbath.

111   *If only girlies sweet and fair*   This is Derzhavin's (see note to p. 85) bawdy 'Joking Wish' (1802).

112   *the Latyr Stone*   'a legendary altar stone that is often mentioned in Russian songs' (James Bailey, *An Anthology of Russian Folk Epics* (Routledge, 2015).

112   *frenetic incantations*   These passages draw on Russian folk incantations and spells.

115   *night's darkness is trained on you like a thousand binoculars*   Lines from Pasternak's poem 'Hamlet' (1946).

115   *the magnificently oxymoronic 'festival of labour'*   In 1918, following the Russian Revolution, May 1 was declared International Workers' Solidarity Day.

116   *a tale is sooner told than a deed is done […] whether long or short, whether near or far*   Stock Russian folkloric formulas.

117   *Mikhail Afanasich, answer me!*   Mikhail Afanasich is Bulgakov (Afanasich is the shortened form of Afansyevich).

117   *Elena Sergeyevna*   Elena S. Bulgakova (1893–1970) was Bulgakov's wife.

117   *stormy Chagallian exaltation*   Marc Chagall (1887–1985), Russian-French artist. This is a nod to paintings such as *Over the Town* (1914–18) and *Bouquet with Flying Lovers* (1934–37), which feature exultant gravity-defying couples – a leitmotif in the artist's oeuvre.

121   *that wondrous Russian novel*   Ivan Goncharov's (1812–1891) *Oblomov* (1859), whose eponymous protagonist, Ilya Illich, is famed for lolling perpetually on the sofa, clad in his dressing gown.

121   *All hail, thou dwelling pure and lo-o-owly*   A cavatina from Gounod's *Faust*, which Bulgakov loved, and which exerted a considerable influence on *The Master and Margarita*.

121   *Give me your hand, gentle reader*   A quote from Ivan Turgenev's *A Sportsman's Sketches* (1852).

122   *At life's beginning [...] I remember school*   The first line of an untitled Pushkin poem (1830), in which the narrator, recalling his time at the lycée, speaks of being tempted by two 'demonic' statues: one of Venus and the other of the 'Delphic idol' Apollo.

122   *Ivan Vladimirovich Michurin*   The real-life Michurin (1855–1935) was a practitioner of biological selection.

122   *Trofim Denisovich Lysenko*   The real-life Lysenko (1898–1976) was a Stalin-endorsed biologist and agronomist who appropriated Michurin's practical ideas and used them as an ideological argument against genetics, the 'whore child of imperialism'. Lysenko was an all-powerful 'Stalin of science'.

123   *Przhevalsky*   In reality, Nikolay Przevalsky (1839–1888) was a Russian geographer and explorer of Central and East Asia; unsubstantiated rumours have it that he fathered Stalin (there is certainly a facial similarity).

124   *Soso*   Stalin's childhood nickname (the Georgian diminutive form of Ioseb/Iosif).

124   *a daring escape from Kutaisi Prison*   The real-life Stalin was indeed incarcerated at Kutaisi, in western Georgia, in 1903, but he actually escaped from the village of Novaya Uda in Irkutsk Province the following year, having been exiled there from Georgia for his revolutionary activities.

124   *His surname was Dzhugashvili*   Stalin's birth surname.

124   *My school friend Troshka's mother*   Troshka is the diminutive of Trofim, which hints strongly at what may have been bestowed upon Troshka's mother by the munificent leader.

125   *Ivan Nechuy-Levitsky*   Nechuy-Levitsky (1838–1918) was a second-rate novelist and prose writer.

125   *Ivinskaya [...] the best and most talented poet of our age*   Olga Ivinskaya (1912–1995) was Pasternak's friend and lover. In real life, it was Mayakovsky rather than Pasternak who was thus described – by Stalin.

125   *some expeditious journalist [...] dashed off* Batum In reality, Bulgakov did, in fact, author this 'playlet' (1939), whose treatment of the character of Stalin, as well as the circumstances of its composition, still generates controversy among critics.

126   *in the words of Zyuganov* Gennady Zyuganov (born 1944), first secretary of the Russian Communist Party.

126   *Lenin, supported by Stalin in his fight against Bogdanov* Alexander Bogdanov (1873–1928), politician and prominent Bolshevik who was expelled from the party in 1909 after his ideological disputes with Lenin came to a head.

127   *the Lysenko Constitution* In this chapter, the analogue of the real-life Stalin Constitution of 1936, which, with its provisions for universal suffrage and civil rights, was nothing more than a propaganda instrument.

128   *the great hyperrealist Laktionov* Aleksandr Laktionov (1910–1972), socialist realist painter. In reality, the 'famous portrait' is of Stalin.

128   *The soul must labour / Day and night, day and night* Lines from 'Don't Let the Soul Grow Lazy' (1958), a poem by Nikolai Zabolotsky (1903–1958), one of the founders of the avant-garde collective Oberiu (Union of Real Art).

132   *inspired in flight, transforms the probable into the right* A paraphrase of lines from an untitled poem (1931) by Pasternak.

133   *In guise at once androgynous and marble-white* 'Lines to Accompany the Portrait of A. A. Blok', by the early symbolist poet Innokenty Annensky (1855–1909). Alexander Blok (1880–1921) was the greatest of the second-generation Russian symbolists; the portrait in question is by Konstantin Somov.

153   *the somewhat strange pseudonym of M. Glubakov* An anagram of M. Bulgakov.

153   *His real name [...] is Nikolai Kazanov, and not Khazaner, as some of his ill-wishers liked to call him* Khazaner being a Jewish-sounding surname.

154 *Friends and acquaintances called her Ritochka, and I – I called her Margot* Ritochka is the Russian diminutive of Margarita; Margarita is addressed as Margot by various characters in Bulgakov's novel.

158 *Alexei Konstantinovich Tolstoy* Poet, novelist and historical dramatist (1817–1875); a member of the Tolstoy family and a relative of Leo.

160 *'Letter to the Amazon'* The title of a French-language philosophical essay written by Tsvetayeva in 1932–34 and addressed to the French-American writer and feminist Natalie Clifford Barney (1876–1972); the essay, a response to Barney's *Pensées d'une Amazone* (1920), deals with lesbianism and, specifically, with what Tsvetayeva calls a woman's 'innate need' to give birth, which, she claims, ultimately causes lesbian relationships to break down.

161 *Just like Vertinsky* Alexander Vertinsky (1889–1957), artist, poet and singer who exerted a profound influence on the Russian art-song tradition.

161 *they say [the dash] is a characteristic of feminine punctuation* Adele's fondness for the dash recalls Tsvetayeva's frequent and idiosyncratic use of the same.

164 *The wax of immortality* A phrase from an untitled poem by Mandelstam (1918).

164 *Dear Vasiliy Vasilievich* Adele's third letter is addressed to the philosopher Vasily Rozanov (see note to p. 103); Rozanov being long dead, the letter form is merely a convenient literary device here.

165 *I wear literature like I wear my trousers* From *Fallen Leaves*.

165 *I feel no constraints in literature* Ibid.

166 *I myself am forever berating the Russians* From *Solitaria*.

166 *I am a most unbearable Shchedrin* Rozanov is comparing himself to the satirist Nikolai Saltykov-Shchedrin (1826–1889), whom, perversely enough, he actually detested for his criticisms of Russian society and the Russian state.

166   *Where, then, can truth be found?*   From *Solitaria*.

166   *Peoples of the world*   Ibid.

167   *Shklovsky*   Victor Shklovsky (1893–1984), writer, literary theorist and one of the founders of the Russian formalist movement, best known for his notion of defamiliarization (*ostranenie*).

169   *lovers are children [...] children don't have children*   The quote is from 'Letter to the Amazon' (see note to p. 160); the musings in Adele's fourth letter closely echo the thoughts expressed in Tsvetayeva's essay.

173   *It's not Rome the city that's eternal, but man's place in the Universe*   Lines from an untitled poem by Mandelstam (1914).

173   *as in Gogol's 'A Terrible Vengeance'*   A horror story (1832). The allusion is to the following phantasmagoric passage: 'An unheard-of wonder appeared near Kiev. All the nobles and hetmans gathered to marvel at this wonder: the ends of the earth suddenly became visible far away' (tr. Richard Pevear and Larissa Volokhonsky).

173   *And died in Rome, befittingly enough*   Gogol actually died in Moscow (in 1852) – this is another mystification on the part of the author.

176   *her wrist joints achatter*   An allusion to Pasternak's poem 'The Substitute' (1917).

177   *make sure you dont* thuffer   An allusion to the stammering Alexei Alexandrovich in *Anna Karenina*, who, in a confrontation with his wife, finds himself unable to articulate the word 'suffering'.

178   *anyone who charges at her with an inkdipped quill*   A paraphrase of a line – 'Whoever comes at us with a sword shall die by a sword' – (wrongly) attributed to Prince Alexander Nevsky (1221–1263), a key military figure in Kievan Rus', and itself a paraphrase of Matthew 28:52.

178   *no better (worse?) ploy could he concoct*   An allusion to, and potential inversion of, the opening lines of Pushkin's *Eugene Onegin*:

> *My uncle, honest, righteous mortal,*
> *Won high opinion when he knocked,*
> *In deadly earnest, on death's portal:*
> *No better ploy could he concoct.*

178 *no one can learn from his example*   An outright inversion of the next line of the same stanza ('May his example be a lesson').

179 *where once a feast was spread a coffin lies*   A line from Derzhavin's poem 'On the Death of Prince Meshchersky' (1779), tr. A. Wachtel, I. Kutik and M. Denner.

179 *there[']s rapture on the battleground & where the black abyss is found*   Lines from Pushkin's verse drama *A Feast in Time of Plague* (1830), tr. James Falen.

179 *the cosmos breathes on her breast*   A paraphrase of a line in 'Don't Wake Her at Dawn' (1842), a poem by the lyric poet Afanasy Fet (1820–1892); the original line reads 'The morning breathes on her breast'.

179 *a cruel romance*   A variety of Russian romance (urban folk song), with lyrics typically focusing on tragic love.

180 *flung into the deep of space must we destined to expire pine for sweet devotions grace and to constancy aspire*   The final quatrain from an untitled poem (1915) by Mandelstam, which, lineated and properly punctuated, reads like this:

> *Flung into the deep of space,*
> *Must we, destined to expire,*
> *Pine for sweet devotion's grace,*
> *And to constancy aspire?*

180 *betrothed to that extraordinary kind of freedom [...] never took off the crown she wore so lightly*   Paraphrases of lines from the same poem.

180 *old wives['] wittering of Fate*   A phrase from Pushkin's poem 'Lines Written at Night During Insomnia' (1830).

181 *mouselike scuttling of life*   A phrase from the same poem.

181 *phonetics is the seraph[']s handmaiden* A phrase from an early untitled poem by Mandelstam, published in 1913 as part of a collection entitled *The Stone.*

183 *Alexei Konstantinovich Tolstoy* See note to p. 158.

183 *Anichkov Bridge* The oldest (and most celebrated) bridge across the Fontanka River in St. Petersburg, built in 1841–42.

184 *the patriotic heart / Finds pleasure in this yellow colouration* In the nineteenth century, yellow was the colour of officialdom and imperiality in Russia; this is especially true of the neoclassical architecture of St. Petersburg that the narrator appears to deride in this stanza.

184 *Inheritors of Batu and Mamai* Batu Khan (c. 1207–1255), Mongol commander and founder of the Golden Horde who oversaw the invasion of Rus' in 1237–40. Khan Mamai (1335–1380), a powerful military commander within the Golden Horde. The implication is that 'we' (that is, the Russians) are the inheritors of barbarians.

184 *Our forebears' style we've newly recreated* A reference to the Rococo Revival of the mid-nineteenth century, which revived the foliate and floral forms of the original eighteenth-century Rococo movement.

184 *The barrack style* A severe classicist style in which the role of ornament is downplayed; developed under Tsar Nicholas I (ruled 1825–1855), lover of military parades.

184 *while here 'twas Arakcheians* Alexei Arakcheyev (1769–1834), influential statesman, military figure and aficionado of the minutiae of military drills whose name has come to be associated with despotism and arbitrary rule. The ideology of 'Arakcheyevshchina' was reflected in the era's predominant architectural style.

186 *The principle of S-shaped lines* The narrator's tutor seems to be an advocate of the aesthetic theories of William Hogarth (1697–1764), English painter and denizen of Chiswick, that 'finest of London's western

Environs'. In his *Analysis of Beauty* (1753), Hogarth declares that 'the Serpentine line hath the power of super-adding grace to beauty'.

188   *Potyomkin's glittering, resplendent ball*   Prince Grigory Potyomkin-Tavrichesky (1739–1791), military leader, statesman and favourite of Catherine the Great. Tolstoy is referring to a lavish masquerade ball thrown by Potyomkin in honour of the empress at the Tauride Palace in April 1791.

189   *Classicism*   Here, the term *classicism* refers not only to classical antiquity but also to a philosophy of education opposed to so-called 'realism'. While proponents of classicism favoured (predictably enough) the study of Greek and Latin, the realists emphasized mathematics, natural sciences and modern languages. These conflicting approaches were embodied in the institutions of the gymnasium and *Realschule* respectively.

190   *By Stasyulevich may I be forgiven*   Mikhail Stasyulevich (1826–1911), historian, publisher and editor.

190   *More schools of the 'Real' persuasion*   That is, *Realschulen* (see note to p. 189).

190   *My namesake*   Count Dmitry Tolstoy (1823–1889), Tsarist statesman and Minister of National Enlightenment between 1866 and 1880. His education counterreforms, which reversed much of the liberalizing legislation of the early 1860s and emphasized classicism as an anti-liberal, anti-radical measure, were passed into law in 1871.

192   *Derzhavin, master of the ode*   See first note to p. 85.